The
Inscrutable Americans

Anurag Mathur was born in New Delhi and educated at
Scindia School (Gwalior), St Stephen's College (Delhi), and
the University of Tulsa (Oklahoma). He stayed in the US
for three years before returning home to India to embark on
a career in journalism and publishing. He now lives in New
Delhi and contributes regularly to leading Indian magazines
and newspapers. He is also the author of a travel guide called
22 Days in India. A fanatical cricket player, he also plays
tennis and enjoys travelling.

The
Inscrutable Americans

Anurag Mathur

RUPA

Published by
Rupa Publications India Pvt. Ltd 1991
7/16, Ansari Road, Daryaganj
New Delhi 110002

Sales centres:
Allahabad Bengaluru Chennai
Hyderabad Jaipur Kathmandu
Kolkata Mumbai

ISBN: 978-81-716-7040-6

60 59 58 57 56 55 54 53 52 51

The moral right of the author has been asserted.

Typeset by Mindways Design, New Delhi

Printed at HT Media Ltd., Noida

This Book is Dedicated to my

Father and Mother

1

Beloved Younger Brother,

Greetings to Respectful Parents. I am hoping all is well with health and wealth. I am fine at my end. Hoping your end is fine too. With God's grace and Parents' blessings I am arriving safely in America and finding good apartment near University. Kindly assure Mother that I am strictly consuming vegetarian food only in restaurants though I am not knowing if cooks are Brahmins. I am also constantly remembering Dr Verma's advice and strictly avoiding American women and other unhealthy habits. I hope Parents' prayers are residing with me.

Younger Brother, I am having so many things to tell you I am not knowing where to start. Most surprising thing about America is it is full of Americans. Everywhere Americans, Americans, bit and white, it is little frightening. The flight from New Delhi to New York is arriving safely thanks to God's grace and Parents' prayers and mine too. I am not able to go to bathroom whole time because I am sitting in corner seat as per Revered Grandmother's wish. Father is rightly scolding that airplane is flying too high to have good view. Still please tell her I have done needful.

But, brother, in next two seats are sitting two old gentle ladies and if I am getting up then they are put in lot of botheration so I am not getting up for bathroom except when plane is stopping for one hour at London. Many foods are being served in carts but I am only eating cashewnuts and bread because I am not knowing what is food and what is meat. I am having good time drinking 37 glasses of Coca-Cola.

They are rolling down a screen and showing film but I am not listening because air hostess ladies are selling head phones for 2 dollars which is ₹26 and in our beloved Jajau town we can sit in balcony seats in Regal Talkies for only ₹3. I am asking lady if they are giving student discount but she is too busy. I am also asking her for more Coca-Cola but she is looking like she is weeping and walking away. I think perhaps she is not understanding proper English.

Then I am sleeping long time after London and when I am waking it is like we are flying over sea of lights. Everywhere, brother, as far as I am seeing there are lights, lights. It is like God has made carpet of lights. Then we are landing in New York and plane is going right up to door so that we are not having to walk in cold. I must say Americans are very advanced. And as I am leaving airplane, air hostess is giving me one more can of Coca-Cola. Her two friends are also with her but why they are laughing so much I do not know. I think these Americans are strange but friendly people in their hearts. I hope she was not laughing for racial. Perhaps she was feeling shy earlier.

Then I am going to long bathroom. As I am leaving I am making first friend in America. This is negro gentleman named Joe who is standing at door and as I am opening it he is holding out hand so I am shaking it and telling him my name and he is telling me his. I am telling him if he is ever coming to Jajau he can ask for National Hair Oil Factory. If I have not returned from Higher Studies please tell Father that if negro gentleman named Joe is visiting Jajau he may kindly do needful.

In this way I feel each and every one of us is serving as ambassador of our beloved motherland. Joe is doubtful I feel because he says 'Far out, man, far out,' but I am reassuring him that India is only 16 hours away by plane and that is not very far. I think he is accepting this because he is not saying anything any more.

Next I go to place marked 'Baggage' as Father has advised and suddenly place I am sitting starts to move throwing me. It is like python we once saw in forest, only rattling and with luggage bouncing on its back and sometimes leaping to attack passengers. I am also throwing myself on bag before it is escaping. I think if I am not wrestling it down it would revert to plane and back home to India. I am only joking of course.

Before this I am meeting very friendly gentleman at Immigration desk. I do not know why all relatives had warned against this man, because he is so friendly. He is talking English strangely but is having kind heart because he is asking me about nuts and I am saying that I am liking very much and eating many on plane. 'Totally, totally nuts,' he is saying, which is I feeling American expression for someone fond of cashewnuts.

Before this he is showing friendliness by asking, 'How is it going?' I am telling him fully and frankly about all problems and hopes, even though you may feel that as American he may be too selfish to bother about decline in price of hair oil in Jajau town. But, brother, he is listening very quietly with eyes on me for ten minutes and then we are having friendly talk about nuts and he is wanting me to go.

At Customs, brother, I am getting big shock. One fat man is grunting at me and looking cleverly from small eyes. 'First visit?' he is asking. 'Yes,' I am agreeing. 'Move on,' he is saying making chalk marks on bags. As I am picking up bags he is looking directly at me and saying, 'Watch your ass.'

Now, brother, this is wonderful. How he is knowing we are purchasing donkey? I think they are knowing everything about everybody who is coming to America. They are not allowing anybody without knowing his family and financial status and other things. And we are only buying donkey two days before my departure. I think they are keeping all information in computers. Really these Americans are too advanced.

But, brother, now I am worrying. Supposing this is CIA keeping watch or else how they can know about our donkey? Anyway please do not tell Mother and Father or they are worrying, but lock all doors and windows. If CIA wants to recruit me to be spy in Jajau, I will gladly take poison before betraying our motherland.

Then I am going out and cousins are waiting and receiving me warmly. I will write soon after settling down.

Your brother,
Gopal.

It was midnight and cold, with an icy wind that New York sends to the airport in winter to greet passengers. Gopal had barely got into the car, he had hardly touched American soil, or more accurately American concrete, and already he was in love.

She was the classic American beauty; hair like flowing gold framing her face, eyes blue as Arctic lakes, she lay stretched in a negligee some thirty feet long, with breasts of a size that made you expect to see rock climbers clambering on them. The spotlights on the words below her urged everyone to use her favourite tampon. As they drove away from the billboard, Gopal craned back desperately.

'Don't worry,' said Sunil, one of the two Indians who had come to receive him, patting Gopal with a grin, 'you'll meet lots more like her.'

'The only people,' commented Sushant who was driving, 'who actually look at American ads, are visiting foreigners.'

Gopal settled back in the seat, not at all convinced that he would meet anybody else who had such eyes that promised things he had only vaguely heard of with disbelief in his twenty years in Jajau, but he didn't want to make a scene. He had been sleepy on the flight, but now that he was actually here, after all those months of filling forms and taking exams and waiting uncertainly, he felt excitement spread in his chest like a pleasant cactus.

The car in which they moved seemed a little world in itself, racing silently through the night. There were numerous glittering dials and the car seemed to move nearly intuitively at Sushant's touch, somewhat removed from the manful grapplings that Indian cars demanded before reluctantly yielding. They seemed in a completely sealed cocoon, able to move swiftly and smoothly for eternity. No rattles erupted in the engine, no blasts of outside air made their vicious and victorious way through minute gaps, no opposing headlights malignantly blinded him, and most of all no horns assailed him at every turn. His ears began to feel numb in the unaccustomed silence.

'Brother,' he said and his voice was like a trumpet, far too loud and he knew it, but he had been accustomed too long to combating loud noises, mechanical and manmade, to be able to lower his decibel level immediately.

'Brother,' he tried again, still unsuccessfully, 'how far is New York'?

'About half an hour,' answered Sushant, switching on the radio, perhaps in self-defence.

Gopal looked around intently. More billboards sprang at them out of the dark, like demented salesmen hurling themselves on a customer pleadingly. Then they fled past as though in sorrow and Gopal wondered if it wasn't a little pathetic that he had such little time to see so many happy faces.

They went past occasional houses with handfuls of golden light thrown softly on the lawn. They were pretty houses: large, clean and with a basket hung on each one. Gopal wondered at those baskets. They went past a row of houses and each one had the same basket hung outside. Perhaps, he speculated, it was some religious symbol. He wracked his brains for an appropriate Christian saint who would explain it, but nobody fitted. Perhaps a lightning conductor, but it was hardly the right shape. Maybe for garbage, but why would anyone want to throw his garbage upwards? It was a real mystery and Gopal would have asked his friends, only he didn't want to look silly.

Then in any case he forgot everything else, because New York rose before him like a vision of God.

'Brother,' roared Gopal making Sushant swerve, 'can you park quickly?'

Hastily Sushant eased the car on to the shoulder, praying Gopal wouldn't throw up his airline dinner all over the upholstery. He leaned across and opened the door, waiting for Gopal to leap out. Gopal gazed ahead transfixed.

'What's happened?' asked Sunil groggily from the back seat. Gopal just gestured ahead.

'Ah, New York,' said Sunil, snuggling back, 'I felt that way too the first time.'

In amusement Sushant pulled the door shut. 'The first time,' he grinned, thinking to himself, 'may be Cosmo should do a round up of The First Time I Saw the Big Apple.' He waited tolerantly for Gopal to recover, who looked like he'd seen a visitation. 'Well, he is a small town boy,' mused Sushant. 'Bit of a hick actually.' He was himself a Bombay boy and quite used to big city lights.

'Can I drive now?' he asked.

Gopal nodded, still mesmerised by the city swathed in platinum glitter. They turned a corner and it was hidden; then passed under some trees and there it was again. Gopal felt as though the city had known he was coming and was playing a little game of hide-and-seek with him. But the closer they came the less it hid, until finally they joined a thunder of cars that seemed fused together like a long sheet of metal, curving and swerving as one.

Sushant, who had been relaxed was alert now, braking and accelerating, changing lanes till they reached the exit point and swept out of the stream into a quieter street.

'I'll give you a quick tour of Manhattan,' he said, as the car rose on a little mound and then plunged into those tar streets that carry such treacherous promises, always around the next corner.

Wall Street, Times Square, Greenwich Village, the Empire State Building, the UN complex, it was all too much for Gopal to take after a sixteen-hour flight. What was even more distracting was a dawning realisation as they sped along an interminable tunnel, that made Gopal blurt.

'Brother, you are driving on wrong side of street.'

'Nah,' reassured Sushant, 'it's how Yanks drive.'

'Why?' asked Gopal.

'I think they just like doing things directly opposite to the way we do them in India,' grinned Sunil.

This made sense to Gopal and he subsided.

'Here we are,' said Sushant as he pulled the car into a slot.

'Where we are?' asked Gopal as they dragged his baggage up a wooden flight of stairs that thumped at every step.

'A little outside New York,' said Sushant, opening the apartment door and turning on the light.

Gopal was startled.

'That light switch is upside down,' he exclaimed. 'You are putting it up to turn it on.'

'I told you,' chortled Sunil. 'Even their taps turn the wrong way from ours.'

Taps reminded Gopal he was thirsty.

'Where is the boiled water, brother?' he asked, heading for the fridge.

The duo roared with laughter.

'Use the tap, it's quite safe.'

'You're sure?' asked Gopal uneasily.

'Yes of course,' cackled Sunil. 'Here, you sleep in this room. Good night.'

Gopal sat in the dark in his pyjamas in the moonlight, finally alone. He was actually and really here. The excitement made him shiver. It was all so alien, so wonderful, yet so scary. Would he adjust, would they like him, would they be friendly, would he do well in class, where would he get vegetarian food cooked by Brahmins?

Tomorrow evening he would be flying to Eversville. What would that be like? Today he had been to New York through streets known to every literate person on earth. So in a way he was part of the legend and the glamour too. He felt a deep, and yet he recognised yearningly, hopeless empathy with all New Yorkers. He wondered if Brooke Shields would like him. The central heating hummed its lullaby and Gopal fell into an exhausted sleep.

The next morning he came slowly awake. For a moment he was going to call for someone to bring him his tea when he remembered where he was. Excitement sat him straight up on his bed and he looked out of the window. He saw a long double-storeyed building opposite, obviously the twin of the one he was in and between them a parking space already nearly empty. He stretched luxuriously and padded out. Sushant and Sunil had already left for their office. Gopal opened the fridge and gaped at the collection of colourful cardboard boxes. He picked out one that read 'orange juice' and was pondering on the mystery of how to open it when suddenly loud music erupted from his room.

Panicking, Gopal looked wildly around for something with which to defend himself. Nobody had been in the room when he left it. Clearly a burglar had climbed in and while trying to carry away the radio had turned it on. Worse still, perhaps there was something supernatural in there. Some unthinkable horrow. Perhaps some racist ghost that hated his presence. Visions from *The Exorcist* which he had seen four times on the video at home dripped like cold lead from his veins into his brain.

'Hey, hey, hey,' laughed a voice in the next room. 'Woiza, woiza, woiza. What a night and what a day. Hey, hey, hey.' There was something hypnotic about that choice. Like a demon trapped inside a box enticing him to come and release it.

Gopal stilled his pounding heart. Nobody had emerged from the room and if there was a burglar he would have fled by now. Picking up the kitchen knife he crept to the door and flung it open. There wasn't a soul, the windows were still shut and the demon in the radio was talking now about the weather. Edging around the supernaturally alive radio, Gopal reached the window and peered out. Not a soul. He sagged weakly against the sill. Then flinging the knife down he strode furiously to the wall phone. He dialled the number written on the sheet pasted alongside and as Sunil picked it up erupted:

'Bloody radio is bloody screaming,' he complained. 'Oh sorry,' said Sunil contritely. 'Did that scare you? I set the radio alarm for ten so that you'd wake up. I'm coming over to pick you up in about an hour and we can go get a bite to eat. Can you be ready by then? We'll go to New York and then to the airport. So keep your bags packed.'

Sunil duly arrived an hour later and first went and turned off the radio which Gopal had circled several times but refused to touch.

'Let's go,' he said and went thumping down the stairs with Gopal's suitcases. People going downstairs in India made a different sound, thought Gopal. It was a sort of scuffling rhythm, maybe because the steps are made of cement, while here each stair seemed a giant piano key that emitted a distinctive, woodenly musical tonking sound muffled in carpeting.

He opened the door and stepped outside. The wind leapt at his face with knives. He reeled back.

'Oh shit, sorry,' said Sunil opening the car door and bundling him in before scampering across to his own side. 'I keep forgetting you're not used to life here. Actually it's not so cold, it's the wind chill factor.'

If Gopal hadn't been so numb he would have given him a baleful look.

'Anyway,' said Sunil, 'you may as well get used to the American way. I'm taking you to a McDonald's for a burger.'

Gopal nodded, starting to thaw. A few minutes later they pulled into a McDonald's and made a dash through the door to escape what Gopal was starting to think of as 'Sunil's wind chill factor'. Gopal thought the interior looked like it had been furnished with a child's plastic building-block-set in reds and yellow. They edged into two chairs.

'What'll you have?' asked Sunil.

'Anything vegetarian,' replied Gopal, not wanting to be difficult.

Sunil regarded him thoughtfully. 'You're going to have a really great time here I can see. How about some French fries?'

'I have never eaten French food. Is it vegetarian?' asked Gopal. 'I think, brother, I will have a vegetable hamburger.'

Sunil looked even more thoughtful. 'The Yanks have much to learn from our ancient civilisation,' he said, 'most of all how to reconcile such contradiction as vegetables and hamburgers. Why don't you have an egg instead?'

Intimidated by the teenagers screaming instructions to each other behind the counter, Gopal agreed. He also had seven Cokes, not including the one he brought back to the car.

'Still no Cokes in India, huh?' asked Sunil.

Gopal shook his head between making bubbles in his glass. 'We have our own,' he explained. 'But Coke is Coke.'

They drove past trees and shrubs so green and clean that they nearly hurt the eye. Gopal's own hometown, on the other hand, wrapped itself in a blanket of dust and grime, much of it, sad to admit, contributed by the National Hair Oil Factory. Some inkling of this difference seemed to occur to Gopal.

'It is all so quiet and green, brother,' he complained. 'We should start hair oil factory here. Good market, no?'

Sunil winced. Gopal's eye was attracted to a little town lying below the ridge on which they were driving.

'What's that, brother?'

'Oh, that's a town – Riverdale.'

'Yes,' nodded Gopal knowledgeably, 'Archie and Jughead are living there.'

Startled, Sunil pondered on a McLuhan world and wondered if the publishers of Archie comics ever imagined that boys in dusty towns in remote parts of India earnestly pored over the doings of that quintessentially all-American group.

'I thought it was only comics,' said Gopal, 'but they are actually living?'

'Anything,' said Sunil feelingly, 'is possible in America.'

'Let us find out. Can we go?'

'Some other time,' said Sunil hastily.

They went over a bridge Gopal had not noticed in his confused state last night. Through the steel girders slashing past alongside, Gopal got his first daytime look at New York. It looked serene, cool and blue. In the distance the towers of the World Trade Center rose in effortless insolence, heedless of the smaller buildings clumped like barnacles around its base. And then they were on the edges of the city, with its red brownstones looking down on the river. Sunil was once again like a fighter pilot preparing for a dogfight. He turned right and eased into the traffic.

'I have some business near Times Square,' he said. 'You can check it out.'

'This is where *Time* magazine is?' questioned Gopal.

'No, that's further down.'

'Then why it is called Times Square?'

'Beats me,' said Sunil, turning into a parking lot. 'I'll be back in fifteen minutes; so don't wander too far.'

Gopal, tall, lanky and bespectacled, peered interestedly at the street as he strolled around. The wind wasn't very strong here and he felt quite elegant in the new overcoat his mother had bought for the trip. There was a bounce in his step and he grinned at passersby who eyed him warily. He was walking with the most exciting people in the most exciting city in the world and even if they all rather quickly averted their eyes from him and hurried away, he was anxious to be accepted as nearly one of them.

A very tall, very good-looking black man, dressed in a breathtakingly beautiful grey overcoat, sauntered past. When Gopal tried his we're-all-New Yorkers smile, he smiled right back. Gopal was thrilled at being accepted by one of the elite New Yorkers.

'You looking for some fun?' the man asked politely. His voice was low and husky. It felt like a cat rubbing its fur on Gopal.

'I am having very good time, hee hee,' modestly acknowledged Gopal, sniggering nervously.

'I knew it. I knew it right away,' said the man putting a brotherly arm around Gopal's shoulder. 'The moment I saw you I said "Here's a man who knows how to have a good time."'

His voice had a sincerity and sibilance that inserted itself into Gopal's skin and began to spread itself warmly. 'Now you come right along with me and we'll have a little old party, won't we? Yes, sir, just a lil old party, ain't that right?'

'No, no,' said Gopal, starting to shake himself loose, 'I have to wait for Sunil.'

'Hey, man,' said the black, the velvet voice starting to harden, 'don't gimme none of that.' His voice softened again. 'You know what I got for you. You know what I really got for you?' His voice was so soft it fell like candy floss over Gopal.

He shook his head, suspicious, wary, but curious.

'Well, my man, my main man, what I got is some real live pussy for you. How about that now? Isn't that what you'd like? Some real live, wild pussy just for you? Let's go get some of that, man,' he urged, guiding Gopal with his hand.

'No, thank you, sir,' said Gopal, shaking himself loose but not wanting to be impolite, 'but I'm vegetarian.'

'That's right now,' soothed the tall man bending over him. 'What I got is prime stuff. So clean and fresh, my man, it's just pure vegetarian. You'll just love it, brother. You just go eat it to believe it,' he urged.

Gopal shook his head and walked away rapidly. Something was obviously very wrong here, he sensed. But as his heart and pace slowed he began to wonder. 'Vegetarian cats?' he puzzled in bewilderment. He reached the parking lot just as Sunil did.

'You had a good time?' asked Sunil.

'Oh yes, brother,' said Gopal, his spectacles shining enthusiastically, 'I met friendly man selling cats.'

'Well anything is possible here,' said Sunil. 'Just don't buy nothing.'

'But they're really so advanced brother,' Gopal said in admiration. 'Vegetarian cats.'

They began to drive through the city, heading towards the airport. Gopal was looking with fascination out of the window. After a while he commented, 'Lot of advertisements, brother. Everywhere.'

'Yeah.'

'Mostly women in them.'

'Yep.'

'Mostly with no clothes, brother.'

'Makes it more attractive.'

'What do their fathers say?'

'Nothing terribly complimentary I imagine,' said Sunil. 'Um, Gopal, you know I don't want you to get me wrong, but America is a very different place. Now I know that in the big cities in India it's pretty much the same as here where dating and drinking and stuff is concerned, but what was it like in your town?'

'It's very small town, brother. No dates, nothing, no chance. One boy quietly went on date with girl but their parents made them marry afterwards. But I am knowing America is very different, brother, so I have read one very good book. I am knowing all about it now. So don't worry.'

'Oh good, excellent,' said Sunil, relieved. As an afterthought he asked, 'What's the book, by the way?'

'*Collected Letters from Penthouse.*'

The car again swerved dangerously. 'Oh shit,' said Sunil. 'Ah Gopal, that may not be the most accurate account of life here. You know I suggest that before you actually start socialising with people, maybe you should first settle down a bit, get to figure out what's what, you know, check out the whole scene. Are you planning to date girls?'

'Oh no, brother,' erupted Gopal with excessive force. 'Never, brother. I am promising everyone that I am not meeting girls or drinking or smoking, brother. I am only going to study, brother,' he swore piously.

'Yeah, sure,' said Sunil with some scepticism. 'But even if you do go out with some girls, don't pile on, all right? And don't promise to marry them on the first date either. It's an old line.'

'Brother, you are talking like fool,' protested Gopal. I am only going to classes, library and home. Nothing else.'

'I bet,' said Sunil. 'Another thing. The girls here are very suspicious of foreign guys because they think the guys are all trying to lay them. I don't know why they're so damn wary considering that Yank guys do nothing except try to lay them too, but since we're foreigners we've got to take it easy a bit. Okay?'

'Oh, yes, brother. I think you are cent per cent right. I feel that we are all ambassadors from our country to America and if we are behaving well then they are having us in their good books. I feel,' said Gopal, clearly warming to his theme, 'that because of our superior culture and all that we must set an example so that the Americans will improve their behaviour and I feel that relations and things like that will also improve and trade and all that also, so I feel ...'

'I see, I get your point,' broke in Sunil somewhat hastily. 'Er, Gopal,' he floundered trying to change the subject, 'how old are you?'

'Twenty, brother.'

'And you spent all your time in, er, what's its name?'

'Jajau. Yes, brother.'

'Didn't you go out to do your college studies?'

'No, we are having local college and father is wanting me to also work in factory and get experience. So in morning I did college and afternoon I was in factory.'

'And what are you going to study in Eversville?'

'Chemical engineering. After that I am returning to use new technologies in our factory.'

'Well, I'm sure you'll do really well. Their educational system is really very easy compared to ours. But I must admit I'm still a little worried about how you'll manage to adjust to the life here. Didn't you go out to the big cities in India at all?'

'Yes, brother, to Delhi, but only very quickly to meet relatives and for weddings, because Father is spending mostly time at factory for expansion and he is taking me with him since I am ten years old.'

'You really must know a lot about the business by now.'

'Brother, I am not showing off or wanting to and all that, but last year All India Association of Hair Oil Dealers is naming me "Most Promising Young Man of Year". I am having certificate with me to put on wall. Do you think,' asked Gopal cunningly, 'the Americans are liking it?'

'I am sure,' assured Sunil, understanding Gopal perfectly. 'The American girls will be very impressed with the certificate.'

They entered another bridge leading out of Manhattan in the direction of JFK. 'This is one of the oldest bridges in America,' explained Sunil, trying to educate Gopal a bit. 'It has a really fascinating history.'

'Yes,' agreed Gopal, '*Saturday Night Fever* is shot here.'

Again Sunil was startled. 'They showed *Saturday Night Fever* in Jajau?' he asked incredulously.

'No, no,' said Gopal pityingly. 'I am seeing on video. I am seeing many realistic and educational American films on video.'

'Which was your favourite?'

'*Deep Throat.*'

'Holy shit, you watched *Deep Throat* at home on video?'

'No, no, at friend's house when his parents are away.'

'Where do you get these films anyway?'

'Many good video libraries in town now.'

'And where do they get the films from?'

'Delhi. Good business in pirated video prints.'

'Don't the cops do anything about it?'

'Brother,' said Gopal patiently, 'you are talking like damn fool.'

Yes, thought Sunil, I certainly am. He'll probably be absolutely fine. In any case why the hell should I worry. This is the second time in my life that I've met the guy. 'How exactly are we related?' he asked.

'Your cousin sister is married to my cousin brother. Don't you remember their wedding? You had come to India for that.'

Cousin sister and cousin brother, mused Sunil. I've really been away a long time. He remembered the wedding and the vast crowds of what were apparently close relatives. He recalled reading somewhere that all cultures developed a variety of names to distinguish the shadings of any element of which there was an abundance in the environment. So the Eskimos apparently had half a dozen names for snow and Indians similarly had names for a nearly endless number of specific relationships. The name for a father's elder brother was different from that for his younger brother and so were the names for the mother's brothers. It probably developed from the joint family system where everybody lived together, thought Sunil. When a kid wanted someone, he couldn't just yell for his uncle. The house was probably crawling with uncles. He had to specify which uncle.

It's probably a good indication of the areas in which a society lays the greatest emphasis, he thought. I wonder what it is that has the largest number of synonyms in America?

'Brother, look,' said Gopal pointing to a billboard, 'whole family is naked.'

Sex, thought Sunil with sudden inspiration. The sex act has more names in America than anything else. Well, he thought wryly, well, well, well, so what else is new. The problem though is that not only are they obsessed with sex, they're making the rest of the world equally crazy. Look at this poor guy, he pondered, he's read *Penthouse Letters* and seen *Deep Throat* and he thinks that's America. Well maybe it is, at least more than Yanks are willing to accept, but how's he going to cope? He's probably been the most sedate, conservative, godfearing guy in his hick town. I mean how much trouble can you get into in a hair oil factory, for God's sake. But almost from the moment he's arrived, he's started to perk up. I don't think he's seen pictures of as many naked women in all his life as he has after driving half a day on America's streets. It'll be a bloody miracle if he doesn't turn into a raging sex maniac. And what's that going to do to his head which must be full of his father's preachings and mother's warnings and a lifetime of the straight and narrow? Well, he concluded, if it doesn't kill him he'll go back a new man. God help Jajau then.

He squinted with affection at the earnest, bespectacled figure beside him. 'How long will you be in the US?'

'One year only. I am finishing diploma course and returning.'

They reached the airport, parked alongside the kerb and got off. Sunil got a trolley while Gopal took out his bags. 'I'll walk you to the airline counter, but I'll have to rush back because I'm illegally parked,' said Sunil. 'Who's going to receive you at Eversville?'

'University said there will be chap with sign,' said Gopal, distractedly walking towards the row of counters.

'Thank you, brother, for everything. Very nice of you and all that. I hope you will come and are visiting me at Eversville. Please say my goodbyes to Sushant.'

'I will,' said Sunil, feeling an unaccountable fondness for this hopeless, gangling, earnest young man so far from home and his natural surroundings. He dumped the bags on the scale, gave the ticket to the lady attendant, took back the baggage tags, ticket and boarding pass and put them in Gopal's hand. 'Off you go,' he said to him gruffly. 'That's the way to your gate. Don't get into the wrong plane.'

'No, brother,' said Gopal obediently, though clearly extremely distracted, and set off down the corridor.

Sunil watched him go, feeling somewhat helpless at what lay in store for him. Then suddenly Gopal turned and loped back.

'Brother,' he asked surreptitiously, 'this may be wrong time to ask, but lady who gave tickets is having red hair. Brother,' he whispered even more conspiratorially, 'I am wondering suddenly. Are red-haired ladies having red hair,' he fumbled desperately, 'all over?' he blurted out.

'I'm sure,' said Sunil giving him a hug and nearly weeping, 'you'll have lots of opportunities to find out.'

Visibly cheered, Gopal strode eagerly back towards the departure gate.

2

Gopal trundled the trolley carrying his luggage in front of him as he came out of the arrival area of the airport. He looked anxiously around for someone carrying a sign with his name and to his relief he spotted one immediately. 'Welcome Gopal Kumar,' it said in large red letters. Underneath it added, 'To the Dullsville Capital of USA.'

The sign was being waved by a tall, cheerful-looking American with curly brown hair who was eyeing the arriving passengers eagerly. Just looking at him made Gopal's spirits rise, which had been considerably crushed by an exasperated stewardess who snapped, after his request for an eighth Coke, 'Why don't you buy yourself a factory,' before ignoring him for the rest of the flight.

Gopal headed for the American youth who sized him up as he approached. He saw a young man with a slightly pockmarked, sallow complexion, about six feet tall, with thick black-rimmed glasses and longish hair that were so oily that they reflected light. But the most immediate characteristic was his enthusiasm and excitement. 'Here,' thought the American, 'is a guy who's glad to be here.'

'Hello, hello,' roared Gopal causing nearby passengers to shy away nervously and the American to flinch. But not to be outdone he boomed back equally loudly, 'Hello, hi, hellow there,' his hand grappled with Gopal's arms before they met and shook. 'I'm Randy.'

Gopal recoiled this time. 'Why?' he asked nervously.

Randy looked at him in amazement. 'Er, why not?' he finally laughed. 'Anyway, let's get out of here and head for the town that time forgot,' he said, seizing Gopal's trolley and wheeling it down the carpeted corridor. And so, eyeing each other a little warily, they emerged into the open.

Almost immediately Gopal began to hurt in the icy wind. He hugged his overcoat around himself and looked in awe at the young American who was dressed in jeans and a plaid shirt and striding briskly behind the trolley. 'My car's just a bit ahead,' he said with a backward, sympathetic glance at Gopal who was shuffling along miserably. 'Here we are,' he announced, opening the door, flinging in the suitcases and ushering Gopal into the front seat. 'My most humble chariot,' he announced, settling in and starting the engine.

They drove out of the airport and Gopal began to unfreeze. 'Thank you for picking me up and all that,' he said awkwardly, remembering his manners. 'Is the college near by?'

'No such luck,' grinned the Yank. 'It's about an hour away, not just from here, but from any place civilised.' He roared with laughter. He had a very infectious laugh and he laughed a lot, thought Gopal, who was beginning to like him. 'It is,' Randy continued, 'a real one-horse town.'

'I see,' said Gopal, interested but confused. 'Whose horse is that?'

'I love it,' shrieked the American, pounding the wheel. The car swerved and another car overtaking them jerked wildly away. Its horn blared and the driver could be seen yelling with his mouth opening and closing rapidly.

'Yeah,' yelled back Gopal's new friend, 'and I hope the next time you meet your mother she barks at you,' he screamed. Grinning, he turned back towards Gopal. 'First rule of survival in the US of A,' he informed Gopal who was all interested immediately, 'Never take no shit from nobody. They give you shit, you give back *two* buckets of shit. You know what I mean?'

Gopal certainly did, though it wasn't a very pleasant thought. The American put on the radio. 'Anything special you want to listen to? he asked.

'No, actually I'm still very sleepy. Jet lag and all that. Can I go to sleep?'

'Sure, this is America, you can do what you like. I'll wake you up when we get to Eversville. You're staying in the dorm tonight. They're supposed to have saved some dinner for you, though I wouldn't bet on that. But you go right ahead and sleep. Here, I'll lower the music.'

Gopal leaned back and dozed. Outside in the early dusk, the trees were slipping into the twilight. A mist was starting to shade the land grey, then a light drizzle swept in the blurred what little could be seen. It is all so different, thought Gopal. I wonder what is happening at home now? They must be wondering about me too. But at least the people seemed friendly. At least this one who had come to fetch him did. Maybe too friendly, he thought with a twinge of uneasiness. He said he is randy. I know from *Penthouse Letters* about that, but there only girls are randy. Maybe he is one of those. Boy types. I must be careful. And then he was asleep.

He barely remembered arriving at Eversville, or getting out at the dormitory, or falling into bed. The non-stop travel, the excitement, the newness, all finally pushed him into an exhausted sleep.

The next morning he stirred sleepily awake. He looked around through gummy eyes and struggled up, wondering where he was. He thought of calling for the cook to bring in his tea and then suddenly he remembered why he was in this grey, cell-like room, and he fell back into bed. A feeling of total fright went through him as though each cell in his body had been touched with ice. He really didn't want to get up. He worried about what lay ahead. Monsters with American faces materialised in front of him waiting to perform unimaginable cruelties.

He heard footsteps outside and wondered if they were waiting beyond the door to laugh at him. Maybe now that he had arrived they had decided that they had made a mistake and were going to kick him out. What would he tell everyone at home? Maybe even now big and tough policemen, hefty-defty, were on their way to drag him out. What would his parents say? He missed them. By this time of the morning his mother would have arrived to get him out of bed. He missed her. He missed her fat waddling figure and the thumps she gave him to wake him up. Sometimes he used to pretend to be asleep until she got near enough, then he would suddenly leap up and scare her. Maybe the Americans would think he looked funny.

Gopal would have carried on fantasising if he hadn't felt the urge to relieve himself. Wearily he swung his feet on to the floor and pushed himself off the bed. He looked around for the bathroom, found a door, opened it, and discovered coat hangers hanging there. Impatiently he went to the other door, turned the handle and looked into a long corridor. Thoughtfully he came back, considered the situation, sat down on the bed, got up again, walked twice round the tiny room, opened the closet door and carefully checked it in case it led into a bathroom. It didn't. He then came back to sit on the bed and think some more. There was no getting away from it, he decided, there just wasn't a bathroom here.

His sleepy mind refused to accept this. Forcing down a feeling of panic, he tried to examine the situation logically. Awful thoughts about unspeakable toilet habits practised by Americans kept leaping into his head. Finally, he abruptly decided that the only reasonable conclusion was that the college had given him a room without a bathroom. It was simply impossible that the entire nation took to the fields in the morning in search of release. After all they are the most powerful nation on earth. What about Ronald Reagan, does he get a bathroom, or in the morning does he go out to the lawns followed by security guards? I am thinking like sick man, he told himself sternly. He dashed out of the door.

A kindly soul he met in the corridor, seeing his overwrought state, escorted him to a door with the sign 'Men'. There he beheld, with the sentiments of a weary knight glimpsing the Holy Grail, a procession of glorious, glittering, welcoming pots. However, his joy was shortlived, since he also found that there wasn't a shred of privacy around any of the pots. It was as casual as a row of marble thrones expecting a regiment of kings for dinner.

A glance at the door showed there was no way to lock it. He peered outside but no inspiration rounded the corner. He looked wildly around inside but nothing presented itself that could be used to jam the door. Suddenly remembering, he dashed to a toilet paper roll, dragged out a handful, folded it quickly into a square and stuffed it under the corner of the door. It was a trick he had read about in *Penthouse Letters* where a young man had met a lady who apparently was unable to restrain her affection for him for a single second longer.

As a much-relieved Gopal went out, having laboriously taken the paper out piecemeal, he accepted with unreserved admiration that *Penthouse Letters* was the finest possible guide to surviving in America. He decided to obtain a copy at the earliest so that he could have an invaluable adviser at hand for the doubtlessly difficult days that lay ahead.

He returned to his room and began to gather soap, shaving kit and other equipment preparatory to having a bath. There was a loud banging at his door. 'Open up,' shouted a familiar, cheerful voice outside. 'This is the FBI. Surrender or die.'

Gopal cautiously opened the door. 'Hi, there,' grinned the friendly face outside. 'Remember? I'm Randy.'

'Still?' asked Gopal, stunned.

'Of course,' said the Yank. 'Do Indians change the names overnight?'

'Oh,' sighed Gopal in understanding and relief, 'your name is Randy.'

'Sure it is, I told you that.'

'Of course, of course, come in, I'm going for bath. Where it is?'

'This way, this way to the most exalted place.' Heralded by Randy, they made their way to a room lined with showers. Once again, Gopal noticed with foreboding, there were no cubicles, just a series of enquiring shower heads leering at him.

'I think,' said Gopal backing away, 'I will not take bath now.'

'Why? Why?' demanded Randy who had been admiring himself in the mirror. 'Tell all to Uncle Randy, greeter of innocents, protector of the poor. Is it the pits? Does our humble loo offend you? Say the word and I'll tear it apart. Out with it. What's wrong?'

'Well, actually, you know,' admitted Gopal sheepishly, 'there is no privacy and all that you know.'

'Ah ha,' said Randy, 'my computer-like mind sees all. Fear not fair youth, I shall stand guard outside and none shall witness thy noble nakedness, as Shakespeare probably said.'

Hastily Gopal bathed, scalding himself once with a faucet that turned the opposite way from Indian taps. He shaved, got into the clothes he had brought and went out. Randy was waiting outside with three other men carrying towels who flinched as Gopal passed. 'Thank you,' said Gopal. 'How you stopped them from coming in?'

'A secret my grandmother taught me,' airily explained Randy. 'A mere nothing for someone of my talents, brains and sexual ability.'

'Still?' prodded Gopal.

'Oh I told them you thought you had got herpes and had gone in a check.'

'What's herpes?' demanded Gopal.

'Just an all-American signal that you want privacy. Nothing to worry about.'

They dumped Gopal's towel and kit in his room and he began to put on shoes. 'Let's go, let's go,' said Randy dancing around and sparring. 'Breakfast time, chow time. I'm so hungry I could eat a cow.'

Gopal stopped abruptly and raised an admonishing finger. 'No. No cows for me,' he warned sternly.

'Oops,' said Randy, landing a quick left-right to Gopal's suitcase, 'a faux pas, a fucks pass, let's go. Take your sweater and overcoat. We're going to see the Dean afterwards.'

They went into the dining hall. The din reminded Gopal of the shopfloor of his uncle's steel re-rolling mill. They joined a line and Randy picked up two trays. 'One vegetarian breakfast coming up, courtesy the Cordon Bleu chefs of Hank's Delivery Service.'

'I am eating eggs.'

'And so you shall. Dozens of them. You want milk or orange juice?'

'Er, orange juice,' said Gopal, a little uneasy about the religious status of American cows.

They went to a table occupied by two young men. 'Will you move,' asked Randy conversationally, 'or should I pull out your intestines and strangle you with them?'

'Up yours, Wolff,' said one, but they moved.

'Fellow Yanks,' resumed Randy after they had sat down, 'I would like you to meet my friend Gopal. He's the Maharajah of Delhi, his father has eighteen wives and he lives in a two hundred-room palace.'

'Hi,' said one, 'sounds just like my old man. I'm Fred.'

The other American who was extremely fat carried on eating.

'Ignore this animal,' advised Randy. 'The school just keeps him here for his sex appeal. By the way,' he asked, suddenly remembering the shower room, 'how did you manage with the John?'

Gopal paused in mid-chew. 'Who?' he asked.

'Not who, what. The toilet, the loo, el stinko place.'

'Oh that,' said Gopal in embarrassment, aware of the other two watching him, 'I managed. Why it is called John?'

'I'm John,' burped the fat one.

'That's right,' hooted Randy. 'That's why it's called the John. After this guy here. Because he's so full of shit.'

Gopal filed this away and regarded the fat boy with more respect. They are naming rooms after boys here, he thought. Perhaps the way they have streets named after great people in India. He wondered if they would name any rooms after him. I must give no cause for complaint, he thought. Maybe a chemical lab, he fantasised, Gopal Kumar Lab.

'Let's go, let's go,' Randy was thumping his tray. 'The merry Dean awaits us at his morning orgy.'

They went out of the doors, down some steps and into a large oval of grass. Buildings fringed it on all sides. Everywhere there were figures sprinting for various buildings. 'Peasants,' commented Randy, 'racing for their daily slavery. We, of course, shall stroll leisurely like two Maharajahs of Delhi or Bombay? Hi, there, Mary Lou,' he called out to a passing girl. 'How're the blow jobs getting along?'

'Who's she?'

'Oh her,' said Randy pleased with his wit and confident that Gopal wouldn't understand. 'She's the Linda Lovelace of the campus.'

Gopal gave him a cold look. 'And you are Harry Reems?' he asked witheringly.

For once even Randy was at a loss for words. By now they had reached a building marked 'Administration' and a short, red-haired man who was about to enter held the door open for them. 'You must be Gopal, I hope Randy's been looking after you. What was he telling you about just now?

'Linda Lovelace, sir.'

Randy gurgled. Dean Smith gave him an old-fashioned look as they went up the stairs. 'I see Mr Wolff has begun educating you in his area of expertise,' he said drily. 'I hope the college can do as good a job in its own field.'

They went into a small but pleasant office looking on to the oval. Books occupied one entire wall. 'Take off your coat, make yourself comfortable. Coffee? Perhaps Mr Wolff can organise three cups if he can tear himself away from his contemplation of last night's excesses.'

Randy hastily complied.

'Sit down,' Dean Smith waved to Gopal. 'We have hopes that we can learn a lot from each other. We don't normally take people for one year, but your experience and knowledge of specific chemicals was so impressive that we felt we had to make an exception in your case. I just wish you were staying longer. A lot of the learning process is just the entire experience of education and I believe someone from a different culture like yours would benefit greatly before returning to your homeland. America has much to offer and I hope you will participate fully and take back pleasant memories with you.

'I appreciate the culture shock may be tremendous, that's why I specially requested Randy to look after you. Being a very small school we try to make everyone feel at home so they don't get the sense of being lost that I'm told happens to a lot of foreign students going to large schools. I hope you don't misunderstand Randy. He's one of our brightest students in chemical engineering and possibly the only one who can come anywhere near the kind of knowledge you seem to have developed. I must say you have a range and depth of experience that I haven't encountered among many students.'

'My father is teaching me our business from childhood...' said Gopal, shuffling his feet in embarrassment. He had never received such praise in his life and wondered if the Dean was being sarcastic.

Randy returned balancing three plastic cups. Gopal tasted the coffee. It was terrible and he was to discover later that coffee everywhere in America tasted faintly of burnt beans and fried plastic.

The Dean continued, 'Randy, I want you to take Gopal to the bookstore, show him the library and campus, help him check out the classrooms and meet the teachers. We've given him one of the off-campus apartments, haven't we? I believe you wanted one so you could eat Indian food. Do you think you'd like to help him move in?'

Gopal turned to see if Randy was agreeable, but apparently this wasn't a question. He left his coffee unfinished and watched wincing as the Americans drained their cups with evident enjoyment, Randy slurping his noisily. 'Anytime you want to see me just drop right in,' said the Dean in farewell as they shook hands.

'He is very friendly,' Gopal told Randy as they went down a staircase.

'Yeah, but not always. Wait till you get bad grades once, you'd think you'd murdered his mother, the way he carries on. Let's go see the campus.'

Randy took Gopal around the small school. Nothing really made sense, because it was all so alien, but Gopal tried to get his bearings. The tour would have been a lot livelier, Gopal suspected, if Randy hadn't been so chastened by the *Deep Throat* shock. He was proved correct when before entering the engineering building, Randy turned and asked in real wonder, 'How'd you know about Reems and all that stuff?'

'Well, heh, heh,' said Gopal enjoying himself thoroughly, 'I am more clever than I look.'

'I bet,' said Randy pushing the door open. 'Here, hang on, I'll go see if any of the profs are free.'

He strode away. Gopal wandered around the lobby watched by a girl from behind the reception counter. He looked her way and their eyes met. 'Hi,' she smiled, 'how's it going?'

'What to say,' confessed Gopal, touched by her interest and not wishing to let it go unrewarded. 'So many things are happening. First I am not finding bathroom and having to close door and things like that. Then there is vegetarian food problem and I am promising my grandmother I will only eat food cooked by Brahmins in Hank's Delivery Service, though I don't think so. Of course, Dean Smith is very nice and all that but I am not knowing if I will adjust to bathroom problem. But I am really loving Coca-Cola. But how all Americans are using same bathroom I am very worried.'

The girl's eyes had begun to glaze and she had started to cringe backwards when Gopal was interrupted by Randy's voice. 'Don't waste your time on her,' he urged Gopal propelling him away, 'she only puts out on the second date. C'mon, I'll show you around the classes and labs.'

Gopal wandered in bliss through laboratories emitting deliciously familiar potent odours and classes with charts that he knew by heart. The rows of computer terminals fascinated him and seemed the only way the laboratory complex of rooms was different from his college in India. All labs, he thought in a state of ecstasy, smelt the same.

He was introduced to numberous hearty and welcoming teachers who all seemed large and jovial and who he would have to learn to differentiate from each other. He was particularly pleased to see numerous other foreign faces. He commented on this to Randy, 'Lot of foreign students here.'

'Yeah,' joked Randy, but there was a slight edge to his voice. 'I'm the token American here. C'mon, let me show you the pirate's den.'

'Is that restaurant?'

'No, it's what I call the bookstore. Damn thieves.'

At the end of the tour Gopal was completely confused. 'Don't worry,' Randy reassured him, 'you'll find your way around in a week. It's a small place. Now let me show you your apartment. You want to walk or drive?'

They decided to walk so that Gopal would learn the way. They crossed a road bordering the lawn, walked past a few white-painted wooden houses and turned into a double-storeyed apartment complex. Randy rang the bell below the 'Manager' sign and a large lady opened the door. She was wearing a flowered summer dress with massive arms emerging from it. Her face had no discernible features except a tiny nose just managing to stay afloat atop the fat. Minuscule eyes peered like mice from behind the protective layers. Her hair, Gopal thought, was suspiciously jet black.

'My, my, my,' she squealed and her voice sounded like the whistle used to wake soldiers at dawn, 'look who's here. Come in, come in, mercy, you'll catch your death of cold.' Gopal felt even colder looking at her summer dress.

Inside, it was warm. All the furniture was covered with flowery material and dozens of glass vases in different shapes, sizes and colours lay everywhere. 'Mind where you sit,' she warned, 'I don't want you hurting my babies.'

Gopal leapt to his feet and looked around in alarm. 'No, love,' she trilled, 'I meant my vases. They're my babies. My liddle liddle babies. And they love their Momma the way their Momma loves them. Isn't that so, honey,' she cooed to a vase in the shape of a winged cupid about to shoot an arrow.

'If that vase was me,' muttered Randy to Gopal, 'I'd shoot that arrow right into her fat face.' They both sniggered.

'Laugh,' she said, affectionately stroking the cupid, 'that's right, laugh. I love a jolly old laugh, dearie me, yes I do.' She gave a jolly old laugh that started in a low whine and gained in bass as though she was changing her sex while crunched over the cupid vase. The laugh culminated in a vast bellow.

'Oh dear,' she gasped, 'that was good, wasn't it? I just know I'm going to love you. I love all my boys. You do speak English, don't you? Ah, good. Well, boys, upsy up we go,' and to Gopal's increasing feeling of hysteria, she skipped like a schoolgirl to the door. She grabbed a bunch of keys hanging beside the door and waved them forward. 'Upstairs, your little castle's upstairs,' she whined and giggled.

She began climbing the stairs, wheezing and stopping and gasping every three steps. Randy noticed with amazement that she was sweating. 'Oh dear me,' she panted, 'Gloria's no longer the belle of the ball.' She stumbled in triumph up the last stair and supported herself with the rails on the side as she tottered her way forward. At the third door she fumbled with the lock while Randy and Gopal tensed in case she dropped dead from exhaustion, but she got the door open and stumbled in.

Randy and Gopal followed and found her flat on her back on the bed, wheezing like a deflating tyre. Her bosom heaved uncontrollably like a ship in a storm. 'Just doing my breathing exercises dear, one of those days you know. Take a look around,' she urged, 'go on.'

Gopal looked and found one small room with a tiny round table with two chairs, a gallery with a cooking range and sink, and a door to which he hastened. He opened it and rejoiced in the sight of a toilet and shower. An apprehensive look around showed no other means of ingress, so clearly this was intended exclusively for him. He came back beaming to Randy who was fascinatedly observing Gloria who now appeared to be gargling with her spit.

'Do you think she'll marry me?' whispered Randy. 'I mean how could anyone lead a boring life with her around?'

Gloria began to get up, apparently in instalments. First her head, then her neck, then her bosom, and finally her stomach till she was sitting upright. 'Ah me, that was fun, wasn't it, toots? What're you going to study here, love?'

'Chemical engineering.'

'Mercy, what brains! I just love brains. I'm educated too. I write poetry, did you know that?'

'No,' they assured her. 'But of course I'd love to hear some,' Randy urged.

'Well,' she said coyly, her eyes rolling back soulfully. She powered herself to her feet. 'The twitch of my hip,' she sang.

'Can make a man sick.'

She turned around and twitched one hip to demonstrate. The twitch started at one end and rolled like wheat rippling across the vast prairies for several seconds before dashing itself against the far end.

'The glow of my soul can burn a big hole.'

Gloria put one hand on her heart and one hand out and paused. Gopal and Randy waited breathlessly for more and then realised that the poem was over. They applauded wildly.

'Dearie me,' whined Gloria cantilevering her bosom down a few inches in what was meant to be a bow, 'what a good time, what a good time. Well, loveys, I gotter run.'

She skipped to the door and turned. Her eyes glowed like her soul and she looked at Gopal. 'I've made a hit,' she crooned. 'Yes, siree Bob, I've made me a hit.'

They could hear her skipping to the stairs outside like a rhino practising ballet steps.

'This is true love, man,' hooted Randy clutching his sides and rolling on the bed, roaring with laughter. 'Boy, oh boy, oh boy.'

'Oh no, no, no,' grimaced Gopal, 'I am sure she is only just friendly. Most American girls are like this in old age?' he asked.

'Absolutely,' assured Randy. 'She's about average I'd say. What are Indian girls like?'

'I am not knowing much,' confessed Gopal, 'but why you are called Randy?'

'Because I am. That's why, I guess. And I am because that's my name, know what I mean?'

'No.'

'Well hell, aren't Indian guys randy?'

'Yes, some boys, but ...'

'You mean you don't go out on dates and stuff?'

'Well in the cities every one is doing, but ours is small town, so ...'

'You mean you've never been on a date?'

'Well ...'

'Aw come on, you must've laid a couple of girls by now, huh?'

'No, actually ...'

'You mean you're actually a virgin?'

Gopal nodded shamefacedly.

'Well, holy shit, I don't think I've ever met one before. It's not infectious, is it? Stay away from me. Can I get it just by looking at you? Hot damn boy, thank you, you've given my life meaning and a direction and a goal.'

'What?' stuttered Gopal.

'I'm going to get you laid. Yes, sir, you heard me right. I do hereby swear as a red-blooded American, that before you go back to India, I'm going to get you right royally laid from sea to shining sea, so help me God.'

'Hey, heh,' simpered Gopal. 'No, no,' he protested with a noticeable lack of vigour. 'I cannot do all that and all that and things like that.'

'Oh yes, you can do all that and all that and believe it or not, even things like that. Do you have a phone here? I'm going to call Hot Pants holly and get this over with right away.'

Gopal shied away in alarm. 'No, no, no phone yet,' he said in relief. This was moving a little too fast for him. 'How I am getting one?'

'Easiest thing. I'll fix it. Anyway, let's go buy some groceries and stuff for you.'

They walked back across the college lawn to Randy's car. 'Hang on a second,' said Randy racing off, 'I've got to talk to that guy. Oi Mike,' he screamed, 'wait a sec.'

Gopal loitered around. The wind had dropped and he was really quite cosy in his overcoat. He breathed deeply and his nose hurt with the clean coldness of the air. He exhaled watching his breath becoming smoke and then tried to blow smoke rings. Just then a girl who looked familiar walked by. He recognised her as being the friendly one who stood behind the counter at the engineering building. 'Oh hi,' she said in surprise, 'how's it going?'

Gopal beamed at such constant interest. Clearly, the brief introduction he had given her earlier had only whetted her appetite. 'Well, heh, heh,' he grinned walking alongside her, 'I am meeting Gloria and getting apartment and you are really glad to know that now no more problem with toilets, I am having one of my own. Of course I am not using it yet but why to bother because it's of my own, isn't it?'

In answer she dug her hands into her pockets and walked faster. 'Of course if there are any problems Randy is there. But everyone is very nice and no worries. It is nice apartment and Gloria is sleeping on bed and it is not falling under her, heh, heh.' Clearly he had essayed a little joke. By now Gopal was walking as fast as he could to keep pace with her. 'The mattress is looking thin but I am sure Gloria is giving new one if any problem. I am sometimes having problems in bed because of thin mattress ...' He watched puzzled as she fled across the lawn.

He trudged back to where Randy was waiting. 'Woman,' he told Randy with real feeling, 'are strange people.'

'The wisdom of the inscrutable East,' said Randy clapping him on the shoulder, 'but I could have told you that myself. C'mon, let's go loot the shops.'

They drove off. 'Wait till you get a load of this place,' said Randy. 'It's a mall and I never thought much of it, but last year I had this African friend studying here and he said he'd never seen anything like it. I mean when his relatives came to visit and asked to see the sights, he'd, like, take them to check out the mall. And he never got any complaints. Not one.'

They drove into the largest parking log Gopal had seen in his life. Nor, he thought, looking around, had he ever seen such a vast collection of different cars. For one wild moment he wondered if they were fakes put there to impress him. There was every conceivable shape and colour and size and Gopal peered into every car he passed, some in envious amazement at the opulence and luxury visible inside, some in pity when they were less impressive than Randy's car. At some he felt downright derisive and when he saw one with a torn roof, untidy interior and dusty exterior, he felt compelled to warn Randy: 'That belongs to crook. I must get good car also. Big one.'

'Damn right you do,' agreed Randy, 'you're not American till you do.'

It was amazing how rapidly if not instinctively Gopal had begun to equate an automobile's looks with its owner's virtues or their lack. A bad-looking car, he instantly felt, demonstrated a lawless personality. Oddly, he had never felt a similar sentiment in all his years in India. But in America, without anyone telling him so, he had accepted implicitly that the possession became the man. With this came a desperate, nearly sexual sense of urgency demanding that he own a car too. Effortlessly he had decided that since a man's acquisitions defined him, he would like to demonstrate his family's wealth with a suitable symbol. And while the idea certainly existed in India too, it wasn't as clear cut as here, and with good reason. In India the options available to a buyer were much fewer, so a man really bought whatever he could get – often the decision was made for him by whatever was available, while in America a man's possessions were actually a very personal statement of his likes, lifestyle and attitude to life. To that extent his possessions probably did define him far better than any proclamations he might make.

By now they had entered the mall and Gopal was again stunned. He saw that it was a huge double-storeyed building with soft music piped everywhere, discreet lighting throwing an actually welcoming glow, rows of shops, some simply decorated, some bizarre, others with exquisite window dressing. Overhead in the centre of the roof was a transparent glass sheet and below it, a restaurant surrounded by green plants. A waterfall cascaded at one end, but so soothingly that Gopal wondered if the water wasn't domesticated. There was a hush all around except for the house-broken water and discreet music. 'It is quiet as church,' Gopal whispered.

'This is a cathedral for Yanks,' grinned Randy. 'It's the most sacred place we know. We do all our praying here, first to get something and then afterwards when the bills arrive. This is really where all our Gods live. Let's go pray to them for some toothpaste for you.'

Walking through the tinkling silence, Gopal contrasted it with the bazaars at home. There was a constant roar, like a torrent tearing out of a gorge – no tame water there. Pedlars shrieked, buyers screamed in horror at the prices, shopkeepers wailed at the ruination facing them if they lowered their rates any further. Goods spilled everywhere, fruits, clothes, vegetables, books, fish, and the odours were so strong they were almost tangible, they felt as loud as the sounds. People bumped into each other, elbowed their neighbours aside to reach in and squeeze the mangoes, deftly exchanged children who had got interchanged, yelled for the proper change, demanded that the oranges be weighed again with weights that didn't look like they'd been made at the shopkeeper's house, avoided persistent beggars, checked one last time that they weren't taking home a different kid from the one they'd come in with and triumphantly departed. The ears buzzed from the clamour, the throat ached from the haggling, the arms hurt from the packages, the feet ached from the walking, but they felt a genuine sense of triumph at having beaten the shopkeepers again, they hoped, and at a good day work done.

But at the mall, Gopal felt totally helpless at the gentility all around and the effortless ease with which shopping could be conducted. However, he knew shopkeepers well and he felt he had no reason to believe that their basic attitude to customers here would be any different from what it was in India. So when the girl at the counter totalled his purchases for pots, sheets and plates and announced, 'That'll be $37 and 52 cents, sir,' he was ready for her.

'25 dollars,' he replied firmly.

'Sorry, sir,' she replied, 'that's 37 dollars and 52 cents.'

'27 dollars,' Gopal suggested.

'Er, no, sir,' she replied nervously, 'if you've run short of cash we'll gladly accept all the major credit cards, cheques or travellers cheques.'

'29 dollars,' said Gopal firmly, 'no more or I am going to other nice shop. They are saying they are having sale but I am giving you chance first.'

The girl began to look around wildly. 'Excuse me, sir,' she pleaded, 'I'll have to get the manager.' She fled.

Randy, who had been wandering around near by, strolled back. 'What's up?' he asked.

'I am bargaining.'

'Great,' said Randy. 'High time someone did. This should be fun.' He seated himself on an ice box.

The manager arrived. He was short, barrel-chested, dressed in a colourful checked coat and had a pleasant smile on his face at the moment. The girl hid behind him, peering over occasionally.

'What seems to be the problem, sir?' asked the manager suavely. 'Could I be of some help?'

'Prices too high,' said Gopal firmly.

'Ha ha ha,' chuckled the manager, 'isn't that the truth. I often say the same to the wife myself. Now I'll tell you what,' he leaned forward conspiratorially, 'if you've run out of cash, leave behind any one of these items, I'll reduce $5 and throw in free this packet of fine chewing gum. How about that? Is that fair or is that fair?'

'Chewing gum rots teeth,' said Gopal firmly.

The manager flushed. His eyes began to narrow, his smile to fade, but Gopal, who had grown up amidst grocers wailing at the imminent starvation of their children, was unaffected.

'All right,' said the manager through clenched teeth, 'what's the real problem here? Come on, spit it out. You broke or something?'

'No,' said Gopal, 'but this only worth $25.'

'Oh, yeah,' said the manager, 'sez who?'

'Who is setting these prices?' demanded Gopal coldly.

'How the hell do I know? Hey buddy, look, I just work here. I don't want no trouble, all right?'

'27 dollars.'

'Hey jerko, what're you? Ralph Nader send you, hanh? He's an Arab too, isn't he?'

'I am Indian. 29 dollars.'

'I don't believe this. What're you ... nuts? Why don't you just take the whole damn thing free?'

'Thank you,' said Gopal, gathering the package.

'Hey, hang on, wait up. Jesus, I get all the freaks. All right, 30 dollars and that's it.'

Gopal strode out in triumph.

'Wow,' said Randy in wonder. 'I must try that sometime.'

As they walked towards the exit, Gopal beheld a short black man wearing a fur cap, half dancing as he walked. His arm turned half circles and his fingers snapped in time to some invisible music. His feet sprang with each step and his body curved sideways keeping pace with the snap of his fingers. Gopal was astonished. 'What is happening to him?' he asked.

'Oh nothing, just be-bopping his way down.'

'He dances?'

'No, just walks.'

'Dance-walk. Wonderful. No one is walking like this in India,' said Gopal entranced. 'How he is doing it?'

'Easy. Here, I'll show you.'

Gopal watched as Randy demonstrated. 'See, the arm goes like this and there's the snap. You've got to feel the rhythm. Go on, try it yourself.'

Gopal put down his package and tried. His legs got in each other's way more than they sprang and the first time he snapped his fingers he nearly gouged out his eye. But when he tried to concentrate on the snap, his feet instead of springing began to vibrate like they had Parkinson's disease. However, when he tried to bring order into his legs, his snap narrowly avoided castrating a passing shopper.

'Needs more practice,' was Randy's opinion.

'You carry packages, I am practising.'

Randy eagerly picked up the packages and wondered when he had enjoyed himself more and they made their stately way to the exit, with Gopal trying to coordinate the spring with the snap.

Outside, he felt free of the hushed atmosphere enough to become a great deal more adventurous in his springing and snapping. 'Better?' he asked.

'You said it. No question. Just keep it up,' urged Randy.

Gopal be-bopped to the car and practised around it while Randy fished for his keys. 'Keys lost?' asked Gopal.

'I can't stop watching you.'

'Doing it good?'

'Oh boy. You bet. Here are the keys.'

'I think I am walking like this every time. But everyone will stare?'

'No, no,' strenuously assured Randy. 'It's how everyone walks. Do it. Go right ahead.'

Gopal rehearsed a few intricate snaps.

'Food,' he suddenly remembered, 'must get food.'

'Right, nearly forgot. Should we go by the grocery store?'

'No use. Can't cook?'

'Who cooked for you in India?'

'Servants.'

'Well, pardon me. I guess in that case it's back to the mad delights of McDonald's, your Servantile Highness.'

They drove around till they found the familiar arch. They got off. 'Er, I thought,' diffidently reminded Randy, 'you were going to walk like, you know, the way you were practising.'

'Oh yes,' Gopal began to be-bop down, adding a distinctive shoulder twist he had invented while sitting in the car. Hastily, Randy raced in front of him and flung open the door for Gopal. 'Hey, guys,' he whispered inside penetratingly, 'get a load of this.'

Half a dozen heads craned around and watched the door attentively. Gopal walked in perfectly normally, smiled at the perplexed watchers who glared at Randy and sat down. 'Heh, heh,' he waggled an admonishing finger at Randy, 'I am not fool.'

Randy sheepishly sat down. 'So what're we eating?'

'Vegetarian.'

'Right, vegetarian for you. Let's see, let's see, hum, hmmm. This is amazing. There's nothing here except fries.'

'I will have.'

'Nothing else?'

'You say?'

'Yes.'

Randy went to order. 'One Big Mac and six orders of fries.'

The girl looked at him. 'You on a low cal diet?'

'Just get it, okay.' He went back to get Gopal's share of the money and came back. 'And four Cokes,' he added fiercely. 'You say something?' he asked the girl.

'Nothin. But I can think, can't I? I mean that's still allowed, inn't?'

It was dark by the time they got back to Gopal's apartment, loaded with cornflakes, detergents, milk, eggs, bread, sheets, pots, and the entire paraphernalia required for survival. Halfway through their shopping Gopal had felt jet-lag creep up his legs and lay an armlock around his head. He had felt too tired even to haggle.

Now he stumbled up the stairs, dumped the packages near the door, thanked Randy profusely, invited him with transparently fake earnestness to come in and have a Coke. Randy declined out of sympathy and left.

Gopal laid out the new bed sheet, got into his pyjamas and was about to shut off the light when there was a tap at the door. It was Randy. 'Tomorrow,' he said as Gopal peered out, 'it starts.'

'What?' asked Gopal groggily.

'Operation Devirginisation,' laughed Randy, turning away to race down the stairs.

Gopal went to bed promising himself he wouldn't dream of girls.

3

Beloved Youngest One,

How much I am missing one and all I simply cannot say. My head is eating circles with all new new things.

Two weeks are already proceeding and I am not even knowing. I am receiving Respecting Parents' letter and sending reply. You may also kindly assure that I am strictly avoiding traps of divorcees. But, brother, you tell, how I am to refuse meeting divorcees when all here are divorcees? Even respected Landlady who is regarding me as own son is divorcee with three divorces.

Also, brother, I am telling you frankly, Revered Grandmother I am loving and respecting very much but she is becoming nuisance. How I can help it if no Brahmins here? And, brother, she is instructing that I must go to every kitchen before eating and ask if cooks are Brahmins. Brother, here they are not even knowing what caste is! But you may kindly tell her that I am strictly doing needful otherwise I am fearing she is starting to sing Holy Songs again and Mother is getting headache.

I do not know what she is saying if I am telling her that I am also cleaning own latrine. I think she is leaving Earthly Form. Brother, I am not liking, but what to do? No one is having servants here. I am even cooking own food but only eggs. I am grateful to our cook who is telling me how long to boil egg, but why he is not telling me that water is required to be added? Anyway I am learning all many things.

I am happy to say Higher Studies are progressing. They are having all facilities here but standard of studies is not so high as in India. In technical matters they are having very good teachers but American boys are not taking much interest. Mostly my class is having foreign students. Course is quite easy and I am knowing mostly already, so Respected Professor is saying I may take test and move to next class. They are allowing many kinds of things like this here. I think this way is better than in India and if we are also doing then nation will be on march.

Also no one is bothering who you are and you are also not to bother. You are not believing, but I am calling Respected Professors by first name. One is saying to me, 'My name is Sam, not Sir Sam. The British are not knighting me yet.' Good joke I think. Brother, are you imagining if I am going to Great Principal of Jajau College and calling him by first name? I think he is dying of heart attack.

I am making one friend here by name of Randy but that is not what it is meaning and is common name. He is very studious, sober and religion-minded boy you may tell Mother. He is from good family of high status. He is showing me all different kind of ropes as they are saying here.

I am now knowing where to go. Earlier I am getting lost every time. On first day I am going to one class and sitting for half an hour and not understanding one word. First I am thinking it is accent I am not knowing. Then I am thinking I am gone mad. Then girl sitting near is whispering it is French class. Now I am having good laugh.

Brother, in food matters I am having big botheration. Everyday I am eating cornflakes and boiled eggs for all meals. Now when I am burping I am getting cornflakes taste. But what to do? I think Americans are hating vegetarians. But their orange juice and milk is being something else. You are having to try it to believing it.

Well, that is all from my side. Only worry I am having but kindly you are not telling family, is fear of high blood pressure. I am never having before but all Americans I am meeting when they are leaving are saying, 'Take it easy.' Brother, even if I am standing fully relaxed and talking and taking deep breaths they are still saying, 'Take it easy.' Maybe some problem in water is causing blood pressure problems. And more they are telling me, more blood pressure I am getting. Anyway let us see. We are all in God's Hands.

All else is fine at my end. I hope studies and work are progressing and you are doing hard work at your end.

Assuring that I will check you out later.

Your beloved brother,
Gopal.

Just as Gopal finished writing the letter there was a thunderous assault on the front door accompanied by screams of agony alternating with pants of ecstasy. This, Gopal had learned, was Randy's way of announcing his arrival. 'Open the door, let me in,' he screamed. 'I know my daughter's in there. What're you doing to her lovely white body, you filthy foreigner? Oh will no one help me rescue her.'

'Door is open,' yelled Gopal.

'Greetings your Maharajical majesty,' said Randy flinging open the door and bowing like Johnny Carson. 'I have discovered the answer to the most perplexing question confronting mankind today.'

'What question?'

'How to get you laid.'

'And what is answer?'

'It is simplicity itself. A stroke of genius such as could only be conceived by a man of my divine gifts. A man who, despite all evidence to the contrary, pretends to be like all other men. A man who ...'

'You want to eat boiled egg?'

'Oh God, not again. I can't bear it anymore. Oh sob, oh cruel life, everytime I've come to your place I've been forced to eat boiled eggs. I hope you added the water this time when you boiled it. I couldn't believe that. I mean how can a guy who can mentally work out faster than a calculator, the square root of II divided by 1228 and multiplied by 892,000 not know that you need water to boil an egg? Tell me that, oh venerable master of mathematics.'

'Are you giving me answer, or am I making you eat egg?'

'What answer? Oh right, to the question of the ages. Quite simple. You know those three girls you said you liked? The one at the library and the other two at the engineering school? Well, what we do is get you into your fancy new Sears Roebuck checked pants. Then you put on your Sears Roebuck tweed coat. Then you walk up to each girl in turn, put your arm around her waist, with the other arm you hold her hand, look deep into her eyes and say: "Excuse me please. Are you wanting to screw?"'

'No.'

'All right. Talk American. Say "Hey honey. Wanna fuck?"'

'Kindly go away.'

'Hey, why not? Look, Gopal, let's face it, you're not doing too great you know. I mean how long've you been here now? Two weeks?'

Gopal nodded.

'And what's been your strike rate? Zero. I mean zilch. I mean if I had to go without it for two weeks, nothing, and I do mean nothing, would be safe in a radius of 50 miles. C'mon, Gopal, let's face it, you can't do any worse you know. Look at it this way; if they all say "no", you're no worse off than when you started. And if even one says "yes", you're home and running. How d'you like that? Am I good or am I great?'

'You are ass. We are going to school.'

'All right, be that way. The truth is you don't deserve an adviser of such imagination, creativity, daring and stunning good looks. Let's go, let's go.'

As they went down the stairs Gopal tucked in his newly acquired scarf into his overcoat. He had gone back with Randy to the mall and in the same store where he had bargained, he found scarves on sale displayed in the window. He went in, picked one up and strode purposefully to the counter. He met the same sales girl. She paled visibly on seeing his determined face and cowered.

'How much?' demanded Gopal.

'Whatever you like,' she assured him nervously.

'Says $5 each in window.'

'So it does. But for you, anything.' She caught the eye of the store manager who put on his suave smile and headed towards them. Then he saw who was with her and quickly stepped behind a rack of kitchen utensils.

'You pay what you like, mister,' the girl pleaded. 'I'll pay the rest.'

Mournfully Gopal had put down five dollars, disgusted at being deprived of a satisfying haggle.

Now as he came down the stairs, feeling warm and elegant, he felt he had got a good bargain. The curtains in Gloria's living room had been drawn apart and as she saw him she gave a friendly wave and struck a pose with one hand poised on her head and another sticking out sideways. She had told him that she had seen the pose in a book which she showed Gopal, which was one of Egyptian hieroglyphics and had decided for some mysterious reason that the posture was part of some intricate Indian dance. She therefore adopted the pose whenever she saw Gopal, apparently as a way of making him feel at home. Gopal often wondered if, all things considered, he didn't prefer her poetry.

As they drove out, Randy commented, 'That Gloria, boy, has she got the hots for you? You know, she's kind of cute in her own way. You two could make quite a couple you know.'

'Thank you,' said Gopal. 'But I am thinking she is more your type.'

'Well, don't dismiss her. Keep her in mind. Who knows, I mean you might get so desperate one day that overcome by lust you might decide to take the leap. Of course you might never reappear after having taken the leap, but that's a small price to pay. And I really think it's worth paying. I mean if I was deprived for two whole weeks, I would. Now what I mean? How d'you stand it? And what am I going to tell your Dad when he arrives to investigate your disappearance? That you've drowned in rolls of blubber?'

Gopal shifted uneasily at the mention of his father. 'I have managed for 21 years,' he said shortly. 'We are going somewhere in afternoon you said?'

'Yeah. The college football team is playing a game. The Dean thought you might like watching it.'

'What is team name?'

'The Eversville Evergreens. And the only thing evergreen about them is that the dumb shits haven't won a match in recorded human history.'

And so they went that afternoon, participating in one of the sacred rites of America, if only Gopal knew it, a worship of its truest gods. Sex and violence, colour and pageantry, brutality and beauty, and most of all, action. All presented in the guise of a game, of good humour and sportsmanship. Gopal came away shaken, as though he had seen an ugly side of the soul of this vast and awesome land.

The first thing that struck him was the sheer wrongness of it all. How typically American, he thought, to call a game football when it had very little to do with the foot and nothing at all to do with a ball. The object in question here was more like a dinosaur's egg and its parents seemed to have emerged from their pens to fight over its possession with a truly maternal fury.

It was a breathtakingly lovely day for him to begin to discover the dark side of the dream. An afternoon in autumn, when the trees looked like an artist's palette and the wind stung the girls' faces into a rosy flawless strawberry flush.

The young people arrived like banners, in streams of colours, dressed in regulation jeans and jackets of dazzling hues. The flags erected themselves straight in salute as the stadium filled and a hubbub stormed across the stands. Gopal and Randy sat in one of the middle rows on the side. The ball – though nowhere else in the world would it be called that, since a ball is by definition a sphere, a round object – had already been placed in the middle. But Gopal, brooding on this impossibly wrong definition, decided he wasn't really so surprised, since he had recently discovered two astounding facts: one, that while all America celebrated the 'discovery' of America by Columbus, the land appeared to have been previously discovered by at least a dozen other prior visitors, among them several hundred thousand Indians who had been peacefully inhabiting it for a few thousand years. Second, that while Christopher Columbus was universally revered – or reviled as the case may be – for his discovery of the country, America itself was named in what must surely be the most historically severe case of ingratitude, after one Amerigo Vespucci. Mr Vespucci, from what a totally mystified Gopal could gather, had had absolutely nothing to do with America. In the face of such historic misnaming, he concluded, what was a mere ball?

A roar from the crowd, like a pride of lions spotting the arrival of its lunch, announced the team and Gopal settled into his bench. In trotted a line of young ladies who seemed to have mislaid their clothing on this cold and windy day and who were therefore attired in their underwear.

To Gopal's total and helpless mystification, they began to perform vigorous exercises alternating with violent orgiastic motions. To this they added cries of ecstasy which faintly reached Gopal. Not really believing his eyes, he carefully looked around, fully prepared to witness a veritable hailstorm of trousers being shed as the males in the audience responded to the unmistakable invitation extended by the undressed lovelies below, as they prepared to descend for what, Gopal feared, would be a gang bang unmatched since Cleopatra. In a way, he felt sorry for the girls could be said to have been asking for the affections of some 10,000 males simultaneously.

To his added sense of bewilderment, the men around him were totally unmoved. Some chatted, others gesticulated for the beer seller, a few gazed vacantly; none seemed gripped by the emotions that possessed Gopal. Maybe, he thought wildly, they are actually a nation of impotents and that is why they are having so many sexy advertisements everywhere.

Before he could subtly question Randy on this delicate subject, the stadium rose to its feet and two lines of astronauts ran on to the field. And then followed a succession of tableaux that completed Gopal's sense of total bafflement. Sometimes two of the astronauts mated in positions made familiar by porno films, at other times they grappled like amorous gorillas, sometimes there were moments of cultural refinement when they huddled together discussing this and that. But most of the time, he noted with alarm, they merely bashed each other enthusiastically. Even when the ball – he winced at the term – was nowhere near the vast majority of them, they fell upon each other to wreak a mayhem that would have been fearful if it hadn't been so cheerful.

'Hit 'im again,' the crowd howled around him and Gopal cowered, never having seen or heard anything like this before.

After a while, when either the game was over or no one was left alive to carry on any further, they trooped out. 'Don't,' Gopal asked, shaken and tentative, 'they hurting each other?'

'Nah,' reassured Randy. 'It's just a game.'

What, wondered Gopal, quivering, are they like then when they fight each other?

It was dark when they went outside, Gopal noticed with a shock. So absorbed had he been in the gladiatorial spectacle that he hadn't noticed the lights being switched on. But as they stepped out the night was a soft blue. They had been among the last to leave the stadium as Gopal had tried to gather his shattered senses.

'Something else, huh?' grinned Randy sympathetically, sensing his state of shock.

The cars had left, the dueling headlights had finished their jousting. At that point it seemed to Gopal that Americans spent all their waking moments locked in some form of vicious battle – and the parking lot was nearly deserted. A few last cars screeched out, the youthful drivers departing with some kind of obligatory yell.

'You want to go down and get some chow?' asked Randy, somehow feeling a little abashed.

'No, I am going home.'

So they went back, Gopal getting off at the apartment and turning to wave goodbye to Randy. He climbed up the stairs, intent on the sheer, staggering spectacle he had just witnessed.

He was fumbling with the lock when he smelt the liquor before he heard anything.

He turned quickly and saw the huge flowered dress moving towards him. He tensed instinctively.

'Hi,' said the voice, and for once it wasn't shrill.

He hesitated with the lock pretending it wasn't opening, but light showed through. Reluctantly he swung the door open and Gloria waddled in.

'Don't put on the light,' she whispered urgently, sinking into the couch. 'Come here, sit beside me. Please,' she pleaded.

Cautiously Gopal sat down at the far end.

'Come closer. Please. That's all I ask. I won't hurt you.' Her voice was soft and vulnerable in the half light. Gopal couldn't see her face, just her enormous, gross body in its cheap flowered print.

'I know I'm just a fat old broad,' he heard the tears wet her voice, 'but I got a heart too.' Her voice cracked and he could almost see the tears streaming down like rivulets. 'I don't want nothin from no one,' the jagged whisper continued, 'just a friend to listen to me. I ain't got no one. No one at all. Please. Please just listen to me.'

In the dark Gopal heard the wretched misery in the voice and it was as though the image she presented to the world was a mirror and it was cracking in front of his eyes and he could hear the glass break in her voice, falling underfoot as the world walked over it.

Suddenly she got up with a speed faster than he had ever seen from her, shuffled rapidly to the door and was gone in a blast of cold air as the door opened and shut. He heard her thumping down the stairs.

Slowly Gopal went to bed, his head whirling with bits of blood and girls and crowds. And crying voices in a dark room. And girls in their underwear flaunting themselves before heedless stadiums. Girls, he sighed to himself as he turned and drifted off to sleep. Why there is no escape from them in this country?

The next morning Randy hurled Gopal's door open, holding a football in one hand. 'Hey semi-nigger,' he yelled. 'Where're you?'

'Have to wash clothes,' yelled back Gopal from the bathroom.

'Well hurry up. I've got a football. Let's go throw some. I mean it's my duty to teach some poor ignorant heathen like you the finer points of life in Yankee Doodle land. Can't have you going back to your ungodly village believing all Yanks are apes who bash each other – even if it's true.'

'Will take some time.'

'What the hell for? Come on.' Randy cautiously pushed the bathroom door open. Gopal was sitting on the edge of the bathtub, a bucket at his feet half filled with clothes and water, vigorously rubbing a soapy shirt.

'What the shit is this?' asked Randy in amazement.

Gopal gave him a cold look. 'You don't wash clothes? I am not at all surprised.'

Randy began to chortle. 'C'mon you ass, lemme show you the laundry.'

He brushed aside Gopal's protests, picked up the bucket and marched out.

'You are laughing like hen,' reprimanded Gopal severely.

They went down the stairs to the far end of the building, opened a door and walked down into the basement. There Randy patted the first one of the two rows of gleaming white machines. 'This,' he announced, 'is what separates us from the Commies. You open the lid thusly, thrust in the clothes in a smooth yet efficient motion, seize some washing powder left behind like so, sprinkle it liberally, shut the lid with finality, put in 50 cents and voila, as they say in Gay Paree, home of the blow job.'

The machine began to gurgle.

'It is doing something,' admitted Gopal, apprehensive but appreciative.

'Now we wait for half an hour or so. You goof, you mean these last few weeks you've been washing your clothes in the tub?'

Gopal nodded, embarrassed. 'Anyway,' he said quickly, changing the subject, 'let us watch some film.' He gestured to one of the many, large, curiously round shaped TV screens lining the walls. No doubt, he thought, they are meant to keep the notoriously restless Yanks entertained for a full half hour as they waited for their clothes to be washed.

Randy collapsed over a machine. My machine, thought Gopal jealously. Randy beat his fists on the white metal. 'I love it,' he gasped. 'Oh boy, you think this is TV! Oh God, is this weird. Gopal, I'm going to make my million today. I'm going to cut you into little pieces and sell you in cans as the funniest thing alive. Oh, wow. This,' he gasped, 'you ignorant mathematical genius, is a humble dryer. After your clothes are washed, you hurl them in there, put in a coin, turn it on and out they come, soft as your girlfriend's ass. How 'bout that. No wonder we're beating the Commies everywhere.'

'Actually,' said Gopal, seizing the opportunity to escape from his mortification, 'you are losing everywhere.'

'Oh, yeah,' flared Randy, 'well, let me tell you Mr Big Shot From India – hmm,' he acknowledged, accepting the feint. 'Not bad Kumar, not bad at all. Maybe we'll increase aid to India this year after all.'

'You are not,' blared Gopal, his voice rising, 'giving us much aid. It is mostly trade.'

'Well,' said Randy with a small smile of satisfaction, 'what say we go throw the ball a bit while we wait for your clothes?'

Later that afternoon, Randy called Gopal on the phone that had been installed the previous day in Gopal's apartment. The instrument had arrived the day after Randy ordered the phone and Gopal watched disbelievingly as the uniformed man quickly plugged in the pastel box. He attempted to bribe the technician purely out of a habit ingrained from years of regarding the installation of a phone as a joyous occasion second only to a birth. The man thought he was offering a tip and refused. 'I get a salary,' he explained. As he was leaving, he thought, nice guy. Gopal watched him go down the stairs. Strange fellow, he mused.

And now he was startled as the phone whirred politely, somewhat different from the sound of metallic drills that emanated from Indian phones. 'Congrats,' yelled Randy, 'are you knee deep in blood?'

Gopal had learned to wait patiently for Randy to translate his mystifying Americanisms into normal English.

'I mean,' gargled Randy, suffocating at his own wit, 'it's the end of your phone's virginity. So about blood, what I mean is …'

'Yes yes,' hastily interrupted Gopal, 'I am knowing about all that.'

'Well,' said Randy, disappointed at being so rudely interrupted, 'I called because now that you've been introduced to the mysteries of washing machines, you may be ready for a real live American Friday night party. Put on your glad rags. Be ready by eight. I'll come fetch you. That is of course if you're not completely booked for tonight. I mean Meryl Streep hasn't been calling and bothering you, has she?'

'No no,' mumbled Gopal. 'I have to study. I do not know them. Whose party it is?'

'Who cares, I'll be there at eight. Bye.'

'But you know, things like that and all that,' weakly protested Gopal to the burring phone.

He was ready at eight, having polished his shoes twice, worn his new Sears Roebuck trousers and coat and oiled his hair lavishly. He had even broken open the packaging and worn his brand new underwear for reasons he dared not contemplate. He had shaved, showered, put on his aftershave and now he waited patiently. A car horn played a tattoo downstairs and Gopal took a deep breath, got up, walked to the door, took a look around in case there was anything left to detain him, and stepped out into the wind.

The party was at an old, double-storeyed wooden house and from the lights, music and crashes emerging, was already in high gear. 'Looks good,' rejoiced Randy. 'Looks real good. Gopal my man, tonight's the night. What say? I feel it. I hope you're in good working condition, because the women are going to leap on you the moment you walk through the door. I just know it.'

Partly as a result of this prophecy, by the time Randy walked through the porch to the front door and turned around, there was no sign of Gopal. Rapidly Randy raced completely around the house once looking for his missing friend. 'Gopal, you goon,' he screamed, 'come on out, you goddam foreigner.'

Silence.

'Oh all right,' yelled Randy. 'Come on in whenever you're sure Yanks don't eat Indians for dinner at parties.' He went inside.

Gopal peeped from behind a tree, feeling foolish, yet safe. He could look through a window and see all those healthy, scrubbed Americans laughing, talking, rapt in each other's company. They will not want me with them, he thought. Supposing he went in and an absolutely deafening silence fell over them? Supposing they just stared at him with looks of contempt? Supposing they forced the host to throw him out? Or worse still what if the girls actually jumped on him as Randy expected, and instead of being nice, they beat him?

He watched patiently from outside for a while until he saw a girl who seemed to have a kind face. For a moment she looked at the window and though he know she couldn't see him in the darkness outside, he felt that she had smiled in a sympathetic way to him personally. Perhaps what he should do is to rush up quickly to her and engage her immediately in conversation so that maybe she would protect him. Just then he saw Randy appear and say something and it seemed to Gopal that they all turned to look at him through the window as they roared with laughter.

This clinched it. Clearly Randy had dragged him into this trap where all the Americans would form a circle around him and laugh at him all night, the girls loudest of all. Supposing they came racing out just now and jumped on him and – you are being donkey, he reprimanded himself roughly.

He shook himself, trying to remove his fears. His heart slowed its racing. His brand new underwear began to itch. Hesitantly he pushed away from the tree and shuffled his way forward. He was sweating despite the cold. Just before he reached the porch his nerve broke and he scuttled urgently to the rear of the house. There he cautiously made his way up some stairs and slipped into the kitchen.

'Hi,' said a startled voice.

Gopal was equally shocked, but recovered on seeing the girl with the kind face. He dug his hands into his overcoat and beamed awkwardly at her. 'I am friend of Randy,' he explained in a rush in case she was planning to throw him out.

'Well, we all have our albatrosses,' she laughed and he noted with pleasure that she had a kind laugh.

'I am sure,' he blurted, 'that you are having kind walk also. I feel you are kind person.'

'What?' she said, slightly alarmed. 'Well, never mind. Welcome. You must be Randy's friend from India.'

Gopal bobbed his head so vigorously that his eyes shut. When they opened again she had her hand out in front of him and was waiting patiently. Hastily he tried to bring his hand out of his pocket where he found it had got entangled in his wallet which he had been squeezing furiously. He jerked his hand out desperately and part of his wallet's contents came spraying out too.

'Oops,' she said and began helping him gather the coins, papers and notes.

'I am not always doing this,' apologised Gopal, bumping into her as they chased around the floor on their hands and knees.

'Oh that's okay,' she consoled, 'I'm a klutz too. C'mon, let's go in and meet everybody else. What'll you have to drink?'

'Coke.'

'One Coke coming up. And away we go.'

'I will go in later,' mumbled Gopal. 'I am little busy now.'

'Right,' she agreed. 'I can see that. Okay have it your way.' She gave Gopal what he thought was the friendliest and most sympathetic smile he'd seen all his life and away she went. Gopal leaned back against the sink and wondered miserably how he could get back home to his apartment.

He yearned for his little apartment with its flat green carpet and the fridge that made funny noises regularly but which he'd got so used to that he looked up if it didn't hiccup on schedule. And of course he wouldn't mind going and spending some time with the washing machines and dryers and absorbing their mysteries. He wondered if there was a way in which he could keep his self-respect and yet ask Randy if he could show him how the dishwasher worked.

Of course he knew about dishwashers. And had been told repeatedly by his mother of their magical abilities. In fact, she had given him to understand that if there was some way in which he could bring one back, she might well regard herself as repaid for the twenty years she had spent in selflessly bringing up an ingrate like him. Of course if bringing one back proved impossible, she had sighed, she would quite understand. After all her heart would get repaired in due course, perhaps in an incarnation or two, her silence had implied.

Gopal decided he didn't know anyone who had silences as eloquent as his mother's. Somehow she made the air crackle with her vibrations with the grand eloquence of a Shakespeare without uttering a word. And what, he thought in sudden fury, she is going to do with damn dishwasher with four servants in house to do cooking and cleaning? Maybe, he thought satirically, she will put it in living room. He chuckled. A moment's thought however revealed that this was exactly what she probably would do with it, since she wouldn't want any of her friends to miss seeing it, particularly Mrs Saxena who was both her best friend and worst enemy and whose son had gone to England to study, which was only half as far as America from India and which therefore, one of her silences hinted, meant that his education was only going to be half as good as Gopal's.

However the specifics of making a dishwasher – the Taj Mahal of mechanical gadgets as far as Gopal's mother was concerned – actually perform, remained suffused with mystery for Gopal. There were all sorts of interesting knobs and switches on the one in his kitchen which he would have loved to turn on and off and experiment with, if it wasn't for a lurking fear that he might electrocute himself or blow out the power supply of all of Eversville, or both.

In any case, concluded Gopal reluctantly, not only did he not know how to run a dishwasher, but he was using it as an excuse to not go in and meet all the people in the next room. Anger rose in him and before he could change his mind he rushed through the door with his chin high, his chest out, his Coke clutched before him like a shield, ready to brave the storm of ridicule and derision the Americans were waiting to fling on him.

Nobody even noticed his grand entrance. A few people smiled in greeting in the midst of their conversation. The others chattered away. Randy was letting a girl feel his biceps in the corner, the kind-looking girl waved at him, but overall the universe didn't alter its course a fraction. Quickly Gopal stepped behind a rocking chair to recover from this wholly unexpected reception and plan his next move.

While he was considering his options, a female voice spoke behind him: 'Hi, I'm Ann. I know who you are.'

Gopal turned and looked at a rather large girl, dressed in an obviously expensive black dress, smiling at him pleasantly. She wore glasses and her skin seemed rough.

'Myself is Gopal,' he bashfully muttered.

'Yes I know. Randy's told me all about you. Hey, let's go sit down or something, my feet're killing me.'

They found a couple of cushions propped in a corner and sank down. Gopal recognised the colourful cushion material. 'Indian cloth,' he informed her with pride.

'Is that right? Oh gee that's neat. You mean you can just take one look and tell if it's Indian? Boy that's real neat. I wish I could do that. Oh I wish I'd been to college,' she wailed comically, 'I'm just a dumbo.'

'What you are doing?'

'Oh I'm just a hairdresser. Know what that is? Fixin hair and stuff? No big deal, but it's good money and I got me a Corvette. Brand new too. Are there hair dressers in India?'

'Yes, yes,' Gopal assured her, 'we are having many. In fact,' he modestly admitted, 'our company is supplying hair oil to many of them.'

'Oh gee, yeah,' she gushed, impressed. 'You own a factory that makes that stuff, don't you? Gosh, we're so backward here in America, we don't make no hair oil at all. How d'you make it? I mean is it like grown on trees and stuff?'

Gopal began to get intense about the subject. He was in his element. Hair oil was a subject he lived, breathed – and if truth be told – smelt strongly of, and he could do a great deal to educate this nice young lady on its fascinating history and mysteries. He launched forth.

When he stopped for breath fifteen minutes later her eyes were shining. Gopal suddenly realised he had never seen such huge eyelashes on anyone before.

'Wow,' said Ann, 'that was real neat. I mean you really care about the stuff, dontcha? And I just love the way you talk, all serious and all. Talk some more to me. No one ever talks seriously to me.'

Not believing his luck, Gopal obliged. Ten minutes later, he paused for a sip of his Coke.

'Boy,' said a radiant Ann, 'you talk like a real diplomat, dontcha?'

'Well, heh, heh,' modestly acknowledged Gopal, not quite sure of how diplomats talked, 'things like that and all that.'

'And you really like to talk to me, dontcha? I mean all that passion comin out and stuff. It was great. Hey, tell me,' she asked, putting her hand on Gopal's knee, 'how long've you been here in the States?'

'Well, three weeks.'

'Only three weeks? And already you speak such great English? Boy, wait'll my friends get a load of you. Hey, I gotta tell you,

I like you. I think you've got kind of a neat name too. Isn't that where all that gas came out and people died and stuff?'

Gopal looked flabbergasted until understanding dawned. 'No no, that is Bhopal. I am Gopal.'

Ann looked puzzled. 'So what's the difference? Hell anyway, I think it's all kind of neat and stuff. Hey listen, you want to go up and dance and you know, get down. Know what I mean?' Her hand rose above his knee and settled on his thigh. Gopal, not sure if all this was real, didn't breathe. He just nodded. It didn't even occur to him to tell her that he had never danced in his life and his only experience came from watching Hindi films and *Saturday Night Fever*. But clearly, he sensed, good things were coming his way and perhaps, he dared to fantasise, even his new underwear at some point in the evening might be exposed to public display in order to impress his audience and drive them wild with unthinking desire into that last bit over the edge.

'Well, let's go,' said Ann and taking his hand – as Gopal's heart sought to leap out of its cage – she began to lead him towards the staircase. Gopal's entire existence was focused on those few inches where her hand met his. How soft it was. How nice it smelled even at a distance. Could he dare to sneakily grab more of her hand? How white it looked compared to his brown and veiny paw? What did she mean by holding his hand? Good heavens, was she lacing her fingers with his? Just then Randy caught up with them.

'Hey kids,' he lurched into both of them, spewing liquor fumes and the contents of his wine glass, 'having fun?'

Gopal, his intense meditations broken, snarled at him as they began to climb the stairs.

'Oh wow,' said Randy, covering his eyes and recoiling from the glimpse of fang and fury, 'what happened to my docile friend from India? Hey,' he screamed up at their disappearing fee, 'women'll do that to you everytime. I'm telling ya!' He staggered away muttering to himself.

Upstairs the music was much louder. They opened the first door trying to find the right room and caught a glimpse of two people before Ann hastily shut the door. 'Oops,' she giggled, 'wrong room, wrong people.'

'Yeah,' shrugged Gopal with nonchalant coolness. 'Deep throat.'

They opened the next door and the music pounced on them like a black cat that had been coiled to leap. They walked inside and in the darkness there was only the green of the lights of the music system. The air beat to the rhythm of the music. Ann slipped Gopal's hand and he sensed rather than saw her begin to undulate to the music. For a moment Gopal stood absolutely still, his eyes straining, but he could see nothing. He relaxed and since no one could see him, he began to clumsily dance.

He wasn't, he acknowledged, any good at it. He was merely moving without being in time with the music. His arms and legs never quite seemed to be where he wanted them to be at approximately the same time, and his head seemed to have been stuffed with cement, going by its refusal to move. Still, he hadn't maimed anyone and since no one could see him he could dance all he wanted. He increased his velocity and experimented with sticking his arm in the air like the man in *Saturday Night Fever.*

Gopal could scarcely believe it. What a good time he was having. What a story to tell his friends when he got home. They would have had dinner and would be strolling down the moonlit street towards the railway station where all the young men around town congregated to watch the trains go in and out. And he would tell them about this lovely girl – well, they wouldn't know the difference in any case, and how she had grabbed his leg – he would show them the spot, a pity he couldn't brand her fingerprints on it as proof, then taken him by the hand and dragged him into a dark room to dance. And how, brothers, he had danced like a demon, like John Travolta himself. And then, his friends would feverishly ask, 'What then?' Well, he would modestly turn away, what could he say? He was a gentleman after all.

And truth to tell, while dancing with increasing abandon, she had begun to bump into him repeatedly. Except on the last bump she hadn't bounced away. Now she was disturbingly close and Gopal was starting to feel distinctly uneasy. It was one thing to take pleasure in what he would tell his friends at home, quite another to have a woman he had never met before wafting powder and perfume up his nostril. 'Let us,' he blared abruptly in her ear, 'go'. And to her astonishment, he was gone.

4

Beloved Brother,

How I am to tell you of what all things are happening and how I am avoiding pitfalls and keeping Nation's flag flying.

I am going to first party and I think it is full of divorcees who are waiting for me with pitfalls. But, brother, I am saying clearly that due to India's glorious heritage and things like that I am not indulging. I am thinking they are very impressed due to high morals I am upholding on behalf of Nation.

What all to say, brother. This is not new country, it is new world. They are playing game which they are calling football in which they are beating each other without mercies for no reason. But now I am feeling that they should do more beating because if they are beating each other then at least they are not beating rest of world.

I am now feeling I am on top of situations and ridin it good. Now I have been to American party also and behaving with credits I feel I am knowing many all things now.

You are also kindly not worrying about blood pressure problems because I am finding 'take it easy' is only American for goodbye. I am not knowing why they cannot speak like others in world.

Also, brother, you are not telling Mother, but they are having machines here that are cleaning clothes and drying in jiffy. I am knowing about all things now and handling with mastery. My clothes are washing whitest and finger lickin good.

But they are still not having proper servants to clean house and bathroom and I am having to do. Anyway what to do but at least my new television is coming yesterday which I am buying from Safeway. I wish I am knowing earlier that they are my friends right down the street so that I can ask for discount otherwise how they are my friends?

With respects to Respecting Parents,

Hoping you are taking it easy,

Your brother,
Gopal.

Gopal pressed the buttons on his phone and listened with pleasure to their musical response to each jab. Once he found a toll free number in a newspaper advertisement and called it just so that he could have more numbers to jab and more musical notes to listen to. The lady he called, however, was not very pleasant when he attempted to haggle further on the already rock-bottom rate their airline was offering on flights to Alaska and hung up on him. In case she had accepted, Gopal had absolutely no idea what he would have done with a ticket to Alaska, but he had taken the precaution of giving Randy's name and address instead of his own in any case. He was confident Randy could have told them what to do with their ticket to Alaska.

Now he phoned Randy who answered sleepily.

'Hello, hello,' said Gopal. 'You are wanting to come over? I am,' he added importantly, 'putting on television.'

'Why,' asked Randy hoarsely, 'what's on?'

'Television,' answered Gopal in surprise.

'Of course, how stupid of me. Aren't Indian TV shows any good or don't you have TV at all in India?'

'Of course we are having,' roared Gopal with a volume that swept the sleep out of Randy's head.

'All right, all right,' he hastily placated. 'Jesus, you're touchy, aren't you? What d'you want to watch?'

'Advertisements.'

'What? Commercials?'

'Yes.'

'What about the shows?'

'Maybe between ads.'

'Shit, why?'

'More interesting. Shows useless.'

'God, how the corporations would love you. You must think I'm crazy if you think I'm going to sit in front of your new TV set and watch commercials all day. Anyway, I forgot to ask, how'd you like the party night before last?'

'Very nice, very cultured.'

'No shit? What happened?'

'I am dancing.'

'Yeah, like Baryshnikov maybe?'

'No, no, like Travolta.'

'Good for you. How'd you get home? Ann drop you?'

'No,' said Gopal surprised, 'you are.'

'Did I? God I was so wrecked I can hardly remember. How'd you like Ann? You jump on her bones?'

'She is very cultured lady.'

'Ann?'

'Yes.'

'Wow. Listen, I've got to tell you a couple of things about her. If you can tear yourself away from the TV commercials, why don't we meet at the cafeteria for lunch? Huh? Half an hour?'

'All right,' agreed Gopal reluctantly, resentful of the sacrifice involved in missing the commercials. Gopal arrived late at the cafeteria, having been held enthralled by the newest McDonald's advertisement which he had found twice in succession after desperately changing channels. Randy was waiting patiently, still undecided about how to break the news to Gopal that his cultured ladyfriend was legendary in Eversville for her proclaimed ambition of sleeping with one thousand different men. In a span of less than three years, she had, through a wholly admirable perseverance combined with a nearly total lack of quality control, nearly reached her goal. She had only one left to reach the magic figure and she was determined to achieve this through the services of a virgin male so that her odyssey ended, as she put it to Randy, 'with a bang.'

However, a virgin American male above the age when the law, Ann indignantly felt, took an excessive and unseemly interest in his private life, was hard to find. So when Randy had informed her at the party that her quest was over, she had not hesitated a moment before hastening over to Gopal to engage him in conversation.

Matters had progressed so well that she was congratulating herself on the dance floor on the imminent consummation of her dream the moment she got Gopal into the next room, when to her total bafflement he had departed.

When Gopal arrived at the cafeteria, Randy was ready to tell him the entire thrilling story, but Gopal blurted out, 'Ann is just calling.'

Randy thought a while. Clearly, Ann's goal had not been reached on Friday night.

'What,' asked Gopal, 'you are wanting to say about her?'

'Nothing much. What did she call about.'

'She is wanting to apply to some college, so she is wanting to get some help in learning maths.'

'I bet she is,' agreed Randy cordially. 'When's she coming for this maths lesson.'

'Afternoon today.'

'It should be interesting to see which of the two of you learns more. You sure you won't have some meat? You're going to need all your strength.'

After lunch Randy solicitously drove Gopal back, dropping him off with what Gopal thought was a peculiarly ceremonious farewell. He is nice boy but bit strange sometimes, thought Gopal going up the stairs.

After half an hour there was a knock on the door and Gopal opened it to find Ann.

'Hi,' she greeted with a warm charm that delighted Gopal. He had not been blind to the splendid opportunities her arrival would present, if only, he thought longingly, she could be impressed by him. The first thing he had done was to dig out from his suitcase the certificate he had received from the National Hair Oil Dealers Association and prop it prominently on the little table where they were to study. He thought deeply on any other item he could use as part of his long-term strategy of so totally impressing her, that within a few months she would fall prey to his dark desires. He could think of nothing and concluded that he'd have to try and swing it through sheer charm.

As she sat at the small round table, prattling merrily, Gopal examined her closely in the daylight and gloried in her eyelashes that projected from her eyelids like the fans Japanese women use to hide their faces. When she blinked them too rapidly, flakes of powder drifted from her face. Her hair had the colour, sheen and texture of gold. It rose with the rigidity of a Gibraltar in an Elvis Presley-like puff over her forehead. The frozen yellow contrasted with her jet-black eyebrows, but Gopal thought it made a charming combination. Her perfume, or perhaps more accurately her perfumes, would have caused him anxiety about his asthma, if he hadn't been so excited.

'Gosh, it's hot,' she protested, 'shouldn't I take off my coat?'

Gopal leapt to carry it away and put it on the sofa. When he turned she was fanning herself while standing in a red mini-dress that ended, Gopal swallowed, an inch below her panties.

'Well,' she said walking purposefully to the sofa and sitting down, 'this looks a lot more comfortable, doesn't it?'

Hastily Gopal gathered his books as well as his certificate and deposited them on the floor near her feet.

'We are starting,' he informed her in a voice over which he was only starting to reassert his authority.

'I certainly hope so,' she smiled fluttering her Japanese fan eyelashes on which Gopal thought he saw projected various appetising though probably illegal acts.

Gopal commenced with his normal sincerity. Some ten minutes later, though personally rapt in his exposition of the delights of integral calculus, he was forced to admit that his audience's attention seemed to have wavered. She was in fact proceeding to slip slowly but inexorably down the sofa, much like the Titanic in its final act, before gently and firmly settling full length, her legs resting on Gopal. Her dress hiked up even further and from this proximity Gopal could hardly fail to notice a blue, strategically placed heart on her underwear.

Seeing her lying thus, Gopal considered the possibilities and came to the inevitable conclusion. 'You are sick?' he asked.

She looked at him through half open eyes whose expression – perhaps fortunately for him – he couldn't read. She nodded slightly.

'I am getting water for you?' asked Gopal anxious to ingratiate himself with her when she was in such need, perhaps to be exploited with delightful consequences later.

She shook her head rather rapidly.

'Then what is happening?' asked Gopal, discouraged by her rejection of his subtle, though long-term pass.

'My body hurts,' she whispered. 'I think I've sprained my back and leg muscles.'

'How?'

'Playing tennis, I think.'

'You are needing massage I feel.'

'Yes,' she agreed, cheering visibly.

'I will do,' assured Gopal enthusiastically. 'I am giving massage to grandmother's legs at home. You may kindly turn around.'

Sitting astride her feet, he began to chop and pummel her legs and back while severely ignoring those portions of her contained in lamentably ill-fitting underwear. How they would later laugh together, he told himself, when he had finally in the next few months conquered all her defences through persistence and cunning. He could then remind her of this occasion. How easily someone less strategic minded than he could have misunderstood and made a hasty move that would have crushed the fragile blossom of their friendship. How impressed she would be – but laughing all the same no doubt – at his self-control and guile.

After about fifteen minutes she suddenly flipped around. Once again Gopal found himself looking at the blue heart from close quarters and once again he felt as though his heart was sinking like an anchor rattling down with its chain, fathoms deep.

'You through messin around?' asked Ann in a hard voice.

Gopal, who had been mesmerised by the heart, guiltily jerked away. He groped within himself for his voice which apparently had gone down with all hands along with his heart, and salvaged bits and pieces of it at a time.

'Oh yes, yes, yes. Mathematics and all that. You are feeling well? Have Coke. You will feel much better. I am getting.' He jumped off the sofa and scuttled with considerable discomfort to the kitchen galley where he could obtain a Coke and repair himself.

When Gopal returned bearing the Coke like a peace offering, Ann was sitting primly upright. 'I think,' she said accusingly, 'you were going to try something funny, weren't you?' Ignoring Gopal's protestations she went on savagely, 'Oh yes, I know all about you foreign students, don't think I don't. I mean I've really got your number, haven't I? Admit it. You were up to some stuff, weren't you?' Gopal had flushed and his mouth had gone dry. 'Look, Gopal,' she said patiently, 'I know there's a lot of difference between us, I mean we do things different here in America. I mean it might be okay in India with all your harems and stuff, but a girl's got to be really careful here of her reputation, know what I mean? I mean one wrong move and a girl's reputation is gone, just like that. I mean it's weird the kind of things people will say about a girl and there's not a damn thing you can do, not one goddam thing. Well hey, I gotta run. I'll check you out later. Take care now.' And to his amazement she came and kissed him on the cheek before leaving. He could have sworn her eyes were wet.

Gopal sat anxiously on the sofa, worried. Supposing she had a big tough brother and she went weeping to him? Supposing he arrived with ten large friends carrying iron chains? Supposing she went to the newspapers and complained that he had tried to loot her virtue? What if the Dean and the professors arrived in a group waving the newspaper? What if someone sent it to his parents? What if the immigration people were on their way right now, racing madly in their cars, desperate to get their hands on him and fling him out of the country?

Realising that this was unlikely, but concerned all the same, he decided to go to the cafeteria where at least he would hear any rumours of savage immigration raids in the neighbourhood. Gopal walked gloomily into the cafeteria. At the door he met Fred, a friend of Randy's he had met on the first day at breakfast. 'How's it going?' greeted Fred. 'You look like you've got the burden of feeding all of India's starving millions on your shoulders. What's the problem, pal?'

'I am meeting bad people.'

'Ah bad people, eh?' said Fred, eyeing him shrewdly. 'What kind of bad people? I mean are they from the college or what? Not drugs type bad people are they?'

'No, no,' hastily corrected Gopal. 'Brother of girl I know.'

'Ah,' said Fred in relief, 'those kind of bad people. Well, I think what you need is some protection around here. And I know just the man. Let't go meet him.'

Unsure but feeling better, Gopal followed him into the cafeteria. They walked to the far end, and standing there at the juke box was a man, the very sight of whom made Gopal feel better. He was black, about six and a half feet tall, and to Gopal appeared to be at least as broad. He wore green, white and red trousers, a purple shirt with yellow circles on it and gold chains that hung like wreaths around his neck. On his feet were white high-heeled boots, on his head was a kind of a cap with a long brim and on his face were mirrored sunglasses.

'This,' said Fred with some reverence, 'is the star of our football team and the guy who makes sure the campus stays clean. We call him the Peacock. And this is Gopal. He's one of our new foreign students and he's got a small problem he wants to talk to you about. Okay, I'll leave you two guys alone. See you later.'

The Peacock's sunglasses measured Gopal as though deciding whether his story was worth listening to. Finally he seemed to have approved of what he saw, because he regally gestured to Gopal to follow him and started a procession out of the building. Of course the procession was only an optical illusion, but it was a very real one, because the Peacock moved with such disdain that a retinue always seemed about to turn the corner behind him. His chains jangled so loudly, his colours clashed so vividly, that an entire entourage appeared to have collapsed into his person like a kaleidoscope.

He thumped a fist overhead with a passing associate who pleased him, ignored the sycophantic cries of greeting of scattered fans and sailed majestically like a technicoloured warship down the sidewalk. Even the wind seemed to avoid him respectfully since he wore no coat.

Gopal followed uneasily behind, wondering where they were headed. A few minutes later they arrived at a scattering of stores among which was a bar that announced itself with the words 'The Drink Tank.' The Peacock turned in here and Gopal timidly edged in behind him.

There was a strange fusion of golden lights interlaced with music, the clatter of glasses underlaid by the murmur of conversation, the clack of billiard balls being hit across dwarf-sized tables, racks of billiard balls being hit across dwarf-sized tables, racks of billiard cues against the wall and generally civilised faces all around. Gopal noted with relief several people he recognised from the college. There was a mumble of 'how you doins' as they went by and such was his sense of terror at his arrival into the house of sin that he nearly stopped to enlighten a few people, though he had learned that 'how you doin' really had no more meaning than 'drop dead.'

But the sheer force or the Peacock's presence dragged him along in his wake and he joined him in a booth in the corner. Gopal wondered what he would say if his mother smashed her way in just then. Would she believe that he had a good, non-alcoholic reason for being there? Could he tell her about Ann?

That would really clinch it for her. She would catch him by the ear and drag him out into the car park where a helicopter would be waiting and hit him on the head all the way back home to India and – he shook his head to clear it so that he could concentrate on the magnificent, mysterious and hitherto silent presence opposite him.

Gopal cleared his throat. 'You see, I am telling you frankly –'

The Peacock raised a hand the size of an oar to stop him. 'You buy me a beer,' he said in a high-pitched voice that seemed to be generated in his jaw rather than his lungs, 'and I'll lend you an ear.'

Gopal ordered a beer and a Coke and when that arrived summed up the entire situation to the Peacock with as much good taste as he could, while of course ensuring that the lady's fair reputation was not besmirched and the blame fell on his own animal passions. However, he concluded, the result of his indiscretion was that he now feared reprisals from the lady's relatives. Could the Peacock help protect him?

The Peacock's reflecting glasses, which had not been removed, glittered. 'I ain't no greedy,' he pronounced reasonably, 'but I sure am needy.'

This Gopal could understand. Whenever their factory in Jajau had experienced problems, small armies of bureaucrats had miraculously materialised and descended on it, all of them apparently needy too. He went into an instinctive whine about the poverty in India, the sacrifices his parents were making in sending him here, he even invented a sister who took in laundry to help pay his bills.

The Peacock's sunglasses remained impassive. 'No sheen, without green,' he announced with finality.

Gopal sought to interpret this and deduced correctly that the green referred to dollars. He thought with a fleeting bitterness of how completely in character it was for the Americans, when they finally had a phrase that was accurate and not misleading, to have it relating to money. Materialistic people, he thought with pitying sorrow. They are not having our superior spirituality.

He got down to the business of serious haggling.

After many minutes the Peacock's sunglasses remained like ice cubes. Gopal speculated if they had become such an integral part of him that they actually reflected whatever went on inside his head. He decided not to push his luck too far. He couldn't after all threaten to take his business to another shop. And in the absence of that ultimate threat, it was a seller's market. 'How much?' he finally asked in surrender.

The sunglasses glinted. 'When the time comes to roll, make sure you got the toll,' the Peacock intoned.

This, Gopal gathered, indicated that the costs would depend upon the services required. They shook hands on that and Gopal paid the bill and left.

It was dark outside and a thin drizzle fell. Gopal dug his hands into his pocket, put his head down and walked. He had found that he preferred the night. He enjoyed the anonymity it gave him, because during the day wherever he went, people looked at him twice. It wasn't usually a hostile look, merely a startled one. He wasn't white and he wasn't black, he was just a puzzling brown. Once a child had come up to him at a grocery store and swiped his little fingers across Gopal's arm to check if perhaps the brown colour was merely dirt that had congealed. Finding no dirt on his fingers, he trotted back puzzled to his mortified mother.

Gopal had never really thought of himself as being any particular colour while in India. Here it defined nearly every moment of his life. Nor was he used to receiving so much attention and he certainly didn't enjoy it, particularly because it arose from curiosity rather than approval. Yet he was helpless at blending with the others. Often when he walked into a room he felt that his skin had burst into flames. He actually sensed the glow of fire. It was as though so many glances locking on to him sparked a kind of spontaneous combustion. He sensed a few people shrink, others become too friendly, nobody was normal.

His entire life in India had become irrelevant and meant nothing. Not his own achievements, not his family's affluence, everything was beyond the curtain of mirrors with which America bounded itself. Nothing beyond mattered. Here he had to recreate himself, but the basic building block of his new persona was his colour. No matter what he achieved, or however respected he became in the classroom, the moment he stepped outside, his colour came and wrapped itself around him like a clown's clothes that had been hanging outside, waiting for him. In the classroom itself though he felt a sense of being de-coloured; the better he did, the less alien and awkward he felt. He revelled in the sense of attracting respect. But once outside, he constantly felt as though nature had constructed him badly.

But in the dark, his stride was less stilted, his posture less rigid. He felt he could flow with the wind. He walked past the wooden houses, wondering how anyone could feel a wooden edifice with all its signs of impermanence, to be a home. After all a home was a place where generations lived and grew and died. It needed bricks and concrete to withstand the generations. It was a form of forever. But a wooden house was such an insecure thing. It could collapse, or be eaten by insects, or become rotted by rains. Even vigorous visiting relatives and their broods could leave it in a shambles.

But the Americans seemed strangely content all the same. He could see them eating their bizzarely early dinners, cocooned in golden light. That was another feature of theirs. Golden light meant homes, bars intimacy. Tube lights, or any form of white light, was for classrooms, hospitals, large stores, anything public and impersonal. He couldn't recall seeing an exception.

The leaves rustled under him and he kept a wary eye out for dogs. He had already adjusted to the fact that Americans almost never walked anywhere; they either jogged or drove. Therefore their dogs seemed also to assume that anyone who was walking was definitely a burglar and needed to be discouraged.

Once again he noticed the strange baskets hung outside the houses which he had also noticed while driving to New York. Now he puzzled over whether they were one of those fads to which Americans suddenly and virulently became addicted. Someone in his class had once tried to explain to him the pleasure to be obtained from pet rocks and Gopal had been so baffled at trying to comprehend it that by mistake he had wandered into the ladies toilet. Fortunately, to his relief, not unmixed with some disappointment, it was unoccupied.

But nothing in his keen observations gave the slightest clue about those baskets. Perhaps, he speculated, it was a national conspiracy intended to mystify foreigners. They were quite capable of it. His own building lacked one, otherwise he could have hidden somewhere and seen what dreadful use it was put to.

By now he had turned into his complex and had begun to climb the stairs. For the first time since Gloria's nocturnal visit to him, her curtains were open. She sat at the window, slowly raised her hand and shyly wiggled her fingers. Gopal bobbed his head at her and walked up faster, persuading himself that it was because he didn't want to miss the TV commercials.

A few evenings later he was sitting in his apartment, studying and eating a pizza – he had discovered that it was possible to order pizza with exclusively vegetarian combinations, following which he hadn't touched cornflakes again – when the phone ventured its civilised buzz. It was Randy. 'Wanna go to a bar?' he asked.

Gopal felt that he really had to study. On the other hand he was extremely curious about what a real bar was like. 'The Drink Tank', he recognised, was just a college hang-out.

'No, no,' he demurred, nearly begging to be overruled, 'how I can?'

'Great,' said Randy who had clearly developed acute insights into Gopal's psyche, 'I'm on my way.'

Driving along in Randy's car, Gopal felt a sense of grand daring and inexpressible sophistication. 'What kind of bar this is?' he asked.

'Oh, no big deal,' said Randy. 'Just your basic drinks and dancing, you know.'

'Of course,' agreed Gopal importantly.

They drove through a part of town Gopal had never seen before and arrived at a horse-shoe shaped group of buildings, all ablaze with lights. 'Which one is bar?' asked Gopal as they parked in the middle of the U shape.

'Oh all of them. Let's take them one by one.'

They got out and started walking. There were lights blinking everywhere, though there didn't seem many people around. A strange smell of wet socks permeated the air. Randy barged his way through the first door and Gopal followed. He stopped abruptly at the total blackness. In the middle of the room was an empty, brightly-lit stage and it seemed to suck all the light through some gravitational force into itself. Gopal didn't move, afraid that he would bump into someone or something. He felt Randy's arm reach across his shoulders pulling him to one side. 'This way,' he guided. Cautiously they eased into a booth set alongside the wall.

Slowly Gopal's eyes adjusted and he realised the room wasn't as dark as he had thought. He made out the bar and various other tables and chairs scattered about. Randy went away and returned shortly with a pitcher of beer and a Coke.

Gopal waited impatiently for the singer to appear on stage. Suddenly, so abruptly that he started, the music began. In the darkness around the lighted stage, movements began as though something was gathering pieces of itself together preparatory to being born and the most beautiful girl Gopal had ever seen materialised, golden-skinned, blond-haired, like a naked angel. She danced as unselfconsciously as if she were at a party, but she wasn't wearing a scrap, except for a minute bikini pantie.

There was laughter somewhere and Gopal quickly looked down in case they were laughing at him. He refused to look up throughout that first number, though every nerve in his body was screaming at him to look. Never had he felt such a total sense of helplessness. Gone was his feeling of sophistication. He felt like a newborn gazing at a new universe.

When he did look up, it wasn't directly at the stage, but surreptitiously, to one side, then to the other trying to see if anyone was watching him. Nobody's eyes met his and cautiously Gopal began to look at that blazing fireball, not directly all at once, but little by little, like someone approaching a ticking bomb. Every time he looked up his eyes rested fractionally longer through narrowed slits, until taking courage with a deep breath, he defiantly opened his eyes wide and kept them focused on his first sight of a live naked woman.

She wasn't, he concluded many months later, a bad way to be introduced to the specie. She was tall, with no extra flesh and she moved with an eroticism that made him suddenly realise what dancing was meant to emulate. He couldn't begin to describe her different attributes, and whether they were good, bad or indifferent, since he couldn't see her in sections, but as one glittering, breathtaking, unique vision.

The music stopped and she stepped back into the void. Gopal burst into wild applause, positive that his approval would be drowned in the cheers of the multitude. At which point everyone in the room actually turned to look at him in surprise. Quickly he stopped and sank back into his seat, not even sure of when he had stood up.

He looked at Randy, excited yet drained, ready to leave since the show was clearly over. Obviously there couldn't be two different women in America, he felt, who would agree to appear naked on a stage surrounded by strange men. The music began again and another naked lady appeared, so apparently there actually were two such women. However Gopal averted his eyes from her. He felt that since he had given himself so completely to the first one, to look upon the new one would be a form of adultery. Besides which, his by now experienced eye told him, this one was shorter, squatter and less pretty.

Then his woman, as he had begun to think of her, appeared in the twilight in front of the stage. She had put on a loose red robe that was unbuttoned at the neck and her hair was now tied back in a ponytail, while on stage it had waved and tossed like a flag semaphoring a message of lust. Gopal willed her into coming to their table and she headed in their direction like a missile homing into a radar beam. Apparently his applause had not gone unrecognised.

'Why, hi there,' she said in pleasure and her voice made Gopal's head feel like a surf was roaring and dashing against it inside. 'You liked my dance, huh?' she put her hand under Gopal's chin and moved his head forward and back. 'My, but that's thirsty work,' she edged alongside Gopal on the couch and her thigh seared his leg like a delicious flame. 'You going to buy me a drink, honey? Huh? You going to buy both of us a lil drink?'

Oh yes, Gopal's head moved vigorously. As a matter of fact he was going to buy her the Empire State Building if she asked for it.

'A big drink, honey?' she wheedled. A hand pleaded with Gopal by pressing him high on the thigh. Gopal's eyes turned to glassy water. 'A real big lil drink for the two of us, huh? Hey Rosy,' she turned to another girl in a similar red robe carrying a tray, 'two big ones here.'

'He doesn't drink,' warned Randy.

'Aw, but for me he will, won't you, honey?' Her hand returned pleadingly to his thigh.

Oh yes, Gopal's head assured her, he certainly would drink. The entire Mississippi River if she so thought fit.

Hardly any time seemed to have passed, or perhaps it was her hand whose every motion seemed to make time disappear, but two very large and ornate urns were convoyed to them. They were green and over-wrought and filled with a fizzing substance. 'Champagne,' announced their bearer, 'fifty bucks.'

'Oh, love,' breathed the girl into Gopal's ear, her hands leaping up the last few inches from Gopal's thigh, 'make her go away. We got things to do together.'

With shaking hands Gopal paid up and turned breathing heavily to his friend. She took a sip of her urn. 'Mmm,' she said, 'wow. Be with you in a minute.' And she walked away.

'Gone to bathroom,' Gopal informed Randy. He waited patiently. He waited impatiently. When she reappeared she went and sat at another table and seemed to be having an animated discussion with the men there. Gopal gestured politely. He gestured violently. Then pleadingly. Despite his increasingly active importunings she remained where she was. She didn't even look at him.

Gopal glared at Randy who appeared to be meditating. 'We go,' he growled.

By the time they neared Gopal's apartment, his breathing had returned to normal and he was no longer grinding his teeth. 'Friday night,' he informed Randy, 'we go back.'

'Methinks I may have created a Frankenstein,' said Randy.

Friday night they were back. This time the parking lot was full and they could hear the music from outside. They went in and she was dancing again. Two men were getting up from a table set against the stage and Gopal determinedly strode to it and sat down. As Randy strolled up more leisurely, Gopal asked him, 'Got cigarette?'

Randy eyed him in surprise. 'Will impress her,' Gopal whispered to him jerking his head in the direction of the dancing girl. She saw Gopal, recognised him, gave a small nod and sank to her knees in front of him. With legs akimbo, she undulated forward and backward in time to the music, less than a foot from his face, till Gopal, transfixed, was beaded with sweat. The music ended. She got up, swivelled around and strode away with a last heart-stopping twitch, leaving Gopal with eyes staring and mouth agape.

She came around the stage a while later in her red robe. 'Still haven't had enough, huh?'

'I will only buy beer,' warned Gopal with finger raised. He stood up awkwardly. 'You can sit,' he offered with clumsy gallantry.

She smiled, her eyes bright with amusement. 'All right,' she accepted, dragging up a chair, 'let's hear your pitch.'

Gopal gave it his best. He spoke, he gestured, he drew charts on the table using the dew on the beer pitcher. She listened quietly throughout, her face wreathed in cigarette smoke, her eyes expressionlessly on his face, listening to the details of the mammoth and sustained programme that had made India one of the ten most industrialised countries in the world. Only when another girl walked by saying, 'you're on, Mary Ann,' did she stir.

She smiled into his eyes and he saw how blue they were. 'Far out,' she said. 'A guy who likes to talk to me.' She kissed her fingers and put them gently on his cheek.

When she appeared again on stage, she still wore her robe. She waited until Gopal had looked long at her, then dropped it from around her shoulders. Then she danced for him. Gopal was to see many many more naked women dance, but this was the only one he never forgot. She was nearly totally nude, but there was something oddly apologetic in the dance. Certainly she didn't dance as well as she had earlier, but that was perhaps because she didn't once remove her eyes from his. She moved for him, she swayed at him and she looked always deep into his eyes. And when the dance ended, Gopal stood up for once unembarrassed and clapped loud and long.

After that there were other dancers, other women; Mary Ann danced again too, but she didn't look at him. Finally, when all the women began to seem alike, they decided to leave. They stepped outside and the fresh air hurt their lungs till they adjusted to it.

'That was fun,' said Randy, lurching more than he strictly needed to. 'Boy, that was fun. Gopal, you god damned furriner, you're becoming American. I mean you can get a damn go-go whore to fall for you. Hoo, boy.'

They walked laughing into the parking lot, looking for Randy's car. They reached it and Randy began to search for his keys when he felt a powerful hand push him against the door and hold him there. He felt a knife prick his neck and a voice say: 'Don't even breathe, boy.'

At the same time Gopal turned and saw five men already in a semicircle around him. With the flashing lights in the background he could hardly see their faces, but from their checked shirts and caps he thought they looked like the kind of men he had seen driving pick-up trucks.

'Well, well, boys,' said the biggest of them. 'What've we got here?'

Gopal felt cold with fright and hot at the same time. 'What is it?' he tried to put some strength into his voice, but it sounded reedy even to him.

'Oh nothin, nothin, nothin at all,' said the biggest one. 'We jest don't like no Eye-ranians, is all.'

Gopal felt a spring of relief. 'I am Indian.'

'That's right. That's what I said. Get him, boys.'

Two of them grabbed Gopal's arms and pinned them to the car. Gopal smelt the alcohol on them. The big one leisurely strolled forward and Gopal's gut burned when he saw him opening a knife. 'I am Indian,' he gasped pleadingly.

The man was upon him, his face an inch from Gopal's. 'I jest don't like no Eye-ranians, boy. No furrin niggers neither. I jest don't like em. Comin in here, takin our jobs, takin our women. I jest don't like it, boy. Why don't you git back to your camel land while you can? Know what I mean? Know what I'm sayin you furrin fuckin filthy asshole?'

His knife had been busy below and as Gopal held his breath it cut away the front of his trousers completely. 'Well lookey here, boys, he's got a teeny weeny camel pleaser.'

The others guffawed. One of them came over and lifted Gopal's genitals with one finger while looking coldly and with utter contempt into his eyes. 'Ain't got much here,' he announced. 'Not even enough to please them goats, forgit them camels.'

The big one with the knife was moving in again. He will kill me, thought Gopal. Bizzarely, he suddenly thought, and I have never even kissed a girl.

The man's knife slid down again. Gopal gritted his teeth and looked straight ahead into the distance trying not to show fear. He felt snot flow down his nose. He read the flashing lights, hoping that if he concentrated on them he would feel the pain less when the animal stabbed him. 'Sin Land', read the largest of the lights. And underneath in a continuous chain running round like it was the news, ran a series, 'where the sin never sets, where the sin always shines, where every day is sin day,' Gopal wondered if that was going to be the last thing he was going to see on earth.

He was so frightened he couldn't feel the cold. His legs felt as though they were made of metal and bolted to the ground. He felt himself trembling but some reserves somewhere stopped him from pleading for his life. In his quivering brain he felt a thought rattle. 'If I am to die in this urine-smelling parking lot, it is my fate.' The thought gave him courage. He took a deep breath and gathered his voice which felt as if it had disintegrated and fallen in pieces into different extremities of his body. When he was sure he had collected it, he stoked it till it felt full size again. He had no idea how much time had passed, but the man was still looking with a mocking fury into his eyes and his knife was still lightly touching Gopal's naked groin.

Gopal released his voice cautiously. 'How much you want?' He was amazed at its quiet arrogance.

The man drew back his head and roared with laughter. His spittle, smelling like whisky, sprayed Gopal's face. 'I want to cut your thing off, that's what I want,' he jeered. 'Hey boys, d'you think the camels'll miss it?

The others sniggered.

Randy's muffled voice emerged unsteadily. 'Hey you guys, c'mon, the guy's not an Iranian. He's an Indian. You've had your fun, now give us a break. Okay?'

The man nodded slowly apparently in comprehension. Again Gopal felt a match of hope sputter in his chest. 'Don't know nothin about that,' he said, this time shaking his head, 'they's all Eye-ranians to me.'

A large group emerged from one of the bars and began laughing and whooping its way towards them.

'Hey,' said one of the men to the big one nervously, 'c'mon, stick im dead and let's get outta here. C'mon,' he urged frantically but greedily, 'make im bleed and let's go.'

From the other side suddenly a car turned in and for a moment its headlight outlined them clearly. The group heading towards them let out startled yells and began running forward.

'I'll git back to you later,' promised the big man to Gopal. Then he raced to their vehicle which was already moving and was helped to climb into the back. It was, Gopal noticed with a small, frozen hint of satisfaction, a pickup truck. It was gone in a blaze of red lights and shrieking tyres.

'You okay?' The first of the group reached Gopal. 'What the shit is going on? What happened here?'

There were startled cries from the other side of the car where Randy had been found slumped over the hood. 'He's hurt,' said one, 'someone call the cops.'

'I'm okay,' said Randy gathering himself. 'He cut me.'

By now more people had come pouring out and someone lifted Randy's shirt. 'I'm a medical student,' he announced, 'let's have some room here. It's not too bad,' he said, 'it's just a nick. What happened?'

A police car arrived with its maddening lights and a towel, of all things, materialised from somewhere in the crowd for Gopal to wrap around himself. Two ridiculously young police officers who had been speaking to some people in the crowd came politely forward. 'If you'll come this way, sir, I'll need a statement from you.'

Gopal was led trembling violently to the police car where he sat quietly, feeling not so much hurt as humiliated, while Randy recounted the story to the policemen, interspersed with contrite apologies to Gopal.

Slowly Gopal began to feel totally, paralysingly numb. He couldn't make out what was being said, he couldn't remember what had happened, he couldn't think of anything. He couldn't even feel himself shiver. In a trance he barely felt the car start off, stop, and Randy help him up the stairs to his bed. He felt as though his world had become a dark room with nothing except himself in it. No sounds reached in, no lights switched on, there was just him in the dark. He lay alone in this silent blackness and wondered why he hadn't seen Brooke Shields in New York. She must be bigger than in *Blue Lagoon*, he speculated. Then he fell asleep.

5

The next thing he felt was a hand gently shaking him. It
was Randy. 'Hey, wake up, Gopal,' he whispered gently,
'It's noon.'

Gopal stretched languorously and felt wonderful. He
wondered what Randy was doing here and decided to force
him to make himself useful. 'Tea, slave,' he ordered and was
alarmed to hear a familiar whiny laugh outside, followed by
Gloria's vast bulk tripping in carrying a tea tray.

Suddenly all the events of the previous night rose like
black vomit in him and he sat back against the headrest. Gloria
stopped uncertainly and Randy urged him on. 'C'mon, Gopal,
have your tea. The Dean's waiting outside.'

Started, Gopal pulled off the bedclothes and swung his legs
down. He found he was still wearing last night's torn trousers
and hastily got back and covered himself.

'I'll get him,' said Randy and a moment later the Dean
came in followed by two uniformed campus security men and
three other people who seemed to have no other purpose than
to look embarrassed.

'Gopal,' said the Dean setting himself on the edge of the
bed and shaking his hand, 'I can't tell you how sorry I am about
what happened. I can assure you the police will do all they can
to catch these people and I want you to know that –'

Gopal sat quietly and listened to it all. The memory of the events was like a stack of photographs kept face down in his mind and he could as yet only dare to carefully turn the corner of one or two and speculate on which image they contained.

'– and I hope you won't reconsider your decision to stay here at Eversville in the light of the unfortunate incident. I've asked Campus Security to post a man here and if there's anything I can do, anything at all, you just let me know. Now you take it easy for a while and when you're feeling better let's meet on this again and take it from there. Well, I've got to go now, but if there's anything I can do, just holler.'

His entourage followed him out. Randy came back. 'I've got to go home and change. See you soon.' From which Gopal guessed correctly that Randy had spent the night on his sofa.

'How you are feeling?' asked Gopal, touched. 'And your back?' he asked, suddenly remembering Randy had been hurt.

'Oh, that little thing,' dismissed Randy modestly. He flexed his biceps and posed. 'Nothing can harm the man of steel. By the way, have you ever wondered about Superman's sex life? I mean if you're the man of steel, then do women like it or not? I mean in my case of course they love it, but –'

'Out, out,' urged Gopal burrowing under the covers, and gathering it was business as usual.

When he re-emerged Randy was gone but Gloria had reappeared carrying a tray with his tea which she had gone to reheat. Gopal watched warily as she tiptoed towards him and ceremoniously deposited the tray on his lap before scampering out. On the tray was an envelope which he opened carefully.

'Dear Gopal,' it said in a child-like scrawl,

'Some Americans are bad,

And some are good and true,

But this one who likes you,

Is really all true blue.'

(I wrote this in creative inspiration when I learned what happened. I felt it in my soul.)

Gloria

This, thought Gopal sipping his tea, must be the same multitalented soul that burned holes in things. He wondered if it was a trick of the light, or his angle on the bed, or even the time of the morning, but the white roots of Gloria's solid black mass of hair seemed to have grown by several inches. He hurriedly slurped his tea and got out of bed since he had to decide whether he wanted to stay on in this country or get back home where it was duller but a lot safer.

He was wrestling with his dilemma when he walked out of the apartment and headed for the campus. By the time he reached the cafeteria he felt like a diabetic overdosing on sugar. News of his ordeal had obviously travelled fast and wherever he turned he encountered smiles – sympathetic smiles, encouraging smiles, guilty smiles, all sorts of smiles. He could have sworn he saw people race across the lawn just to have the pleasure of smiling at him. A man he was positive he had never clapped eyes on in his life slapped him warmly on the back, clicked his tongue in what he obviously regarded as the ultimate sign of friendship and said, 'Here's my main man.'

Outside the cafeteria door he saw a short, thin, long-haired and swarthy individual who could only be the other Indian on campus Gopal had been told about but had never met. He possessed a moustache like the man in the Camel cigarette advertisements and the moment he opened his mouth Gopal decided he disliked him.

'You must be Goh-Pahl,' he said stylishly, curling his lip and affecting the nasal drawl illiterate Indians adopt when they think they're speaking like Americans. 'I'm Andy.'

Gopal looked at him incredulously.

'Well, my Indian name is Anand, but all my friends call me Andy.'

'Hello Anand,' said Gopal politely.

'And this is my American girlfriend Sue. Her Dad owns a big business up north.'

Gopal recognised her with a start as the girl with the kind face from the party. They murmured polite hellos.

'Say Goh-Pahl, I heard about your accident. You sure you didn't provoke them?'

Gopal sneered at him, not even bothering to answer.

'Well, it could have happened much more easily in India. I mean it was happening to me all the time there, that is why I had to leave. I said, "No way man. I don't need this shit. I'm leaving." And of course the government thought I was too dangerous to them and put spies after me.'

Gopal laughed outright.

'Hey listen, Goh-Pahl, why don't you come over now to my apartment? I've got a colour TV and you can watch it for a while.'

Gopal tried to select from a range of rejections that would succinctly tell Anand what he could do with his colour TV. But Anand cleverly added, 'And I've got some Indian food ready too.'

Gopal hesitated, his craving for home food warring with his dislike of this insufferable fool. The cafeteria door opened and a smell of boiled beef and disinfectant wafted out. Gopal capitulated.

They walked around the cafeteria to the parking lot where Anand's car was parked. They got in with Anand insisting that Sue sit in the back so that Gopal could sit in front and marvel at the car's gadgets. 'Want me to put on some music? I've got classical, rock, jazz, you name it. No Indian of course. I don't go for that shit.'

Gopal demurred and prayed that at least the food would be good.

'Should I put on the heater? You know American cars have these heaters. Man, I used to freeze my butt off in India in the winters and melt in the summers. How long before Indian cars get that stuff, huh?'

'We are already having now. My car has music and heaters, both.'

Anand checked himself. 'Yeah? Really? Oh sure. I heard about these new models. Want me to put on the radio? We can catch eighteen stations here. In India,' he tossed back spitefully to Sue, 'they only have one.'

Gopal sighed deeply. 'There are many channels,' he informed gently, 'but only one broadcasting authority.'

'Yeah, but they're all bullshit, man. Real bull. I used to listen to those and say "this is real bullshit man." You know what India needs, Goh-Pahl? You know what India really needs?'

Gopal didn't answer, believing this to be a rhetorical question.

'Let me tell you what it needs. It needs the free enterprise system. That's right. That's what it needs. It's all fucked up, man. You know they should make me the prime minister, you know I'd fix things and teach them how a democracy should be run. A real democracy. You know what I'd do?'

Gopal practised deep breathing.

'I'd line up all the politicians there and shoot them dead, that's what I'd do.'

Sue commented reproachfully, 'That doesn't sound terribly democratic, Andy.'

'Hey, you don't know these guys, Sue. You know this guy Rajiv Gandhi? Well, do you know what job I had to do when

I was in India? Well listen to this, let me tell you. I was an assistant at a shoe store. Can you believe that?'

'Oh I'm sure Rajiv Gandhi didn't order that,' objected Sue. 'He's kind of cute.'

'Why not? It all comes from the top I'm telling you.'

'What you are doing now?' asked Gopal.

'Well, I study of course, and I sell real estate at the same time. And I can tell you, I wouldn't go back home if Rajiv Gandhi paid me a million bucks.'

'I am sure,' murmured Gopal soothingly, 'Rajiv Gandhi will be very upset to hear that.'

'That's right,' rejoiced Anand, much pleased at the prospect of Rajiv Gandhi's distress. 'Not for a million bucks. And I tell you only I know how to make that country work. You know what I think they should do about the population problem?'

Gopal wondered if he would survive if he opened the door and leapt out.

'I'll tell you what they should do about the population problem. They should just castrate the whole lot of them. That's right, that's what they should do.'

They pulled up alongside a small, single-storeyed apartment complex before Anand could suggest more solutions to India's problems and Gopal was the first to leap out.

'Castrate the bastards,' muttered Anand vengefully, opening the door.

The apartment was comfortably done up and from the cushions, rugs and art objects scattered about, considerable effort had obviously gone into making it homely. Gopal contrasted it with his own Spartan furnishings and concluded that quite clearly this man genuinely intended to make this country his home.

His voice emerged from the kitchen, 'What'll you have? I've got bourbon, gin, wine, beer, tequila, you name it. Not like that inferior stuff you get in India, I can tell you.'

'Coke.'

'You sure? I mean this is America, nobody'll tell your folks.'

'Yes. Coke.'

'Okay, though I'm telling you, you're missing out on something.'

He emerged with a can and Gopal watched as he popped it open. Though he wouldn't admit it to anyone, Gopal thought one of the most glorious sights in America was the popping open of cans. It combined technology, a solicitude for consumers, a deceptive ease and the poetry of the actual pop followed by the Wagnerian symphony of the hissing soda. By comparison, the unscrewing or decapping of bottles paled into ordinariness.

The cans, as well as the machines into which you dropped coins and which disgorged food, enthralled Gopal. It still seemed incredible that machines could be so highly trained that they would not only provide you with different kinds of chocolates and sandwiches, but also give you back the change. One machine even consumed dollar bills with a greedy hum and sucked at your fingers as if it was a venus fly trap wanting more, before digesting your money with a rumble. This was followed by creaks and rattles as it disgorged your food and ended with a silvery tinkle as it returned your change. Gopal was considering tape-recording the entire process and sending it back to his friends, asking if they could decipher what the whole thing was about just from the sound. He wondered what they'd make of it. Once he'd peeked quickly behind the machine when seized by the suspicion that there were people who actually did all the work while maintaining this façade of

Technology as Provider. But no, there was a gap between the wall and the back of the machine. He scrutinised the bottom half of the machine which seemed excessively large, with considerable suspicion, but it seemed unlikely that anybody would push plates up and down all day while lying flat on his back like Michelangelo. To a bedazzled Gopal, the analogy between masterpieces didn't seem so far-fetched.

As Gopal sipped his Coke, Anand returned. 'Sorry,' he apologised, 'I forgot all about the TV. Keep sitting,' he admonished Gopal, 'in America you don't have to get up to put on the TV.'

He lifted a remote control box and switched it on. 'Here,' he said handing him the box. 'Make yourself comfortable,' he added, kicking at Gopal's chair, which to his fright began to undulate under him like the Loch Ness Monster. Gopal found himself stretched almost fully flat, alarmed and wondering with a certain lack of respect at the need for inanimate objects that suddenly and without provocation leapt to life. He remembered the radio in New York on his first morning.

He was still too shaken to check the mechanical configuration that could lead to a small, normal, perfectly wholesome looking little chair, suddenly elongating itself into a basketball-player length. Besides there was Anand to cope with, who was not wistfully demanding to know when colour would come to Indian television.

'Has been since '82 now,' Gopal informed him.

'Oh yeah?' there was a resentful belligerence to Anand's voice. 'Well it can't be as good as American colour. You know I can catch 36 channels on this. I mean it really blows your mind. How many can you get on Indian TV?'

'One,' Gopal admitted humbly.

'One?' Anand chortled. 'Here one channel isn't even television. Well, anyway,' he consoled Gopal, 'India has a lot of growing up to do and America will show the way. Well, the food should be heated up by now. Hey Sue, help me serve,' he yelled into the bedroom into which she'd disappeared.

Gopal began to ungrit his teeth as familiar, delicious, Indian food smells began to comfortably wrap themselves around the room like a halo.

'There we go,' said Anand in satisfaction. 'Come and get it.'

Gopal moved forward with the careful slowness of a person who is restraining himself from bursting into a sprint.

'Help yourself,' urged Anand. 'You know, Goh-Pahl, I find that Indian food always tastes better in America.'

'Oh Andy,' broke in Sue, 'I'm sure it does not too. Why don't we all just eat.'

They started, Gopal reverentially. He had to admit that the food was superb.

'Very good,' he acknowledged.

'The reason,' resumed Anand, 'is that the materials are so clean and pure here. Not like that shit in India I can tell you. Man, that used to really freak me out, all that adulteration. Man, I wouldn't go back if Rajiv Gandhi paid me two million bucks.'

Gopal put his head down and burrowed into the food. He experimented with chewing so loudly that it would drown Anand's voice, which was now urging him to write to all his friends and relatives in India in praise of the free market system.

'I do that all the time,' Anand assured him.

Gopal said something through a full mouth about this no doubt making Anand very popular.

'What? What d'you say?' demanded Anand. 'Well anyway, eat up, eat up. It's good all-American food.'

Gopal let that pass.

Afterwards, replete, he followed Anand to his car and was driven to his apartment. Only when he got in did he remember that he still hadn't decided about returning to India.

Lying in bed, he was astonished at the severity of his responses to Anand's views on India. In India itself he would have paid no attention to them. Here in America he felt himself personally liable for every one of India's policies and answerable for their failures. One evening he had been requested to attend a question-and-answer session with a political science class in which a surprisingly well-informed young man had launched a bitter attack on India's alleged closeness to the Soviet Union – about which Gopal in any case knew nothing and cared even less – ending with a vehement 'Why? Why after PL 480 and the massive cheque write-off are you so close to the Reds?'

Gopal had felt so upset at the young man's passionate sense of having been ill-done by, that he had considered apologising to him while promising never to do it again. In the event, he had merely muttered incomprehensibly.

It had not been one of his more glorious moments. At the best of times his awareness of politics was low, being largely confined to the ritual incantation of 'all politicians are thieves,' which has had inherited from his father. At the class, he was further unnerved by the nearly theatrical languor of the students. So long as he was one of them, it wasn't so apparent, but now that he stood behind the podium and saw this class together, he was nearly struck dumb. One had his thick boots on the table. Another was peering into an empty Twinkie's wrapping as though it was Alladin's Cave that might yet yield treasures. Several were sipping coffee from paper cups. A latecomer arrived and began to disrobe. Two people were diligently helping each other light what Gopal sincerely hoped were cigarettes. A poetic soul was gazing dreamily out of the window as though Camelot had suddenly swum into view. In the face of this pure, unaffected, masterful disinterest, Gopal felt the few facts he had hastily crammed fall into a black pit of panic that suddenly opened inside his head.

He contrasted this with India where the students projected a nearly unseemly reverence for their teacher and an apparently hypnotised interest in his pearls of wisdom. In reality they were probably even more bored than the Americans so candidly demonstrated, but at least, Gopal thought indignantly, they had the decency to hide it.

In any case he had mumbled through his speech as rapidly as he could so that they could all go home. For the sake of courtesy he had asked if there were any questions as he was gathering his papers. To his consternation, there were many. He had fended them off feebly and gone back puzzled as to how he could have gone through life back home while knowing so little about the country.

Now propped up in bed, he again realised that he had to make up his mind. On one side was a sense of humiliation and fear, on the other was the fascinating spectacle of watching a new universe reveal itself. If he stayed, obviously he would grow enormously as a human being by the sheer process of surviving in this enchanted forest where light switches worked upside down, men spoke in rhyme and national conspiracies of silence existed about unexplained baskets outside houses. On the other hand if he stayed, he might not survive at all. Yet also to be considered was the important fact that he still hadn't seen Brooke Shields.

He wondered now about how he had ever imagined that he would meet her, as though she was the lady with the Welcome Wagon he saw in commercials. But all the same the fact remained, he still hadn't seen Brooke Shields. He wondered cunningly if she could be manipulated into seeing him if he sent her a lifetime's supply of hair oil. Perhaps in sheer gratitude she would fly over immediately and there she would be, thumping at his door, coat aswirl in the wind. Gopal gloated at the thought of the look on Randy's face when he heard about it.

The phone burred, nudging him out of his favourite fantasy. It was Randy. 'Today evening. Right. Double date. Be ready. Bye.'

Gopal's decision about whether to go or stay was necessarily postponed. A double date. He rushed to get his underwear to put under his mattress so that it would be ironed by the evening. When the familiar klaxon blared, Gopal was, as Randy often said about himself, 'as ready and as willin as anyone's ever going to be.'

He got into the front seat of the car and Randy sped off. 'I think you already know both the ladies, Gopal.'

Gopal tried to plug in his seat belt, say hello and see who they were at the same time. A miracle prevented his neck from snapping but he caught a glimpse of both. They were Ann and Sue. He smiled hello to Ann, grateful that she hadn't brought her brother along, but said in surprise to Sue, 'Anand?'

'Oh, he's a boyfriend. He's not the only boyfriend,' she laughed.

Gopal laughed back far too loudly. 'Where we are going?' he asked.

'For dinner. Followed by Plato's Retreat.'

'New disco?'

Randy groaned. 'You know, Gopal, I should carry a box with eyeballs in it. And everytime you say something I can just hit a button and the eyeballs can revolve instead of my having to roll my eyes around so much. I'm sure it's not good for my eyes.'

They arrived at an obviously expensive restaurant. As they waited to be seated, Gopal noticed the other patrons looking at him obliquely and then at the two American girls he was with. Gopal looked straight back at anyone he thought was staring at him, but he never quite managed to catch anybody in the act. Everytime he looked at someone, his eyes skittered away like mice. But it was uncomfortable and again he felt his skin begin to burn.

The headwaiter arrived oozing charm. 'Is that a table for three, sir?' he asked looking directly at Randy.

Randy, who had been observing one of the waitresses with more than academic interest, slowly turned and his eyes locked on to the headwaiter's with a nearly audible click. 'Yeah?' he asked so politely and laconically that it was a threat.

'Oh I'm so sorry, sir,' gushed the headwaiter though quite clearly he wasn't, 'I hadn't noticed your distinguished guest. Do forgive me. This way, sir.'

He led the way in a confident stride that simultaneously conveyed servility and superciliousness. 'I hope you'll feel completely comfortable here, sir,' he said with a small edge to his voice that made Gopal feel anything but comfortable. Their table was situated next to the kitchen door and was nearly hidden from the rest of the room. Gopal wished he had the courage to demand a better table, but sat down instead.

'And the young ladies,' continued the headwaiter in a deferential voice that contrasted with his knowing eyes, 'can I get them something unusual?'

There was nothing even remotely objectionable in his words, but his tone suggested that the company they were keeping was unusual enough by itself.

'No nothing right away,' said Randy, deciding to hint about Gopal's affluence, 'but just don't get anything too unusual, or our friend here from India might decide to buy the restaurant.'

The headwaiter tittered politely at the thought. 'Ah from India is he, sir, I thought as much. I always contribute my bit at the church, sir. Shall I get the wine list?'

'No, don't bother,' said Randy. 'Just get us a good white wine.'

The man bowed and left. Randy began talking hastily to cover the awkwardness that was palpable. 'So tell me about your factory, Gopal. Their family owns a company,' he explained. 'Makes great stuff too. So what's the story on that?' he rambled on rapidly.

The headwaiter was back soon. In his hand he held a tray from which he lifted a brown plug which he placed in front of Gopal after reaching over Randy. He waited with a bland smile.

Gopal was nonplussed. He hesitated, wondering if it was an appetiser he was supposed to taste or a relic he was meant to pocket and carry away. Before he could commit some momentous faux pas, Sue picked it up and handed it back to the man. 'Just get the wine,' she suggested firmly. 'Okay?'

'With pleasure, ma'am. Er, how many glasses, sir?'

'Four,' announced Gopal loudly, surprising himself most of all.

The headwaiter bowed his way out.

Another waiter came over and somewhat shamefacedly gave them the menus.

The headwaiter returned and ceremoniously poured out the wine.

'And a specially large one for our overseas friend, sir,' he announced.

'To good times,' toasted Randy. He took a sip of his wine and found that Gopal had already tossed down his entire glass. Gopal stared triumphantly at the headwaiter.

'My word, sir, you must be thirsty,' he murmured, refilling the glass to the brim.

Gopal consumed it in another gulp. The headwaiter refilled it. Randy began telling a long story about the meaning of life which he insisted required all of Gopal's concentration. Sue agreed and pulled his wine glass her way. Groggily Gopal heard something about pink ping-pong balls constituting the real meaning of life and then found himself free to repossess his glass and continue sampling its remarkable contents.

He lost count of how many times he had lifted and put down the glass. Randy had commenced another story which Gopal could hear only sporadically through the buzzing in his ears, but it was obviously a very funny one because he found himself laughing uproariously with the others. Then Ann and Sue took turns telling even funnier stories and they were all so amused that they were barely able to eat their food which had mysteriously arrived. Later they discovered that Ann had ordered for everyone since the waiter's repeated pleas had been ignored by the other three.

Gopal told them his favourite story about the Japanese tourist group in Delhi that a lazy tourist guide had conducted around a hotel named Taj Mahal instead of going through the bother of taking them on a four-hour trip to Agra to see the real thing. The tourists had apparently not even realised there was a difference, or perhaps they had been too polite to mention it. But somewhere in Japan there were various neighbours being shown vacation slides, who were probably convinced that the Taj Mahal contained reception counters, restaurants and elevators.

'You mean it doesn't?' asked Randy. They all roared.

There were numerous other equally amusing stories and Gopal, through his foggy head, couldn't remember when he had had such a wonderful time. The others declined dessert, preferring coffee, but Gopal opted for the largest ice cream available. As the plate of ice cream with its accompanying fruits and nuts began to finish, Gopal's head began to think again, somewhat.

When the headwaiter arrived carrying the bill, Gopal was faintly able to hear his murmured polite 'hope that you enjoyed the food'. 'Yes, yes,' enthusiastically acknowledged Gopal, 'very good. But,' he paused, a thought starting to glow in his mind like an ember on a foggy day, 'what I am eating?'

The others collapsed again in merriment and Gopal joined them too, the ember drowned in laughter. When they surfaced for breath, he dimly heard the headwaiter's amused answer, 'Why, steak, sir. That's what madam ordered,' he gestured to Ann.

Gopal accepted this while wiping tears of laughter from his eyes with his sleeve. He fought loudly with Randy over the bill and they finally decided to split it. They began to unsteadily lurch their way out, helped by various waiters, as though they were batons being passed from hand to hand. As they recovered their coats and scarves, the headwaiter came to bid a final goodbye. By now he seemed to have become quite fond of them.

'Do come again, sir,' he urged.

'Certainly,' promised Gopal, preparing to step out.

'By the way,' he asked casually, 'what kind of vegetable is steak?'

'Oh that's not a vegetable, sir,' said the headwaiter quickly, anxious to make up for his earlier rudeness, 'that's beef.'

Gopal froze. The fumes fled from his head. His heart seemed to stop. He looked stupidly outside.

'Oh shit,' said Randy, suddenly quiet.

'Why? Why?' demanded Ann. 'It's great beef here. I mean I've eaten here lots and it's the best red meat you can buy. That's why I ordered steak. I mean didn't you like it, Gopal?' she asked, genuinely concerned.

'I can assure you, sir,' added the headwaiter, 'I personally select the choicest cuts. There's nothing to be concerned about, sir, livestock is specially grown for slaughter.'

'Shh, shh,' Randy hushed him, 'sacred cows.'

'Oh dear, oh dear,' bemoaned Ann, awareness dawning. 'I'm so sorry. Oh gosh, how stupid of me.'

'Oh good heavens, sir,' apologised the headwaiter, rattled by this development and then even more stricken at the look on the paralysed Gopal's face. 'I'm so sorry, sir, we've never had this problem here before, sir. Oh wow, but, but ... I can assure you, sir,' he was stammering as he sought desperately for something to say, 'I can assure you that, that ... that American cows aren't as sacred as Indian cows, sir.'

Randy and Sue, despite their concern for Gopal, relapsed into howls of laughter, and even Gopal began to feel himself thaw at the explanation. He felt Randy and Sue each put an arm around him and giggling, propel him forward, out of the door. After a last wild look behind and around in case his grandmother was lurking around somewhere and had witnessed one of her many dire predictions come true, Gopal allowed himself to be led to the car.

The next morning Gopal woke up, his head feeling as if the Americans and Russians were exchanging thermonuclear devices inside its premises. His tongue felt as though a constipated alligator was waggling its scaly tail and he suspected smelt like one too. The business end of the alligator seemed to the deep in his innards helping himself to a snack.

Gopal staggered out of bed, stumbled to the bathroom and violently threw up in the tub. Sweating and panting, he groped his way back to the bed and lay there gasping. His breathing began to ease and he started to feel much better. He went back to the bathroom and cleaned out the mess. The nuclear war inside his head had subsided, but an active insurgency still seemed under way, characterised by a nearly continuous burst of machine gun fire across the centre of his head.

He brushed his teeth and found to his surprise that it had a therapeutic, if temporary, effect. He got himself an icy orange juice carton and sitting down on his bed, he opened the curtains on the little window alongside. The view wasn't much, just a chain link fence and beyond that a short path through some trees, but Gopal thought it was a wonderland.

It had rained at night and the glass had frosted slightly. But through it he could see how clean the air was and the water dripping off the metal on the fence. The trees shivered in a sudden wind and the branches were iridescent with light. Gopal had found that one of his greatest pleasures was getting up early and looking at such an ordinary, such a quintessentially American, such a breathtakingly beautiful scene.

There was a hammering on his door and the howl of a werewolf outside followed by yaps, screeches and bow-wows. Gopal gathered that Randy had arrived. He went to open the door.

'Get dressed, ponder,' announced Randy striding energetically in and heading straight for the fridge. 'We're going to church.'

'Feeling sick,' said Gopal collapsing on the bed.

'You got a hangover?'

'Yes,' said Gopal with unmistakable pride.

'I'm not surprised. You had your first date, your first drink, and your first beef. And all in a night's work. You've got to expect to pay some price for it. C'mon, get off your butt. If you go to church maybe God'll forgive you for eating beef.'

'Christian God,' said Gopal. 'Doesn't count.'

'Well, what'll help get you forgiveness then?'

'Holy water from the Ganges.'

'Yeah, well, won't Budweiser from Milwaukee do as good? I mean, who'd know the difference. What're you supposed to do with the water in any case?'

'Bathe in it.'

'Well that sure rules out Bud. You coming or what? I've told them you'll give a talk on modern India after the service. You can't let down your Fatherland, can you?'

'Motherland.'

'Whatever. Parentland. Now get dressed for Christ's sake.'

As they drove down, Randy asked: 'You been to a church before?'

'Yes, sometimes.'

'You have? I mean you have churches in India?'

'Yes, yes, many. Also many Christians.'

'How'd they get there?'

'British converted many.'

'And so what were you doing in a church? You're not Christian, are you?'

'No, no, Hindu. But school where for some time I studied had Christian Fathers as teachers. We had to go to chapel.'

'No shit, what denomination?'

'What?' Gopal was puzzled. 'Christian of course.'

'Right, right. How come they didn't convert you?'

'I am high-caste Hindu. Conversions were among lower castes.'

'Yeah, I guess that figures. Say, Gopal, what caste would I be in India?'

'Depends on what ancestors did.'

'How far down? Which ancestors?'

'Not sure.'

'Well,' recollected Randy, 'I know my grandpa's name, though I'm not sure what he did. How far back can you go?'

'Oh about fifty ancestors.'

'Whaaat? You know the names of fifty ancestors? I don't believe it.'

'Yes, yes, quite true.'

'Jesus. What'd they do?'

'Sold hair oil.'

'You're joking. You're kidding! I'm going insane! This is crazy.'

'No, no. Actually not only hair oil, sold other things too. But mostly hair oil. Long history in India of hair oil. Mentioned also in *Kama Sutra*.'

'Jesus! Supplied by your family no doubt.'

'Probably.'

'Well don't give them a lecture on hair oil or the *Kama Sutra* at the church. They'll freak. Here we are.'

The church was a modern-looking structure with a high curved front where the steeple should have been. But the interior was familiar, as were the stained glass windows and cushioned benches. The service was a rite he remembered from his childhood, as were the songs.

Everything passed off smoothly except for a brief moment when Gopal joined in singing *Lead Kindly Light*, only to have Randy nudge him urgently with the news that they were singing *Abide With Me*.

Afterwards those interested, or intimidated beforehand by the priest, retired to the Committee Room and in exquisitely polite silence heard Gopal expound on India's industrial achievements, its satellite programme, its computer software exports, its mammoth armament manufacture and other good stuff.

While most people smiled encouragingly, and a few had nostrils flaring periodically along with dilating pupils and clenched mouths, one little old lady furiously scribbled notes and nodded intelligently every now and then. Gopal directed his speech at her.

At the end when he asked if there were any questions, her hand shot up immediately.

'Yes, madam,' he encouraged her.

'Young man,' she rose creaking to her feet, 'tell me. Do you drive elephants in the daytime as well as in the night time? I mean do they have headlights and tail lights that blink when they turn at night?'

6

In the months that followed, Gopal remembered her vividly as one of his symbols of America. Virtually every literate person in the world has a few symbols which for him mean America. For most of those who have never visited, it is the Statue of Liberty, Niagara Falls, skyscrapers. But those who have stayed in the country for a while invariably have their own personal lists. Gopal had added the lady to his, which he had drawn up based upon the total inscrutability displayed by the symbol. To gain admission into his list, a symbol had to be completely and uniquely American, and so baffling that any right-thinking foreigner would swoon on encountering it. So far he had listed vegetarian cats, the baskets outside houses and now the old lady.

Gopal was wondering what else could qualify for the honour. He was sitting one dark evening by a window high up in the tower of the library. It was his favourite place. He could look down at a scene of nearly pastoral serenity. There was the lushness of the lawns, a few trees rustling quietly, as though content to watch from the background the periodic small army of eager rushers. Gopal wondered if the souls of dead professors came finally to roost in the trees where they could continue to watch over the campus, changeless and everchanging.

He wondered what it would be like to be a professor in this place, with its quiet beauty, its civility, to see the young faces finding love, sorrow and sometimes a little learning, to grow old gracefully like the trees, rustling in amusement at youth discovering the old verities every new semester. It wouldn't be a bad life, Gopal mused, so far from the clamour of commerce. He had come a long way, he suddenly thought, from the night when he was trying to decide whether to leave the country that very minute. Finally he had decided it would be too much of an admission of failure if he went back without a degree. What would he have said that his friends wouldn't disbelieve? What's more, what would his mother have said to her friends, especially Mrs Saxena, whose son was still in England and apparently untouched by Skinheads. He had decided to stay, but to take as many courses as he could so that he got his degree as soon as possible.

The days had sped in a blur of classes and libraries. Having once already eaten beef he had decided that he couldn't be doomed more than once and had descended upon hamburgers as though he had invented them. Perhaps that was the turning point in his adjustment to American life. No vegetarian ever made it fully. They were always having to inspect menus minutely and explain their preference somewhat defiantly.

And now here he was a few brief months later, wondering if he should abandon a family business that was so old that it was nearly genetic. His father used to joke, 'We don't have blood in our veins, we have hair oil.'

There was an old history book in Gopal's house which had belonged to his grandfather. Gopal often picked it up to smell its mustiness, to feel its engraved hard cover, the brittleness of its paper that cracked like biscuits. And as he read the long and ancient saga of India's endless history, whenever he turned a page and found some small unexplained stain on it, he fantasised that the stain marked a spot in history where the family business was present in some tiny way, perhaps as a head massage for some mighty king the night before a fearsome battle. They were a vial of oil in the torrent of history.

Could he leave all that? Could he ever really leave India? Would he ever be anything but an alien in any other country? With his head here, his heart in India and his skin set on fire by the gaze of strangers, could he ever leave forever the smell of woodsmoke and jasmine on a winter's night? The stars, often so many of them that there seemed a rainfall of light. And the night itself spread like a dark blue wanton. Dawn and the sun rising like an explosion of softness. A hundred ruins weeping silently amidst the thunder and dust of everyday life. The sheer bliss of being home, of walking the streets amidst littered scraps of humanity, amidst cows and garbage, yet totally content at being home, being where you belonged, where no man looked at you twice on the streets in question.

And yet here there was tranquility, efficiency, a certain new-world courtesy and civility all their own. There were amazing facilities to study, unimaginable in India. The business of living was made easy, so you could get on with doing more than surviving. Ye gods, the very phones worked. Initially, Gopal grimaced at the memory, he used to pick up the phone and listen to the dial tone as if it was music sublime. Food, drink, transport, communication, housing, clothing, the essentials were cheap and easy. In India you clawed your way through the day, through dirt and glamour and people who seemed to strip the skin off your bones when they dealt with you, leaving every nerve raw. Here it was all so much more courteous even at its worst, hushed, gentler. They spoke to you with a respect that wrapped you in cotton wool. You didn't feel that every man coveted your property or your self-respect or was otherwise desperately straining to find ways to humble you.

It was a failing, Gopal knew, of village folk. This overwhelming pride, this need to be arrogant with very little really to be arrogant about. And India was still actually only a generation removed from the villages. Everyone still demanded to know who you are, what you do, what your parents did and whether they did so legally. Here, he exulted, no one seemed to care. True, it was initially annoying not to be able to bask in your ancestral glory, but gradually he felt a great sense of deliverance. You were not responsible for some totally forgotten yet deeply resented past, you were responsible only for your own actions and often not even that. No one cared. After the initial sense of puzzlement, Gopal had come to be extremely proud of the fact that he had no idea who his next-door neighbour was. He was merely a constantly changing set of music heard indistinctly through the wall.

In India, Gopal shuddered as he thought of his neighbours who seemed to have no other occupation in life then to look burningly into his house all day. And his neighbour's neighbour did the same to him. And his neighbour to him. And so on, until Gopal could visualise India as one endless chain of neighbours, each fanatically and sleeplessly obsessed with what was happening in his neighbour's house and life.

At this exact point, as Gopal was visualising this nightmare nation of neighbours, he felt a gun touch the back of his neck and a voice hiss. 'Move and you die.'

Either, thought Gopal, it's the Vietnamese finally arrived in America for revenge, or it's Randy.

'Beat it, Randy,' he said concentrating on his book. 'I am studying.'

Randy came across and sat on his table.

'Thanksgiving weekend's arriving,' he announced. 'I'm going home. What're you doing?'

'I will stay here and study.'

'You want to come home with me for the weekend? Might be fun.'

Gopal was touched.

'Really?'

'Sure. I asked the folks. No big deal. Matter of fact they're all pretty excited.'

'Very nice of you and all that,' thanked Gopal formally, shaking hands. 'I am very happy and all that and ...'

'Oh shut up,' said Randy hastily, 'I'll pick you up Friday morning. You don't have any feathers and bows and arrows, do you?'

'No,' said Gopal nonplussed, wondering if this was regulation wear for Thanksgiving.

'Well, too bad. My family's never met an Indian before and they think you'll come dressed in war paint. Bye.'

Gopal was ready early on Friday morning, excited at his first real trip out of Eversville into America. He had found from Randy that he lived about three hundred miles away in a town called Springfield. Gopal had got an atlas and went through it, trying to find Springfield. To his consternation, he found not merely one, but literally dozens. Virtually every state seemed to have several. Another phone call to Randy elicited that it was the Springfield in the neighbouring state. Further research revealed that it had a population of about 7,000. Thereafter the sources were strangely silent on its notable features, tourist spots and rich history. Among places you must see, it mentioned only 'Noodle Factory'.

As they were driving out, Gopal hesitantly mentioned this strange lapse on the part of the guide book.

'No, no, nothing wrong with the guide book,' Randy assured him. 'There just isn't anything else to see.'

'Nothing?'

'Nope. Just the noodle factory. That's why we call ourselves the noodle capital of the South Central United States.'

Gopal sniggered.

'And I don't want any of your lip, Gopal. I mean your town, what's its name? Jajau, Jesus, what a name. I mean that can't be much better. But at least we're honest. What'd you say you guys called Jajau? 'The Paris of the state of Madhya Pradesh. Wow!'

Gopal settled back, refusing to be provoked. 'We are asking both towns to become sister cities I think,' he suggested.

They were out of the town soon and Gopal began to take in the magnificence of the American countryside. Generally, he had been told by well-travelled relatives, the countryside of Europe, though undeniably pretty, required a bit of fog or mist to display them in their best colours – anything that hid them a bit. But looking through the clear cold air that appeared to magnify rather than conceal the American scenery, he was taken aback by how lovely it was. The sparkling greens, the rich gold and rusts, yet all of it so controlled. Though clearly untrimmed by human hand, it all seemed so intrinsically civilised.

In India, he contrasted, when it was arid you could practically see the parched lips of the people, when green it was so monstrously lush and tangled that the trees seemed to have writhing snakes instead of roots. And poisonous snakes at that. The extremes were too harsh, they made you wary. There was too much history coiled under every rock. He had never been able to admire wholeheartedly some old structure or even some part of India without later finding that it contained in its bowels some history of horrow, or as often, the abject disgrace of some Indian defeat at the hands of a few foreigners.

Here he sensed there was nothing in the landscape but itself. He was delighted at this liberation from history. The trees, the meadows, the houses were just themselves; attractive, healthy, often beautiful, civil in their lack of extremes, open in what they had to offer. There were no poisonous snakes crawling here. How curiously like Americans themselves, he thought. Obviously the characteristics of the land seemed to have entered into the people too. Perhaps, he thought with a start, that was true of India as well. The extremes of kindness and cruelty, the brooding patience, and always, behind the smile, a slithering something.

Suddenly Gopal noticed a strange aloneness. He looked carefully all around and confirmed that there wasn't a human in sight anywhere. Again, he thought, in India, no matter how deserted a place appeared, if you looked diligently you would always spot a distant farmer, or someone herding his cow, or even one of the many souls nature had created with the apparently express destiny of gaping at life. And if you stopped the car in the midst of sublime silence, within minutes a bush would rustle and someone would drag his sheep away, a distant tinkling would herald a bicycle, or one of the gapers would materialise from thin air to gawk at you.

But here, Gopal was absolutely sure, there was nothing except nature. Even the road, with its straight lines, its empty sleeve reaching endlessly forward, seemed more organic then manmade. On an impulse, Gopal asked Randy to stop the car and went out to relieve himself behind a tree. This was the ultimate test to discover if there actually were any life forms around in the undergrowth or behind the trees. In India, a bare minute after you stopped for such sensitive and urgent requirements, a cow would emerge to observe you with philosophic sadness, as though reluctantly reconciled to the appalling toilet habits of mankind. Or a dog would appear to compete for space on that very same tree. Or a child materialise from a bush behind which he had apparently been waiting patiently all his life with the solitary ambition of gazing upon you at that delicate moment.

But again, Gopal reconfirmed, nothing stirred except the wind, the leaves and a few birds. Gopal shivered, zipped himself up and hastened to the car. Such solitude was, was – he groped for a word – not unnatural exactly, but, but – un-Indian, he thought triumphantly. That was the correct word.

'You through fertilising the fields?' asked Randy.

Gopal got in and urged him on.

'Well,' said Randy as they drove off, 'at least there's one part of America that's forever Gopal.'

There was a loud buzz in the car.

'You've forgotten your seat belt again, Gopal.'

Gopal began to buckle it on. He had never understood this national mania for seat belts. In India, he thought, cars didn't even have seat belts. And if a manufacturer did install them, the driver would probably merely assume it was a useful device with which to strangle opposing drivers during one of their numerous fights.

Certainly there was great merit in seat belts. But typically the Yanks had made such a fetish out of it, that it annoyed every right thinking person. It was like cigarettes. Gopal, who smoked very rarely, found himself defiantly lighting up in rebellion against the implicit national demand that he not smoke in public. It had come to a point now where he only smoked in public; he felt it was a democratic protest against the forces of fascism.

Thus occupied, they drove along. Eventually they came to an overhead bridge festooned with names in the characteristic white on green. One of them, Gopal noticed with astonishment, claimed that Beirut lay 11 miles to the east.

'Driving very fast,' Gopal commented.

'Not really. Barely over the speed limit. Why?'

'Sign says Beirut only 11 miles away. You are reaching Asia.'

'Very funny. But Beirut's not the only one. We've got the names of all the big cities in the world here in the States. We even have a couple of Delhis.'

Gopal was thrilled. 'Let us go.'

'Nah, the one I know about's in California. Anyway, we're nearly home. Don't blink too long, otherwise you'll miss the town.'

Shortly they saw a sign announcing Springfield and after turning right, drove immediately past a row of white wooden houses. They seemed small but clean and several had children's cycles and toys littered in front. They drove a little further, turned into another road and went up to the garage of a house indistinguishable from the others.

'The Wolff's Lair,' Randy announced.

They unloaded their luggage, walked into the garage and through a door there into the kitchen. Gopal was struck by the way nearly all American houses had garages intermixed with them just as they had bedrooms. It was as though a garage was an extra room for a valued member of the family, which in its own way it probably was. Everywhere else in the world people kept their garages at a proper distance from their abodes out of a healthy respect for the petrol fumes and grease smells they contained. In America, even though there was no shortage of space, the garage, with all its accumulated litter, lay as naturally inside the house as the baby's nursery. Gopal speculated on the scene in case the family baby and the family car were left parked outside the house one night. Certainly there would be anguished cries of 'My baby!' but which would Mr and Mrs America rush to first?

He shook himself out of such idle reverie and tried to gauge from the sounds where Randy's parents were. He suspected they were hiding in case he shot an arrow through the first one who came through the door. He waited alone awkwardly in the kitchen since Randy had gone to roust his family. In a while there were the familiar wooden thumps that seemed the background accompaniment to all American living and Randy returned with his parents.

His father was short, red-faced, balding, wearing a pair of well-used overalls and obviously very shy about their visitor. But he shook hands bravely enough and retired quickly to the refrigerator. The mother was nearly as tall as he, extremely plump, wearing an apron over her blue dress. She had fat, rosy cheeks with tiny, shrewd, yet merry eyes and she obviously laughed a lot.

'Well, mercy,' she said and her voice seemed to fill the room, 'why have you left the poor dear in the kitchen?'

She wiped her hands on her apron and putting a motherly arm around Gopal led him to the living room.

'Come, come,' she urged, 'you must be starving. I've fixed a light lunch for you. Growing boys need to eat.'

The light lunch turned out to comprise some nine dishes and every time Gopal finished one helping she seized his plate and heaped more of everything on it. Obviously she had been well briefed, because she had somehow managed an exclusively vegetarian meal, some of the dishes being so obviously experimental that Gopal had never seen them before. Nor, he suspected, had she.

Gopal wolfed it all down, encouraged by loud approval from Mrs Wolff along with the most severe admonishments to Randy for not imitating the example set by his nice young friend. Finally, when Randy threatened to throw up all over the table, she allowed them to stop. Gopal sat back groaning and replete.

'This is a good boy,' chuckled Mrs Wolff noting his blissful state. 'One more little scoop of ice cream?'

Gopal could only clutch his stomach and gurgle a refusal. Much pleased, Mrs Wolff bustled off, clearing the table.

Moments later they heard the front door open and close and stealthy footsteps begin to climb the stairs. Like an overfed panther, Randy hobbled to the door and leapt out. There was a scuffle and screams and he reappeared with an armlock around a wriggling, blond-haired girl of about ten who was giggling, trying to get free.

'This,' he announced, 'is the Wolff cub. Responds to the name of Tabatha and is known to bite. Say hi to my friend Tabby.'

The girl buried her head in his shoulder and peered back giggling.

'She has rotten manners,' said Randy, 'I can't imagine where she gets them from.'

'I have small present for her,' said Gopal and captured her interest. They trooped out to a room beside the stairs where Randy had put his suitcase.

Gopal took out a vividly coloured piece of rectangular cloth embroidered with tiny glass pieces and ceremoniously handed it to Tabatha. She was thrilled.

'What is it?'

'Well,' said Gopal, 'you decide.'

Actually it was a table cloth, but after giving a similar gift to numerous Americans, he had found them using it as a wall hanging, a bed spread, and often even as a skirt. He had concluded it was best to let the Americans decide what they thought it was.

Tabatha raced off with the cloth and Gopal collapsed on the bed.

'Your room,' Randy waved around. 'Be it e'er so humble.'

'Nice, nice,' assured Gopal. 'What your father does?'

'Oh, he's a carpenter. Makes stuff you know.'

'Mother works?'

'Oh, yeah. Bakes all this food and stuff and supplies it to a couple of restaurants and families who order it. I mean she's got this menu and anyone who wants something calls her. She's even got this Indian dish on her menu.'

'Maybe we will have for dinner?'

'You just had it for lunch.'

'Oh, yes,' said Gopal trying to figure out which one it could have been. 'Really excellent. Very nice.'

Randy grinned sardonically. 'Hell, what do her customers know. I don't think anyone in Springfield's been out of the state, much less to India.'

Gopal began to doze.

'You want to catch a few z's?' Randy pushed himself off the wall. 'There's nothing wildly exciting happening in Springfield this century. Yell when you wake up. Sleep well.'

Gopal began to fall asleep. It had been months since he had been near any family environment and the simple, unaffected aura here of a home gave him a pang of homesickness. He wondered what was happening in his own home in India. His father would be away at work, his mother would be bustling around ordering the servants about – suddenly he wondered with his American experience of handling everyday chores, since their cook cooked, their gardener gardened and the cleaner cleaned, what did his mother do? Well, anyway, she was probably hassling his brother right now, he thought with a fiendish grin. Wanting to know why he wasn't studying, and if he was, why he wasn't eating, and if he had, why he hadn't eaten enough. Serves him right, thought Gopal, for being younger. And there would be his grandmother pottering around the courtyard to her holy tulsi plant before which she mumbled prayers or sang loudly, depending on whether she had remembered to put in her dentures or not. Warmed by the sense of being again with a family, he fell asleep.

When he woke again he saw that it was nearly 6 o'clock. From the cookie smells that were insinuating themselves into his nostrils, he feared that Mrs Wolff had organised a light tea.

He wandered out and met Randy's father who mumbled an embarrassed 'Hi' and dashed into the dining room. Gopal followed and as he had suspected, found Mrs Wolff heaping the table with sandwiches, cakes, doughnuts and other unknown delicacies.

'This one's Indian,' Mrs Wolff pointed to a plate.

Gopal gingerly bit into a piece. It tasted like aluminium.

'Excellent,' he enthused. 'Really, really, very very excellent.' He tried to edge out of the room so he could find a place to dump the offending object.

'You stay here and eat,' ordered Mrs Wolff. 'Mercy, you're thin as a stick. Just like my Randy. Well never mind. I'll put some meat on those bones soon. Sit you down.'

Gopal wondered if his mother's soul had somehow transmigrated across the globe and though visa-less, evaded the vigilance of the Immigration Service and settled within Mrs Wolff.

'Have to go to bathroom,' he excused himself, knowing that this was a reason against which even the most skilled mothers were helpless. He retired to the bathroom and flushed the unidentified object down the toilet. He lurked there for a while, wondering how he could escape eating some more of these rare Indian delicacies that Mrs Wolff had prepared with such considerateness. He couldn't think of a way out and manfully concluded that he would just have to risk food poisoning in the cause of Indo-American relations.

He returned to the dining room and was relieved to see Randy already there stuffing food into a bag.

'We're going to catch a movie at the drive-in,' he explained, 'and Mom wants us to take this stuff along so we can eat it later.'

'Eat eat,' urged Mrs Wolff, 'it's good for you both. You're thin as walking sticks. It's a mercy you don't blow away in the wind. What d'you want for dinner when you come back?'

'Ah nothin, Mom, we'll just pick up a burger or something,' hastily said Randy.

'Well, I was thinking of making a completely Indian dinner so your nice friend here can eat lots. I bet he's so thin because he doesn't like American food.'

'No, no, I am loving,' protested Gopal, aghast at the prospect, 'really loving all American foods.'

'Let's go, let's go,' urged Randy carrying out a small sack full of food.

They raced to the car and drove off.

'Mother,' grumbled Randy.

'Mine is worse. She used to make servant catch me while she stuffed food in my mouth.'

'Ah,' chuckled Randy, 'childhood confessions.'

'Till day I left for America.'

'Don't tell that to my mom, she'll get ideas. Oh boy, mothers. Anyway, we're picking up these two girls and going to the drive-in. You like drive-in theatres?'

'Never been.'

'You don't have them in India?'

'In one or two cities. Not near my town. Who are these girls?'

'Oh, Jill and Bernice. Bernice is a wild one. She's your date.'

Gopal salivated and sniggered nervously. 'No, no, heh, heh, heh,' he protested. 'I am sure she is nice girl. And Jill?'

'Well, she and I've been a twosome around here since grade school. Nothing new about us.'

They parked in front of a modest house. Its lights had been switched on in the dusk.

'You want to come in?' asked Randy getting out.

'No, no, I will wait.'

Randy strode off. Gopal watched him ring the bell and the door instantly open to swallow him. He heard cries of welcome. He could see figures going back and forth behind the window and then a flood of farewells whose force seemed to fling the door open. The parents appeared waving at Randy and the two girls and trying to peer into the car to see if they could make out what he looked like. Though Gopal knew they couldn't see him, he tried to look as civilised as he could and not at all the sort who had misplaced his feathers and tomahawk or whatever it was that Americans thought of when they thought of Indians.

He was tempted for one wild moment to leap out and emit war whoops, ending with pouncing on Randy and biting him. But it wouldn't do any good, he concluded. Randy would probably persuade them that this was a normal Indian greeting. He could almost hear his sincere voice '– and because there are so many starving millions, to allow yourself to have a bite taken out of you shows that you are ready to share your food with the person and leads to the highest form of karma.'

To Gopal's regret, no amount of persuasion had been able to convince Randy that there weren't starving millions in India any more. Gopal had once told him in desperation, 'now even beggars are well-fed,' but to no avail. Randy remained positive that Gopal was lying on behalf of his country and that not only did everyone starve there, but Gopal's first square meal must have been eaten after he came to America. Usually he selected the most public places in which to embarrass Gopal with loud statements of his views. And sure enough as he opened the door he announced, 'And heeeeere's Gopal. Brought straight here, ladies and gentlemen, for your entertainment and edification from famine-stricken India. Don't be surprised, folks, if you find a bag full of food around. Let's face it, our friend needs it. Right?'

A red-faced Gopal muttered his hellos. Jill, who was rather pleasant-looking with her hair tied in a ponytail, was obviously very friendly. She smiled at him and Gopal decided that she was good wife-material for Randy. Bernice, on the other hand, he noticed with a silent shiver of pleasure, was chewing gum.

While there was nothing inherently remarkable about chewing gum, after all nearly the entire population did, to the wild delight of dentists, there were ways and ways of chewing gum in America. Girls, especially, had developed it into not just an art form, but a very personal and eloquent language. It was astonishing how much they could convey just by the way they chewed the gum.

Sometimes they were merely chewing. At other times their chews suggested they were interested in whoever they were looking at, but weren't sure. Sometimes they were contemptuous of what or who they saw. While still looking at the person, their masticating jaws clearly stated that they had turned their face away.

When angry, they didn't chew – they bit. If they stopped chewing altogether, it was a sign of the most extreme displeasure preparatory to an explosion of wrath. At the other extreme, a sign of great approval was a chew slowing so that the gum could be gathered to create a gentle bubble. However, the cognoscenti were aware that an excessively large bubble displayed not extra-approval, but either flirtation or a patronising contempt. Gopal was positive he had seen high school girls conducting intense conversations purely through the medium of chewing gum at each other.

On some happy occasions the chewer communicated that a certain erotic interest was rhythmically powering her jaws. And such, decided Gopal, certainly seemed the case with Bernice.

'Well, hi there,' she exclaimed with such pleasure that Gopal wondered if she had heard of his mathematical prowess.

'Yes, yes, very well and all that. Very good,' Gopal felt himself gibber like an idiot.

She had, he noticed, hair so golden, so wavy, so shimmering, that it undulated around her like waves flowing into an ocean sunset. Her eyes were like blue fires, and Gopal, like a little boy in the dark who had gazed too long into the flame, couldn't look away. When she smiled, it was an act of unspeakable intimacy. The rest of the night flashed before his eyes. Her skin shone as if it had been rubbed with diamonds. And that American smell of cleanliness, soap and perfume, with just a hint of the tang of chewing gum, was heady in the little car. He breathed deeply and like so many visitors to that mysterious country, was intoxicated and in love.

'Movin right along,' chortled Randy driving off, much amused at the effect on Gopal. 'Bernice, why dontcha tell Gopal about drive-ins. He ain't been to none.'

'Oh, yes, yes, I am,' objected Gopal loudly, anxious not to appear like a hick before this vision.

'Well anyway,' drawled Bernice, slowly eyeing Gopal up and down with a gaze, he could swear, that burned the clothes off his skin wherever it rested, 'they're real fun places. I mean all the neat guys go there to make out. You know what I mean, make out and stuff?'

'Certainly, everything, yes, yes,' Gopal assured her, his mind racing. 'Make out.' He turned the words quickly around in his head like they were a Rubik's Cube, twisting them this way and that to see if he could find a pattern. Something to do with making things, he speculated, like sandcastles on the beach in Archie Comics. No doubt this was some form of socially meaningful construction work that the young elite of Springfield performed during a movie. It seemed a bit far-fetched to him, but he had learned to withhold judgment of things American. Or perhaps they endeavoured to 'make out' the finer nuances of some deeply relevant and artistically significant film. This seemed more likely considering that 'making out' something was a visual and intellectual process, as were movies.

Reassured at having deciphered the enigma and pleased at this sign of devotion to art in his lovely companion, he asked: 'What film it is?'

'Who cares?' said Randy.

'I know,' said Jill. 'It's *Texas Chainsaw Massacre* Part III.'

Once again Gopal was plunged into thought. But he couldn't think clearly for long because of the proximity of Bernice. Though she wasn't actually touching him, he was positive the heat from her arm was tanning his hand like a microwave oven.

Then they reached a gate and beyond it Gopal saw the familiar screen with those magical pictures. But he couldn't hear any sound and he wondered when they were going to switch it on and deafen the countryside. They drove in and Gopal saw that it looked exactly like the parking lot outside the mall in Eversville, except that each space was marked with poles. They drove into one slot and Randy got out, picked up a speaker hanging from the pole and stuck it into the window. The sound of a chainsaw slicing into bone sprayed into the car like blood.

Gopal was stunned by this sign of American ingenuity. They are really advanced, he thought, impressed. For a moment he had forgotten all about Bernice. Randy put a speaker into the other window as well and strode off. Gopal saw him walk to a booth at the back and return with huge bottles of Coke.

'Here's the Coke, here're Mom's sandwiches. When you want'em, grab'em.'

Gopal was fascinated at this novel experience. He looked around and saw a few figures dimly in the cars, others sat on the roof even in the cold with the inevitable paper glasses. Nowhere were there signs of construction activity or anybody making anything.

Bernice's hand began to brush against his as she jiggled the glass to shake the ice, so Gopal obligingly moved away. He was still trying to absorb this entirely new sensation. The loudspeakers were loud and scratchy, but he felt a certain sense of grandeur in sitting back in the privacy of a car and watching young girls get murdered while he ate a sandwich and drank Coke. Watching a video at home couldn't compare. It was too common, the box itself so small that it trivialised your interest. Besides anyone wandering past your house could come in and watch, thereby devaluing it to a democratic level. This was Roman. He was Caesar, a Maharajah watching blood sports performed for him while he sat regally in privacy.

Nearly half an hour had elapsed while Gopal sat like Caesar and Randy and Jill had slid so far forward that Gopal couldn't see their heads any more. He wondered if they were able to see the screen. Bernice, his Bernice he thought with pride, was slumped away from him against the door. There was a tap on her side on the window and she sat up.

'Bill,' she squealed and each particle of each syllable of her voice was like a knife thrown into Gopal's heart. 'Who're you here with?'

'Oh, bunch of jerks.'

'Well come on in. It's cold outside.'

'But your friends …'

'Oh he won't mind,' Bernice said quickly, 'he's from India. Come in,' she moved into Gopal making room.

Randy's head appeared over the front seat. 'Hi Bill,' he said without enthusiasm, 'don't you have a date to go to?'

'As a matter of fact I don't,' said Bill, opening the door and edging in without yanking out the speaker in the window.

Randy sighed and disappeared. Gopal was in a ferment. Clearly he had competition. The best way, he decided, to win Bernice was to impress her with his intellect. He would soon send this interloper scuttling by the sheer force of his oratory, he swore.

Bernice was formally introducing them when Gopal began his campaign to woo Bernice.

'I am sure you are feeling very concerned about trade deficits of third world countries,' he suggested.

'Who, me?' asked Bernice in real alarm.

'Well, these are because some very strange problems are occurring because of OPEC price increases.' Gopal noticed with satisfaction that Bernice was leaning back to hear him better, but a sword slid into his guts as he realised she was leaning into Bill who put both arms around her waist.

Gopal redoubled his efforts.

'You see, due to large transfer of funds from developing countries to OPEC, short-term resource crisis is prevailing. But in long term due to developmental needs of OPEC block and manpower and intermediate technology exports from developing nations, reverse recycling is occurring, leading to improved balance of payment position.'

Gopal saw Bill lower his head and kiss Bernice who raised her arms to lock them around his neck. The sword in Gopal's gut multiplied into many more swords that flung themselves into every portion of his anatomy, embedding themselves and twisting cruelly.

'Well,' Gopal began to subside sadly, 'and all that. But cash flow position is more healthy now,' he ended defiantly.

Bill raised his head with difficulty. 'Hey, don't stop now, buddy, carry on. This is great stuff.'

An impatient Bernice dragged his head down again.

Gopal glared at the screen and muttered to himself. While in other circumstances he would have been fascinated to observe in real life and from such close quarters these arcane erotic arts, right then his bloodstream still felt too full of knives cruising endlessly down, pricking his veins from inside.

Bernice was proceeding to get really enthusiastic. Gopal bit something soft in his mouth which he could have sworn was his heart. Bernice adjusted herself and dragged Bill lower whose hands began creeping southwards down Bernice's front. Gopal regarded each crawling hand as he would a cobra. He wondered what he should do.

He leaned forward and looked over the front seat to find Randy's face similarly enmeshed with Jill's. He sat back. The situation was becoming critical because Bill's hands were about to reach unthinkable outposts. Gopal raised his Coke glass and poured its contents over the front seat where he approximated Randy's head would be.

There was a yell of shock and Randy's face appeared dripping brown beads.

'They did it,' said Gopal virtuously pointing to Bill and Bernice who were still engrossed.

'Yeah,' grunted Randy, taking in the scene. 'Okay you two, break it up. Out. We're going home.'

The duo exited, still not completely disentangled, but helped out by a last spiteful push from Gopal.

They drove away and Gopal sulked for a week. He didn't sleep that night, wet smacking sounds flooding his dreams like a dam bursting every half hour. All the little knives in his system gathered themselves into one huge sword on which he felt impaled and which seemed to jut into the roof of his head with its hilt in both feet.

He glowered at young Tabatha who hid from him. He muttered monosyllabic answers to Mrs Wolff's friendly questions. He barely noticed the magnificent Thanksgiving dinner the next day and deliberately refused to praise Mrs Wolff's turkey except to ask if turkeys also gave thanks on Thanksgiving. He glared at Randy whenever their eyes met who winced helplessly. And before leaving he handed out the Wolff's farewell presents with the worst grace he could muster. He was not a very nice guest.

On the drive back to Eversville, he refused to look at the countryside, much less admire it.

7

Back in college, Gopal devoted himself to his work. Though he knew it was an illusion, he thought he sensed his mind flower and expand. The Indian system of education had drilled his mind and beaten it until it was a tight, rigid mass laid upon the fundamentals of science that had been dug deep until they sank into his subconscious. Now from this unshakeable base, he was able to make sorties that his American colleagues couldn't imagine trying, unsure as they were about the basics.

For the first time he began to learn the joy of analysis rather than retention. Based upon the core of fundamentals that had been hammered into him – often quite literally – he experimented with leaps of logic. Often he paused uncertainly, as though in mid-air, waiting for someone to admonish him and demand that he return to thinking by the book. Instead he found encouragement. His mind soared. He felt himself flying. For the first time in his life he gloried in studying.

I came out of India at the right time, he felt. He had got the best of an educational system where the early years instilled discipline and the basics, but the subsequent repetition of the same crippled minds that were ready to take off. In America he found that encouragement, yet simultaneously he found that the American students seemed unable to utilise the truly astonishing opportunities that their educational system offered at the higher levels.

He found himself studying late in the library, staying even later in the lab, not because he wanted higher grades, but because he was enjoying it. He felt that his grasp over his subject had become so thorough, that he was able to go back to the fundamentals, to those dragons of his earlier days, and look at them with a new eye. Why were they constructed as they were? What was the intent and what the result? Could they be improved upon? Such questioning would have been heresy to his Indian teachers, a scandal. But they had done their job and Gopal had left them behind. He often considered amusedly with what horror they would react to his questions and the viewpoints he held now. But now he thought of them, the giants of his childhood, as dusty, shrunken old men with barred minds.

Here, he exulted, they loved questions. They didn't care if they were insane, in fact the crazier the better, so long as they were also intelligent. Even the students, astonishingly, didn't seem to resent his clearly superior abilities. At least, he amended, most of them didn't. They said they enjoyed his sallies and they spoke to him, asked to study with him and expressed their admiration to him with a frankness that was staggering, yet deeply touching. Initially he was so incredulous at their straightforward talk that he suspected they were being sarcastic. But very quickly he realised they were transparently honest.

In India, he sighed with real pain, we could write the definitive book on envy. For centuries outsiders had exploited this fatal flaw, using it to divide and rule. And even today, rumours of a person's success caused demonic leaps of fury in the breasts of nearly everyone who heard about it. The immediate response was to either belittle him, or, if possible, to find ways to actively impede him. Using a simple contrast, Gopal suspected he received more compliments in one month in America on his abilities and his work, than he had received in all his life in India put together.

And then they wonder why there's a brain drain, he thought. It wasn't often any longer out of a desire for a more comfortable life in America – in India an affluent person usually lived better than one in America – but it was also for the sheer bliss of a friendly, supportive, well-equipped, encouraging work environment. It could be to get away from the fierce, eternal, all-encompassing hatred with which colleagues in India battled each other and everybody else, usually for no discernible reason other than habit. Transplanted to America, however, they were transformed into paragons of efficiency and tolerance, mused Gopal.

He closed his book as the lights in the library began to be turned on and off as a sign it was closing. As he stepped out into the night, the wind seemed to have a colder thrust to it than usual. He had hardly walked fifty feet when he felt a soft white dandelion rest on his cheek. He brushed it away and to his surprise it felt cold. He looked up and there were many of them floating gently downward. They looked like the little blossoms of a tree, but when they touched him they turned to water.

Snow, Gopal thought with a shock. Goodness me, they are having snow.

He had never seen snow before except in photographs where it lay like the skin of some dead white beast on the ground. He had not realised that it danced with such joy through the air, with the beauty of a ballet dancer. Its touch upon him was hesitant as a child's. And as Gopal raced under each flake trying to catch it in his mouth, he could have sworn each was alive as it playfully evaded him and settled on his hair or his coat. One enterprising fellow made his way on to the back of his neck and rested there for quite a while.

Gopal ran about, his ungainly legs pumping furiously, trying to swallow as many snowflakes as he could. It wasn't easy. Some bumped into his nose, another on his jaw, but it was exhilarating. He dashed about, his overcoat flapping, sucking in the air so clean and clear that it felt like a miraculous new drink. He snapped at a flake, leaping up for it, and his teeth clicked on themselves. A flake fell on his eye and stung. He blinked, trying to clear it and then brushed his sleeve over the eye.

When he could see again he saw with embarrassment that one of the security guards was sitting near by on his scooter and had been obviously watching him for some time. He was a burly, cheerful, red-faced man and Gopal wondered what he made of the sight of a foreign student leaping like a deer at midnight on the lawn, attacking snowflakes.

The guard started his scooter. 'Feels good to have a full stomach, doesn't it?' he remarked kindly, driving away.

Worse was to follow. There was a rustle among the nearby trees and Gopal realised that obviously there had been another witness to his infantile behaviour. A figure moved towards him in the dark and Sue's amused face came into the moonlight.

'Some exotic Indian night dance?' she suggested.

'What you are doing here at this time?'

'Coming out of the library. Same as you. Some of us Yanks work as hard as you guys do, believe it or not.'

Gopal heh heh'd in embarrassment, scuffling his feet.

'Well,' asked Sue, 'are we going to have a cup of coffee or are we going to freeze here?'

'Certainly, certainly, oh yes, coffee.'

Sue took his arm and they began walking. Her normally friendly face was particularly soft tonight and she looked incredibly amused.

'You've never seen snow before, have you, Gopal?' she said so gently that it wasn't an insult or a put-down.

'Well, only snow in India is in Himalaya mountains. I have not been.'

Sue put her arm through his and they walked closer together, seeking warmth in the cold. Gopal gathered from the direction that they were going to his apartment, but they walked past it, past a hedge to a tiny cottage next door.

'You are living here?' asked Gopal in surprise.

Sue smiled and nodded. Gopal was surprised he had never noticed the place, perhaps because it lay on the side away from the college. Sue went up the porch stairs and was fumbling with the lock. A sign alongside the door said 'Weizensacker.'

'What this is?' asked Gopal.

'Not what. Who. And the who is me.'

'Your name.'

'Yep. Step right in,' she invited pushing the door open.

Gopal walked in, careful but curious. He found a single room with a sofa, a small dining table with three chairs and a staircase on the side, going up. The carpet was threadbare and the furnishings were worn. Whatever cloth was visible was faded. A few brightly coloured cushions lightened the room. Even the lights were dim.

'Well,' said Sue, a little uncertain how all this would look to Gopal, 'home, sweet home. Why don't you sit on those cushions, they're near the heater. I'll turn it on.'

Gopal went over and watched her light up a contraption that looked like petrol cans joined together. A blue flame appeared and it began to hiss and emit a reluctant kind of warmth.

'It'll heat up,' she assured him. 'I'll go make some coffee. Make yourself at home.'

Gopal looked around again. It all seemed so simple and poor. A few prints hung on the wall and a spray of flowers sat in a vase on the dining table. Opposite the sofa was a small television set. Gopal switched it on and found it was black and white. He watched it unseeingly for a while, feeling sorry for Sue's obvious poverty. She seemed such a nice girl and he wondered why she hadn't married and moved out to some place better.

Sue returned with two steaming mugs.

'So,' she said handing one to Gopal, 'what d'you think?'

'You are having money problems?' Gopal blurted out. And was then horrified.

Sue didn't seem offended. She laughed. 'Yes, indeed. You can say that again.'

Gopal wondered how to frame the next question. Finally he asked, 'Why?'

'Ah why. You want the whole story? All right, I'll tell you.' She settled back against the sofa. 'No big deal here. I was married and now I'm not. He doesn't pay alimony and I don't care where he is. He walked out one night and now I'm trying to put myself through college so I'll be self-sufficient before I get married again. I have a part-time job that helps pay the bills and that's about it I guess.'

Gopal thought the most heart-breaking parts were the things she hadn't said.

Sue put her hand on his arm. 'Please,' she asked softly, 'no questions, okay? I don't want to think about it. It's all behind me. Okay?'

Gopal hesitated and then nodded.

'And now tell me about you, oh mysterious stranger from the East. What ancient secrets lie behind your inscrutable smile?'

Gopal giggled loudly at the thought.

'Hair oil,' he trumpeted with a rare burst of humour. Her solemnity dissolved too. 'You actually make hair oil?'

'Yes, yes. Many.'

'And you actually make money on it?'

'Oof, oof.' Sue gathered this meant yes.

'Well, tell me all about you. I mean how'd you get to Eversville of all places?'

'I am applying to many places and getting admission to five. Eversville is cheapest.'

'Yeah, but why come States-side at all? I mean your life seems a dream back there with servants and stuff.'

'Well, seeing world and things like that is making me broader before I am settling down to do business.'

'It's certainly making you broader,' tartly commented Sue. 'You're twice the size you were when you first came.'

Gopal chuckled, highly pleased. He started telling her about how plumpness was greatly respected in India as a sign of prosperity and from there on the conversation went on to the different sizes of his numerous relatives. Gopal had never found anyone so easy to talk to before and he astonished himself by his volubility and frankness. A bottle of wine had appeared somehow and was nearly exhausted before Gopal was. Finally he felt sleepy, dizzy and intoxicated, both by the wine and by Sue.

He tried to stagger to his feet and got on his knees, swaying.

Sue pushed him back gently.

'Sleep,' she said, putting a cushion under his head, 'I'll get you a blanket.'

Gopal lay still, the brightness of excitement combating the alcohol urging slumber. He heard Sue come down the stairs and the warmth of a woolly blanket all over him.

Sue got up and switched off the lights. There was just the hiss of the heater and the blue glow of its flame.

'Sleep well,' said Sue.

He felt her tuck the blanket under him. Her lips touched his for a while.

'Good night,' she said and he heard her on the stairs.

Something inside him burst like a flare and he was bathed from inside with white light. The excitement surged in him like a swell and then subsided. Before he fell into a deep dreamless sleep, with sudden clarity he thought, 'I am in love.'

The next thing he remembered was Sue's hand gently waking him. Groggily he woke. The wine felt as though it had accumulated inside his head and was sloshing there. Sue smelt of soap and nice things. It was still dark but the light was on. It was cold.

'I'm going out camping, Gopal,' he heard Sue say. 'But you can stay till you get up. When you leave, just make sure the door latches shut behind you, okay?'

'What? Who?' Gopal mumbled trying to struggle up.

'Go to sleep, sleepyhead.' He felt her kiss again. 'See you when I get back.'

He fell back flat, his heart pumping so loudly he was afraid he would have to hold it with both hands to control it. He heard the door open and close behind Sue and went instantly back to sleep.

When he woke again it was 11 o'clock in the morning. I will miss classes, he thought. He remembered the night and warmth began to flutter in his chest as though his breastbones had chrysallised into butterflies and were trying to fly away. One kiss, he slowly counted to himself. Two, he exulted aloud.

He leapt up from the makeshift bed and did a few steps that he persuaded himself were like Michael Jackson's moonwalk. How to celebrate? He thought in excitement. Push ups. I will do push ups, he decided. Dumb, dumb, how dumb, he berated himself. You cannot do push ups to celebrate.

He picked up his overcoat and rushed out.

The town had turned white. The streets, the houses, the trees, all were a clean glittering white. Gopal saluted this with the moonwalk too. A passing couple turned to stare at him, and not caring for once, Gopal added the be-bop he had learned from Randy at the mall, to his moonwalk. The couple had stopped to watch, so Gopal decided to sing them a song of joy as well.

The only song that came to his mind at that moment was the Indian national anthem, so he burst into that, keeping time with his moonwalk and punctuating it with his best be-bops.

Since Gopal sang about as well as he danced, the couple turned and fled. Gopal hastened after them as fast as his moonwalk would allow, holding his heart at the higher notes, till they sprinted away in panic. Gopal returned, winding down the anthem to a hum as he climbed the stairs to his room. Only after he got in did he realise that he hadn't put on his overcoat at all.

A hot shower cleared his head and some cornflakes made him feel more settled. He strode off purposefully to class and greeted all the surprised teachers and students with boisterous hellos and handshakes. He laughed unnecessarily at everything, and far too loudly in any case and called everyone he knew by wrong names. Then he settled himself in his chair, piled his books in front like a fortress and got down to some serious day-dreaming.

By the time it was evening he was extremely restless. The moment the last class finished he gathered his books and without waiting to dawdle for a chat he galloped to her house. He knocked on the door, rattled it and waited. Nothing stirred. He knocked even more loudly and reluctantly concluded that she hadn't returned yet.

Slowly he went back to his apartment and sat down at his dining table which was piled high with books, since he never used it for eating. He drew the curtain and saw that he could see up to the hedge dividing his apartment complex from Sue's house. He could even see the top of her house.

He opened his books and tried to study. Every hour he went down and knocked on her door in case she had driven in from the other side. The house remained silent.

At about midnight he began to really worry. So far he had told himself that it was probably some kind of Girl Scout's picnic with bonfires and singing and clapping, but now he wondered if something had happened to her and her friends. Perhaps they had met with an accident. He wished he had seen their vehicle before she left. If it had been a bus then the other vehicle must have been pulverised, serves them right.

At two in the morning, he looked down with surprise at the number of pages he had read of his book though he couldn't recall a word. He went down to check again and coming down her porch suddenly found the ground had turned to ice. He slid feet first, landing with a jar.

Shaken, he told himself he was being foolish. No woman was worth the trouble, his experienced friend Prakash used to always tell him. They are like taxis, Prakash never failed to add. If one goes away, another comes along. In any case, Gopal told himself, still lying flat on the ground, she is probably sleeping in some silly tent being mother to schoolgirls who were scared of the creaks and sighs in the dark outside.

Gopal picked himself up and went back home, annoyed with Sue and determined to get a good night's sleep. The next day was Saturday and he looked forward to a long rest. Hah, taxis, he gloated.

He was up at six tapping at her door. As the day wore on it became progressively more embarrassing to make a pilgrimage to her unyielding door every hour. Gloria had begun to notice and had placed herself by the window where she could watch the staircase. To add to Gopal's worries, it looked like she was writing another poem.

He thought of walking past Sue's house and around the block till she arrived, but he was afraid of the slippery streets. He fantasised that he would go to the house across the street and so enthrall them with his charm that they would let him sit at their window all day and keep watch on her house. Finally he just stayed behind his own window.

He was there all day, believing that a big yellow bus would rattle into view any moment and she would emerge amidst a chorus of adolescent goodbyes. By accident he would happen to be walking down the stairs and coincidentally would bump into her. How casually he would say hello to her, graciously acknowledging the stares of the appraising school girls, how casually he would pick up her little packing case and walk her to the door. And once inside, she would melt into his arms. He refused to speculate any further than that just now.

He sustained himself on cornflakes, orange juice, peanuts, cookies and potato chips from his larder, refusing to take the time off to go and eat. He didn't want to order a pizza because for some perverse reason he decided it would be a bad omen to eat and would delay her arrival.

The day dragged itself like a bag lady with overfull paper sacks. The sun set and there was no sign of her. Finally at 8.30, according to two sets of watches that both seemed to be functioning with abominable slowness, Gopal gave up in disgust and decided to walk down to the grocery store to replenish his stocks.

He trudged down, wondering what it was about her that he could have found so interesting. Aside of course from the fact that her name didn't begin with the letter J. It was amazing how many American names did. There was Joe, John, Josephine, Joanna, Joyce, Jack, Jake and probably hundreds of others, he thought. He bought the groceries and holding the bag with both hands began walking back. But aside from the J factor, he thought critically, there was nothing special about her.

She was back! His heart raced. There was a car in front of her house and several lights were on inside. The groceries weighing him down now felt the weight of a tennis ball. He thought of hurling them from this spot through Randy's window in the men's dormitory. He thought of charging into her house and scaring her. But he restrained himself and decided the strategy of coolness would pay the greatest dividends.

He went up to his apartment, carefully deposited the bag on the table, wiped his shoes with the curtain, dusted himself thoroughly and otherwise prepared and improved himself in every manner that did not require him to leave the window from where he could see her house.

Regally he thumped down the stairs. Fortunately no car drove away from her house, otherwise he would have had to abandon his quiet dignity and fling himself down with wild cries. Breathing deeply and evenly and smoothing his coat, he reached her porch.

Before climbing up he peered curiously into the car and noticed it was a two-seater. He stopped. A sense of alarm rose in him. He backed himself into the hedge and then crept along it till he reached the back of her house. He stood in the short space between the house and a dark wall. He stood against the wall and looked into the lighted room where he had slept the night some centuries ago.

Suddenly a face appeared at the window and Gopal froze. He realised that the face couldn't see him in the dark, but he dared not breathe. The face, he noticed, was young, male, with a red moustache, freckles, red hair. While apparently looking at him, it was combing its hair.

The sword that rose in Gopal's throat now felt like an old, familiar enemy. He watched aching and motionless as the face finished its toilet. Gopal was certain it winked at him. Then it turned and Gopal saw the rest of the body to which it was attached walk back, shout a goodbye up the stairs and leave. At least, thought Gopal, after two days and a night together, the least the face could have done was to wait till she came down the stairs to say goodbye.

He felt alone, more alone. The face had been company. He dragged himself away. Each leg felt like an elephant's trunk, his spine as if it had become an eel and he couldn't seem to lift his arms above knee level. He could scarcely recollect getting to his room, so engrossed was he in the sword stuck all the way up his chest, now slowly twisting and turning itself to cause the greatest hurt.

He punched Randy's number on the phone with fingers that didn't want to leave the buttons.

'Bar?' he suggested as Randy answered.

'You had one of those days too, huh? I'm on my way.'

By the time Randy arrived, Gopal had three empty beer cans in front of him and was stubbing out his fourth cigarette.

Randy held out a sheet of paper.

'It was stuck on your door.'

Gopal read it.

On the stairs today you went up and down
I hope you don't fall and break your crown.
You make my heart go pitter pat,
So don't fall and break your nat. (nut)
Gloria

Gopal handed Randy a beer.

'We are both needing.'

Carrying their beer they went out. The wind turned their breath to smoke and Gopal remembered his childhood when he would try to make smoke rings on winter nights. He refused to look at the direction of Sue's house. As they drove through the neighbourhood, he recalled how annoyed he used to feel at their stopping at every alternate street.

'Why you are always stopping?' he had irately asked.

'Well, there are all these stop signs you know. It's the law.'

'You are stopping only because sign is saying to stop?' Gopal had been amazed.

'Yep. Don't they in India?'

'Ha, never. No one is bothering with signs and many not even with red lights. If government is liking stop signs so much, then let them stop.'

Randy had tried to unravel the logic of this. 'But doesn't that kind of lead to a lot of traffic accidents?'

Gopal was even more surprised. 'Of course.'

'Then why don't they stop?'

'Because it is all in God's hands.'

'Wow.'

'You see, it is in His hands when we are going up and for how long we are staying here on earth. Isn't it?'

'Yeah, well I guess that's finally true.'

'Then who is damn government to tell us what to do?'

Randy sometimes reminded Gopal about that conversation along with solicitous questions about the 'damn government'. But today neither of them was feeling humorous. Both drank steadily and quietly from their cans.

'Which bar we are going?'

'You haven't been here before. A lot of young people come here. Mostly singles.'

They parked on the street. There seemed a large number of cars on both sides and they had to walk for a few minutes before reaching a house. Randy walked down a few stairs. They came to a door with a guard outside who hesitated almost imperceptibly when he saw Gopal.

'It's really crowded tonight, sir,' he apologised, 'I'm not sure you'll even find standing room.'

Randy stood his ground. 'We'll manage.'

The guard opened the door and the music screamed its welcome and the darkness swept out an arm and pulled them into its fold.

Only thing that welcomes you in America, groused Gopal to himself, is darkness. He was relieved to be out of the light and the guard's hesitancy. The music was so loud and so alive, that it actually seemed a living thing. Randy seemed to have disappeared into it and Gopal hastened to stumble his way to the wall and wedge himself into the corner against the bar.

He looked around cautiously. There really were a very large number of people. He noticed they seemed older than the students Gopal knew and were certainly better dressed. There seemed more women than men. They were all displaying that unique American gift for holding suave, sophisticated, apparently witty conversations in the midst of music so loud that nobody from any other country can hear a word. Gopal wondered how they did it.

Maybe they're pretending, he speculated. He saw a girl sitting a foot and a half away from him throw back her head and laugh at something that had been said by a man sitting with his shoulder against Gopal. Gopal hadn't heard either the man's words or the laughter. But obviously the girl had heard him because she would hardly risk a glorious laugh on a wild guess if she couldn't hear him at all. Supposing he was informing her of his mother's death.

All around there were people chatting, laughing, as though the music that was driving nails into his ears didn't exist at all. Maybe they lip read, thought Gopal. In any case nobody seemed to have come singly, because everybody seemed to be extremely good friends. After all can everyone lip read a stranger? Not unless they're a nation of lip readers. He thought about this for a while. Could there be another national conspiracy? Armies of kindergarten children being made to talk to each other while disco music blared through earphones clamped over their ears?

He felt a thump on his back and turned to find Randy mouthing soundlessly at him. Gopal laughed politely. Randy tried to pull him away towards two girls standing a little behind him waiting patiently. Gopal hugged the bar as if it was the last life raft on an empty ocean. At the best of times he felt paralysingly shy of girls. Even when he knew them well and could hear them perfectly, he had great difficulty in doing anything other than mumbling at them. Now he sweated at the prospect of trying to converse with strange women whose every word would be inaudible. Finally, when it became clear that the only way to prise Gopal's fingers off the bar would be by seeing them off, Randy gave him a disgusted look and walked away.

Gopal huddled over the bar top with enormous relief. He found himself looking into the laughing if dilated pupils of one of the bar girls. She said something and filled a tall glass with beer from a keg and put the glass before him. Gopal pulled out a note from his picket, saw it was a ten dollar bill and gave it to her. He gestured to his glass and then to the keg and she nodded that she understood that she should keep his glass filled till the dollars ran out.

Gopal concentrated on finishing as many beer glasses as he could, afraid to look around in case Randy pounced on him. Soon his ears began to buzz and he felt even more deaf. The bar girl kept his glass full and smiled at him every time. She had a nice smile and she was pretty. He began to drink his beer faster so that he could see her smile more often. He realised that she had been trying to talk to him while he had grinned back inanely. He wondered what she was saying but the thought was too difficult to hold.

Then suddenly she disappeared. He gazed intently down the bar trying to find her, and suddenly she was at his shoulder, a coat over her waitress costume. Wonderingly he allowed her to lead him out, but even his non-existent senses had enough awareness left for him to give Randy a kindly smile on the way to the door and to note the look on his face whose expression Gopal would remember to his grave.

Outside, the guard looked at the two of them leaving together as though his worst fears had been confirmed.

'Have a *very* good night, sir,' he wished them sadly.

The wind had dropped as they stumbled to her car and got in. Gopal had to try several times before he could locate his bottom on the seat.

'Drunk,' he muttered explanatorily.

'Don't apologise,' she giggled, 'I personally follow the policy of one glass for myself for every five glasses to the customers.'

They had hardly gone a few streets when she stopped in front of an old red brick building that was now closer to black. They staggered up the stairs, thanks largely to the handrails which Gopal used like a rope-climber and staggered into her room. They collapsed on her bed.

Before Gopal could struggle upright she was all over him. He plunged back and closed his eyes as he felt her lips and teeth on his neck. A red curtain undulated behind his eyes. Slowly the earth began to heave. Even in his drunken state Gopal sensed that the earth was scheduled to heave much later. Besides which he could only dimly feel where she was now on some extremity of his body, much less be aroused by her.

He felt himself begin to surge like the sea. The alcohol began to rise and fall in his veins like black waves in a storm. He felt as though his body was going up and down on crests and troughs, as though he was immersed in an ocean. I am feeling seasick, his mind gasped. He began to sweat as he lowered internal sluice gates against torrents of sickness. But the bile rose further and further with each attack, until with overwhelming force it flung aside his restraints and poured out in a gush of vomit.

The two nights of drinking, the junk food, the excitement and the despair, the worry, the most recent binge, all came pouring out till he felt his guts would come out through his throat too.

He had still retained enough awareness to turn his face away from where the girl was, so she was more concerned than angry.

'Aw gee, I'm so sorry, I didn't know you were sick, aw gee,' she apologised, rubbing Gopal's chest with a soothing circular motion.

'Okay, take it easy. You'll feel much better now.' She stroked the panting Gopal's sweaty head. The hair oil was melting but she carried on patting him.

Gopal's breathing eased. His chest began to feel cool. His brain, which had felt as if it was trying to emerge through his eyes and ears, fell back into place. The rest of his insides began to settle down. His ears stopped singing. Cautiously he waited until the feeling of well-being became a slightly permanent one. Then he began to feel embarrassed.

'I will help in cleaning,' he told the girl, pushing her away.

He tried to get up. To his shock the same feeling of rising and falling, making his head swim, making him feel seasick again, came over him. He tried to push himself up and felt himself sucked back as though he was lying in quicksand.

He felt the girl take his hand and pull him to his feet. He turned to look at the bed and he thought he was reeling because the bedcover was undulating towards him as though it intended to capture him and drag him back to its depths.

Gopal staggered back in alarm. The girl put a supporting arm around him.

'Whoa there,' she said kindly. 'It's only a water bed.'

Everything suddenly became clear to Gopal. He had heard of these depraved inventions before. His sense of being underwater, his feeling of seasickness, all became understandable. He was even able to look at the device with cautious curiosity, though it was hard to believe that it wasn't alive, a large, round, protoplasm, quivering hungrily for its prey.

Now he could smell the vomit and his own bitter taste.

'Clean up,' he suggested again.

'Nah, that's okay. No big deal. I'll take care of it,' the girl reassured him with exaggerated casualness, probably relieved that he wasn't dying in her room. 'Want me to drop you someplace?'

'I am staying near college.'

'Well, if you're ready to move, let's go. You want some coffee or something?'

'No, no,' said Gopal, heading out.

All the way to his apartment he kept quiet, his face averted from her so that she wouldn't have to breathe his smells.

Embarrassment made him vibrate like, he thought, the water bed. Since nothing could really condone his behaviour, he decided against saying anything at all. He felt as though he was no longer a man. He felt disgraced, as low as the vomit he had left behind.

He began to worry if the girl and he knew anyone in common and if news of his traumatic failure might get to the college. He began to wonder how best to protect himself. At least she didn't know his name, he thought with relief, so the chances of her pinpointing him as an embarrassment and failure were remote.

In a friendly, reassuring voice she asked, 'And where're you from?'

Gopal's mind raced like a rat. All could be lost here. 'From Pakistan.'

'Aw gee, that's great. And I've forgotten your name.'

Gopal struggled with himself. 'Myself is Abdul.'

They had arrived at the campus.

'I am getting off at corner here,' said Gopal.

'That's okay. I'll drop you to your place.'

'I am staying in men's dorm. They are not allowing visitors at night.' Gopal was astonished but pleased at his fluent lies.

'Oh okay,' she pulled over. 'Maybe we can get together sometime, huh?'

'Certainly. But I am returning to Pakistan next week.'

'Aw gee, that's a real pity. Well, take care now. By the way, my name's Cindy.'

They shook hands in greeting and farewell, but briefly. Gopal got out and watched her car till it had disappeared, to make sure she couldn't see which way he was going. Then he tramped home.

When he got there he found a sealed envelope taped to his door, saying 'To Gopal, from Sue.' He tore it up unread and tossed the scraps over the rails. He watched them float away, like lost souls, luminous.

8

The next morning Sue called and the moment Gopal heard her voice he put the phone down. Sue called again and he did the same thing. She called a third time and Gopal now kept the phone off the hook. He refused to think of her. He felt all his emotions about her boiling inside him and he firmly gathered them together, stuffed them into some kind of internal box and put a lid on them. It felt like a pressure cooker.

Must study, must study, he told himself, rushing around and gathering his books. He slammed the door behind him and set off for the library. He had discovered that thought was sometimes an antidote for emotions. Whenever he felt himself particularly distressed and hurt, he dashed inside his head into a room reserved for mathematics.

There, amidst familiar symbols and predictable logic, he performed mental calisthenics until he was exhausted. It was calming, absorbing and when he felt more in control, he cautiously opened the door and peered out. Often the monsters of emotions were gone for good. At other times he could see them hiding near by, so he would return to the room and immerse himself in its strange, incestuous beauty till he felt it was safe again.

The worst was when he thought it was safe and would walk out and take himself somewhere when suddenly, some hidden animal of emotion would leap inside him and sink its teeth into his guts. It left him feeling utterly helpless. And it seemed to happen much more often in America where girls were concerned. Perhaps the fact of living alone made him concentrate much more on such emotions, sharpening them. In India there were many friends to share them with and many relatives to keep him diverted, besides which he had never been in position of such intimacy with girls.

Even when he did meet them in India, there were the armours of politeness, of common friends, fears of society, to protect him. Here he felt emotionally naked within minutes. The girls went under his skin as if it was made of paper, made themselves at home deep inside him and sharpened their nails on his bones.

With Sue, he had sensed that she touched a part of him that he had never known existed. She had barely grazed something that had lain dormant if not dead all these years in India and whose existence he wouldn't even have suspected all his life. But the reverberations of that little caress had rolled through him so loudly, so ominously, so painfully, that he had realised that if Sue actually began to play on whatever that thing was within him, she would control his life totally. He would alter direction, become a different person, anything could happen.

Even after just their fleeting moments together, he felt so betrayed by her weekend with another man, that he couldn't bear to think of them together. He felt numb at the consequences to him in case he spent more time with her and she then wandered away with somebody else.

Strange creatures these women, he thought warily. Looking so soft and weak, but what troubles they are causing!

He hastened towards the refuge of the library. Footsteps squelched behind him.

'So what'd I do wrong?' her familiar voice asked.

Gopal shook his head and walked on.

She stayed in place behind his shoulder. He could sense her thinking. 'You're making me feel cheap. Is that what you want?'

Gopal didn't answer. The pressure cooker in him was boiling and he had to sit on it.

'I'm sorry,' she said softly. 'I know it was wrong, but he's an old friend and I had promised him. Forgive me this once, okay?'

The pressure cooker overflowed scalding his insides, but he still had it under control. Just about. Gopal ran from Sue. From her voice and its softness and need and hurt. From the lovely promises it held. From the future that being with her would first cause to crumble and then reshape.

He felt his eyes grow wet but he kept running.

Once again he dived desperately into the always welcoming world of books, of words, of logic. Once again books were the balm for his shredded heart. Sitting again in his eyrie, in the nook he had made his own, he thought for the first time in his life of his heart.

Though doubtlessly a vital portion of his anatomy, he had to confess he had never given it much thought as it went about its lawful business. Now he had to adjust to the fact that it wasn't just a basic heart, it was also some kind of serpent in disguise. It lay there all asleep, then when you least expected it, the damn thing leapt up and bit you in painful areas. It had never, he thought bitterly, behaved like that in India.

It was so easy and so tempting to think of American girls as sex objects, but his own ability to handle the emotions that accompany a relationship was certainly in doubt. Gopal sensed that his own development in this area was so primitive that he probably had the emotional state of an adolescent in a junior high school in America. But the women he met were obviously much better able to manage a relationship, as well as several others simultaneously. On the other hand, he, a shaken Gopal felt, merely had the arrogant brashness of the utterly naïve. For a few brief moments he had felt Sue open the hidden box of his emotions and he had glimpsed inside it an overwhelming joy, and coexisting in the same space, the red writhing worms of hurt.

Gopal didn't think he wanted to see more of the box. Yet in this country that didn't seem possible. Not only were they careless of the box and what it could do to them, they seemed to take out its contents and display it on the sidewalk for strangers to examine. Not that they were unaffected by the trauma; they seemed to hurt a lot of the time. It was just that they never seemed to learn. One emotional disaster always seemed to be a prelude to an even bigger holocaust.

He had held long discussions on this with the learned Randy, whose opinions and views on matters relating to sex and its aftermath were, like those of many young Americans, frighteningly experienced for his years. Gopal didn't think that in the rest of his life in India he would experience as many emotional upheavals as he had in these last few months. He couldn't even begin to compare with Randy whose experiments with the other sex seemed to have started as soon as he was able to climb over the cradle walls. He freely and casually admitted to devastating heartbreaks. 'You get used to it,' he grinned. 'You just staple the pieces together and carry on. Just don't try it too often though,' he cautioned as an afterthought.

Gopal was determined not to try it at all. All his broodings about hearts and emotions and boxes of snakes had made him feel uneasily like the heroes in romantic novels that Mrs Saxena's daughter read at an appalling rate. Gopal had flipped through some on visits to the Saxena house and warned the mother that such garbage would turn her daughter's brains into a junkyard. Privately, he believed that Miss Saxena was so ugly that such books were the closest she would ever get to romance.

To now find himself pondering such embarrassing subjects made him feel foolish and irritable. He was quite content to amble along in life without having to see exposed some red wound in his recesses which he had never suspected. A life, he concluded, devoted largely to selling hair oil, was a far more sensible one. Let the Americans keep their obsession with sex and romance and let them pay for it. It would be good revenge for Vietnam. And yet, how curious that they rejected any suggestion that they were a deeply, incurably romantic people, as displayed by everything they did – from the unending pursuit of each other at the individual plane, to the amazing insistence on human rights at the international scale. All of it demonstrated an undying belief that a better world, a more perfect relationship, a rosier future, was possible.

And that was probably the essence of romance, thought Gopal, this belief that things can be made better, that the future will become brighter. India, on the other hand, seemed to believe, based on its past, that the future normally made life worse. At the personal level, Indians didn't even seem to believe in love as an emotion directed at a unique person, as displayed by that monument to pessimism, the arranged marriage. Nearly total strangers were married off to each other on the theory that people from roughly the same background and with a clear idea of the duties and responsibilities of each, would make happy marriages. In a depressing majority of cases, they did.

Gopal slammed his book shut in disgust. He had caught himself brooding about romance again. He decided to go out into the cold afternoon air and let it sweep these mushy thoughts from his mind.

He walked briskly out of the library and saw two people tossing a frisbee. He wondered idly why so many Frisbee players had beards. He had tried to throw one once with undistinguished success. He found himself walking towards the cafeteria breathing deeply, feeling the clean air fill his lungs with light.

Outside the cafeteria two people, a man of about thirty-five and a woman who was much older, were distributing leaflets to everyone who came out or went through the door. As Gopal approached them, both looked awkward. The man looked familiar to Gopal, who waited patiently in front of them till they reluctantly gave him a leaflet each.

The one from the lady was a straightforward request for money by an organisation that said it wanted funds to train soldiers to work for Christ to convert the Godless heathens. The man's leaflet was far more fascinating.

It reminded the reader about the global Communist conspiracy against America and warned that its latest manifestation was the attempt to mix coloured blood with white Americans so as to 'dilute the perfection of the Aryan race whose achievements have taken the world to where it is.'

Gopal brightened visibly at the prospect of an argument. He smiled his friendliest grin at the man who was shrinking visibly in embarrassment but maintaining a defiant hostility.

'We have met?' questioned Gopal.

The man looked even more awkward. Gopal heard him mutter something about restaurants and beef. Suddenly he recognised him as the supercilious headwaiter at the restaurant where he had first eaten beef with Sue, Ann and Randy.

Gopal clasped the man's hand in pleasure.

'How wonderful I am seeing you again,' he exulted. 'Come in,' he beamed, urging him through the door with such courtesy that the man, clearly wishing he was anywhere but here, reluctantly crept in. The lady, looking confused, followed.

Gopal led to the far corner, while assuring the man of how pleased he was to meet such an old friend.

'Sit, sit,' urged Gopal. He had come to believe that though the American personality contained many positive elements, it lacked the essential one of enjoying arguments. People either said 'yes' or 'no' or sometimes a 'maybe'. If they liked something they said so and if they didn't they let you know that too. Sometimes they were even polite about it, but decisively so. If they didn't like something and still didn't walk away, it was a dangerous sign, portending physical violence.

Their attitude was so clear cut, that it left no space, no large chunks of vacant territory on which a person could base an argument, fortify it, launch attacks from it, defend it and when all seemed lost, sneak out in the night to wage guerrilla war leaving the old argument in ruins.

There was a very real pleasure to be derived from such arguments approximating war and Gopal felt its absence keenly. Either Americans were too busy to occupy themselves in such pointless pursuits, or they took the reasons being propounded thoughtfully, not realising that in any mutually gratifying agreement, as in any war, the main purpose was the process of the whole thing, not the logic or its lack in it. Gopal felt disappointed in the Americans for not appreciating this, particularly since they were a nation that had gone into Vietnam, Grenada and reflagged oil tankers and otherwise displayed such a masterful talent for being illogical.

Gopal sometimes pined for his Indian friends among whom he had seen savage fights occur between people who were on the same side of a question. What evenings there used to be! Fiercely contesting this and that and often God alone knew what, but always disagreeing. It was common to find people entering a room vehemently rejecting what everyone else was saying, or had said, or indeed might say.

Americans though never seemed to take such vigorous positions. And if they did and found them so savagely and scornfully attacked, they turned red and Gopal always feared that they might pull out a gun and resolve the matter with a wholly permanent finality, which, apart from being painful, would be dishearteningly terminal.

But today, Gopal exulted, he had found a headwaiter after his own heart.

'Have milk shake,' Gopal urged. 'What is your good name?'

'Ah, I'm Tom.'

'Myself is Gopal. Let us discuss.'

Tom clearly didn't want to discuss and was looking trapped.

'You are knowing that Aryans are coming to India?' Tom looked surprised.

Gopal drew a symbol on the table with ash from the ash tray.

'You are recognising?'

'Yeah, sure, that's something near Hitler's swastika sign.'

'Commonly used religious symbol in India.'

'Is that right,' said Tom relieved that the discussion was over, 'that's a completely new ball game then. Sure is.'

'And Asians are scoring higher in IQ tests.'

'Hey hey hey, time out, time out. Now hold on there for one cotton pickin' minute.' Tom was starting to lose his politeness. 'That's not true and I know it.'

'And no Communist threat is there to America, there is only big Communist threat to Communism.'

'Well, hell, you're one hell of a ball player, I can tell you that. But you don't know nothin about here in America. There's one Commie under every rock as Joe McCarthy said. And I can tell you, we've got to be real careful. Now nothing personal you know, but we've got our own problems and our own way of doin things here and we don't want nobody messin with nothin we do, know what I mean?'

'Children from mixed marriages,' said Gopal thumping the table, 'are having more brains.'

'Well mebbe they do and mebbe they don't,' said Tom placating but determined, 'but we don't want none of them here. We're going to keep America just the way it's always been and that's the only way to keep it great. My grand-daddy died fightin for it, my Dad was wounded in the war, my brother served in Korea and I did my duty in Nam. We've paid our dues and we done all we could for this country, but we didn't do it to turn America into no nigger heaven, pardon my saying so. And we'll do it again if we have to against those Commie rats and anybody else that don't like the way things are. That's the American way.'

'Amen,' burst out the lady.

Gopal tried to interrupt. Tom ignored him.

'And I can tell you it makes me sick to my stomach the way this country's goin to hell and nobody's doin nothin about it. Well I reckon it's time some red-blooded Americans got together and told them all where to get off. Now nothin personal against you, sir, you being a visitor and all, but coloured blood is the real problem we got here. It's the Comunists trying to do us in and it's time America woke up to that.'

'Amen,' repeated the lady.

'And don't think I don't know what's happening,' Tom nodded significantly. 'I got a good head here and I kin use it. I seen the foreign people comin in here and takin our jobs and the factories closing down. Yes, sir, don't think I ain't seen nothin. I know what it's all about.'

'You see,' Gopal explained patiently, 'you are needing foreign investment –'

'Oh no, oh no, no, we're not. We ain't needin nothing foreign. We never did before and we sure don't now. That's not what made America great.'

'Then what you are needing?' challenged Gopal, delighted.

'We need American jobs for American people. We need to tell our people about the Communist menace and warn them about them foreigners. Can you believe,' and Tom's voice suddenly had a wondering softness to it that made Gopal's nerves tingle, 'that men who've risked their lives for this country now ain't got no jobs. And it's all started when them foreigners came in and took our jobs and the factories closed down. Yeah, I seen it all. We've got to make America for Americans again.'

'You were working in factory?' asked Gopal quietly. There was such suppressed passion in Tom's voice that Gopal sensed it was not a college debate any longer.

'Trained mechanic,' Tom nodded. 'Best damn one you ever saw. I could fix a truck in Nam almost as fast as I could kill a gook, if you'll pardon my French. And now I ain't held a job in three years.'

'You are headwaiter in restaurant.'

'You call that a job? It's what high school kids do for pocket money. I got me a wife and kids to support. Sure I fake it real good, but what's a guy to do? You tell me that.'

Gopal was abashed at the anguish in Tom's eyes. It wasn't a harmless argument any more. It was a hurt man and a very real family standing behind him. The children must be small, Gopal thought.

'Any trouble here?' a soft, high-pitched voice asked.

They looked up and it was the Peacock, 6 feet 6 inches, with a new hat, an even more colourful shirt and his reflecting sunglasses. He put his hands on the table and they looked like sledgehammers.

'Nah,' said Tom and a lingering bitterness infused his voice. 'What could possibly go wrong? Everything's just great. Well, sir,' he stood up and adopted his headwaiter stance and language, 'I do hope we'll have the pleasure of your company real soon.'

He bowed and left. The lady trotted behind him, both carrying leaflets that Gopal suspected were really a plea to God or man or anyone to come to their assistance. No one, Gopal felt with a pitying certainty, ever would.

'What'd he want?' the Peacock asked.

'Oh he is not having job so he is hating world.'

'White boy's learnin about life, huh?'

'No, no,' said Gopal defending Tom, 'he is poor, I think so he is writing leaflets and distributing.'

'Writing leaflets, huh,' the Peacock's sunglasses reflected thoughtfully, 'and I suppose you felt real sorry for him.'

'Well,' said Gopal shocked at such hardheartedness, 'I mean of course and I mean things like that –'

'Come,' said the Peacock swivelling on his heel and sailing out, his shirt billowing behind him.

Gopal hastily followed, afraid of the consequences if he disobeyed. The Peacock flung open the door with a sound like the crack of thunder and to Gopal it sounded like the elements themselves fell over each other to provide the sound effects to the Peacock's majestic passage. They reached a sports car with flames painted on its sides and both got in.

It was like being in an aircraft cockpit. There were needles and gauges everywhere, soft green lights lit the instruments, switches caused windows to whirr, all sorts of witchery occurred as they drifted out of the college.

Gopal would have enjoyed the hi-tech wizardry more if he could have figured out where the Peacock was taking him. Perhaps he was going to tie his arms to a tree and beat him. Or he might be, Gopal thought with a wince, a homosexual.

He contemplated the consequences of that with dread. Or he might have a divorced sister he would call to a church and who Gopal woul marry, without the Peacock even asking it, his presence being threat enough. Gopal wondered how he would explain his new bride to his parents. His grandmother wouldn't desist from holy songs for the rest of this incarnation. Gopal was starting to panic. What on earth could the Peacock want with him?

'Nice day,' suggested Gopal tentatively.

The sunglasses turned and looked at him and looked away without comment. Gopal didn't dare say another word in case the Peacock reached across and crushed his neck like a beer can. He tried to breathe more softly so it would annoy the Peacock less.

They had passed through the parts of Eversville that Gopal recognised and were now driving between a vast junkyard. On both sides were stacked piles of rusted objects, cardboard boxes, abandoned cars and inexplicable shapes. It looked, thought Gopal, like what Headwaiter Tom would probably imagine an Indian supermarket to look like.

Gopal saw a few figures carrying sacks shuffling from spot to spot, finding and choosing items they could put into their bags. They all seemed old, or at least it appeared that way from a distance.

Almost immediately after the junkyard ended, they entered what seemed a ghost town. Buildings so weary that they seemed upright only with a heroic effort. A tattered curtain fluttered out of a window like the flag of an impoverished nation. The automobiles, those expressions of an American's self-image, were rusted, battered, tired. The lawns were untended. Windows stared brokenly. Clothes hung brazenly to dry on clotheslines in front of the homes. Clearly the place was inhabited. People became visible, some sitting on house steps, others leaning against walls, all seemed to carry a brown paper bag clutched at the neck. And all of them, Gopal gradually realised, were black.

The Peacock slowly drove through the streets. Such was the languor of the lollers, so listless were they, that almost none of them acknowledged the great car prowling through them, like a tiger among sheep.

Suddenly a fight erupted among a group. There was a fierce uproar for a while, then they dispersed, a few to resume lounging against the wall, some to disappear into alleys, leaving one very tall man standing in the middle of the street screaming at the sun. A trickle of some kind of liquid ran down the sidewalk and over his feet. He ignored it, his ranting increased. Gopal couldn't understand a word of what he said, but he could sense the rage and the frustration of the man which spewed out of his mouth like a tangible flame.

'What is happening to him?' Gopal asked.

'Same thing that's happening to everyone around here. They is born poor, they stays poor and they dies poor. You'd be mad too if it happened to you.'

Gopal shook his head in disbelief. 'It is not even looking like America. No one is working, there is so much dirt, it is so poor.'

'I figure they don't think it's part of America either. The white boys keep the junkyard between them and us and they don't want to see us or hear about us.'

'What work people are doing here?'

'Not much. The most money you make is going through the junkyard and picking up whatever whitey throws away. You wouldn't believe the kind of stuff the white boys got no use for.'

'You are living here?'

'Sure did. And if it wasn't for football I still would be. And if I don't make it big, if someone busts my knees in a game, this is home again. There are a lot of soul brothers who didn't do so good that're still here. The ones that are lucky.'

'And unlucky ones?'

'Dead or in jail. Sure happened to a lot of them.'

Gopal shivered. Even with the gusts of wind he could sense the empty stillness. It felt menacing. One day it will go up like a petrol tank, he thought.

'You wanna go back now?' asked the Peacock. His voice was kind. Gopal nodded.

'When I heard the white boy bellyaching about his problems, I thought maybe I otta show you some real problems. Show you how the black man lives. Ain't as cute as white America, is it?'

Gopal suddenly asked: 'Why you are earlier talking in rhyme?'

'I ain't one for talking much to folks I don't know. When I have to talk, I make it short and sweet and real educated. I ain't having no one laughing at me. Say, what do they think in India of the colour problem? You have much of that?'

'Well,' Gopal fumbled, trying to find a way to explain to this giant young man the complexities of India.

'I mean,' continued the Peacock, 'do they look down on the black man?'

'Well,' parried Gopal, not wanting to give him the bad news, 'actually everyone is brown.'

'It figures,' nodded the Peacock in resigned understanding. 'The black man's the lowest on the pole everywhere, huh?'

Gopal twisted in embarrassment. He tried to frame a brief history of India and the impact of fair-skinned invaders and the final result of two hundred years of British rule. He groped for some American parallel.

'You know,' said the Peacock, 'I really want sometime to get out of this place and go walk among my own people, know what I mean? Not have everyone stare like you're a freak.'

'Yes, that I am understanding fully. I am also wanting many times to go home.'

'Maybe we can both go,' joked the big man. More seriously he asked: 'Is there much football played in India? I mean can I get a job on a team?'

Gopal tried to laugh it off. 'Heh, heh. Maybe we are using Taj Mahal for football matches.'

'Great,' enthused the Peacock, now really interested. 'Is that like the local stadium?'

Gopal looked at him sideways and found him serious. 'No, no,' he placated, 'we are only playing soccer.'

The Peacock's excitement dissipated.

'What your real name is?' asked Gopal.

'Peacock is it. Don't use no other. Like Mr T. Know who I mean? Big, mean mother?'

'Oh yes I have seen on TV.'

'Well, here we are,' said the Peacock drawing up outside the cafeteria. 'I hope you checked out what I had to show you.'

He reached over, took Gopal's hand, twisted and mangled it and ended by bouncing his fist off Gopal's palm.

'That's the soul shake. Keep the peace, brother.'

Gopal got off. His hand ached and he wondered if what he had seen was actually true. It seemed like a part of the dream that America hid from everyone. He trudged home shaking his head in amazement, partly because there existed such dismal poverty in this richest of all lands and partly because such few people knew about it.

The next afternoon after classes had finished for the day he headed for the cafeteria and again saw Tom outside its door, handing out leaflets. They nodded quickly to each other and Gopal walked in.

After some time Tom came in and sheepishly stood near Gopal's table.

'Sit, sit,' urged Gopal.

'Well, just for a while,' Tom conceded, edging in. 'Boy, I really gave you an earful, didn't I? You must think I'm weird or something. I mean I've been thinking about it all night.'

'No, no,' assured Gopal. 'You are patriot. That is good thing.'

'Yeah, but all the stuff I said. I mean you must really think Americans are strange.'

'People are people,' said Gopal. 'Indians are also like this.'

'Really?' Tom was surprised.

'Yes, yes. Everywhere people are same. I am having uncle who is so proud of India and culture that he is thinking all others are inferior.'

'India had culture?' Tom was downright sceptical.

'Going back 4,000 years back. Many palaces, tombs, art and dances.'

'How come no one ever hears of it? I mean no offence, but let's face it, who's heard of India?'

'Well, Christopher Columbus is hearing. What you think he is looking for when he is discovering America?'

'Oh yeah, that's right. Now, that's pretty far out. Never thought of that. But say, ain't it right that only the highest castes can make money and everyone else is treated like shit? I mean I know about all that stuff.'

Gopal was pleased that Tom had at least heard of castes and was genuinely touched by his interest and willingness to listen.

'No, no, no, not true at all.'

'Well,' challenged Tom, now feeling himself on firmer ground, 'ain't it right that all your leaders – d'you call them presidents? – all belonged to the highest caste? I mean that guy in the underwear and bedsheet who kept getting rolled in that movie I saw –'

'Mahatma Gandhi. He was not from highest caste. He was from trader caste.'

'Is that right? And say, how come he didn't waste those guys who were bashing him? Man, he should have got a gun and shot them all dead.'

'He is,' said Gopal with heroic restraint, 'having other ideas.'

'Boy, sure burned me up, watching him get pasted. Say, you're not Christian, are you?'

'No, I am Hindu.'

'Oh, right. Is that like Moslem?'

'No, no. Separate.'

'So do you like to go to churches and stuff?'

'We are having temples.' Gopal wondered what this was leading to.

'Well hey, listen, you seem like a really nice guy. Know what I mean? And this Sunday there's a special prayer service at my church, so if you're not doing nothing, d'you want to like come along and listen to the word of our Lord, I mean take in His words?'

'I am reading Bible many times.'

Tom gaped. 'Well, that's real nice, really great. But you ain't heard nothing till you hear our preacher. Man, is he something else? I mean when you've heard him, you stay heard. Know what I mean?'

Gopal did. The desire to seek converts was a palpable one among all Christian preachers in India despite firm discouragement by the government. In America, where there was something of a shortage of people who remained to be converted, preachers must be starved of heathen souls to save. Perhaps that explained the born again creed. It offered a new challenge, some old souls that could be retreaded.

'All right,' he agreed, reluctant to give offence, and aware that it was a great concession for someone of Tom's beliefs to invite him. 'But I do not know way.'

'That's okay,' assured Tom. 'I'll pick you up. Where do you stay?'

Sunday morning was drizzly and gloomy. Gopal wondered if he could pretend to be sick, but with a sigh got dressed. Tom arrived and Gopal met his wife and two little daughters in the car. The wife was shy and nervous, but the children were not. They told him all about their friends on the way.

They drove till the outskirts of the town and parked outside a plain wooden building painted red. A sign said 'Church of Redemption'. Tom's wife – Gopal couldn't remember her name – scampered away in relief to join a group waiting outside. Obviously everyone had been told beforehand about his visit, because he received many friendly smiles and 'how you doins' from people who didn't look very friendly.

Gopal wondered why he felt an aura of roughness around them. The men seemed large and bulky, the clothes very loud, the accents harsh. The women wore perfumes that smelled cheap. Their eyes had an edge to their glances. Their voices seemed shriller and more savage than what Gopal had become used to. Everyone was looking at him covertly.

They walked in and sat down on the simple wooden benches. The voice became more hushed. The organ started and the service began. Gopal didn't feel as much at home as he had in the first church he had gone to for his speech on modern India, so he didn't join the singing. He watched the minister who was a short, stocky man with thick features and black hair brushed back. His face had adopted a look of such piety that Gopal distrusted him.

As the music died down the preacher began to rock from side to side, increasing the speed until he burst out. 'Satan,' he roared, thumping the pulpit, 'Satan is everywhere today.'

'Amen,' murmured the congregation.

'All round me, I look around and what do I see? I see fornication.' He waved at the walls and Gopal looked eagerly around only to be disappointed.

'I see drugs. I see the demon drink. I see our brothers and sisters being unfaithful to their marriage vows. I see Japanese cars. I see our factories closing. I see our sisters showing their nakedness everywhere.'

'Amen,' said Gopal, attracting severe looks.

'I see the Communist menace all round us. I see the Godless Communists come raining down on us, taking away our jobs, making us slaves, raping our flocks.'

Raping our flocks? thought Gopal incredulously, was he accusing the Soviet High Praesedium of bestiality?

'Yes, my brothers, I see Godlessness everywhere and I hang my head in shame.'

He hung his head in shame for a while.

'And why do I hang my head in shame? Is it because I have done some wrong? Yes, my brothers, because I have sinned. Because we have all sinned. Because seeing Satan and his works around us, yet we do nothing. Therefore we have sinned. Oh there is none so blind as those who will not see.'

'Hallelujah!' said the flock.

'And yet it is our duty, our sacred duty to battle Satan and his Communist hordes.'

'Amen.'

'And do you know why, my friends? Because I had a dream last night.'

'Hallelujah!'

'Yes, brothers and sisters, I had a dream. And in my dream a shining light came and in a voice of thunder it said, "Go forth and battle Satan. Go ye and battle his Communist type empire." And I said, "But, Lord, I am weak and alone. Satan has many tanks." And he said, "Oee of little faith. Speak to your flock.

And their strength shall multiply manifold. My strength shall be their strength. Say to them it is the Lord's work. Get them to distribute leaflets."'

'Praise the Lord,' chorused the worshippers.

'And I said, "Lord, forgive me my trespasses, but many will fall by the wayside and die, slain by the Communists, so tell me, Lord, give me a sign, tell me why we should battle the Communists." And the Lord said, my friends, he said in a voice that made the Heavens shiver. He said: "Because they don't follow the American way."'

'Amen.' 'That's right.' 'Praise be the Lord.'

'And yet many among us today,' the reverend was obviously in great form, 'walk the path going right down to hell. Yes, my friends, going right down to hell. O little do they know of what waits at the end of that path, that terrible path.'

'Say it preacher.' 'Amen.'

'Hell, my friends. Hell waits at the end of that terrible path.'

'Hallelujah! Say it like it is.'

'And the walls of hell are ten thousand miles thick. And whosoever goes in, he surely will never come out again. Because black devils will leap on him and tear him limb from limb. They will cut out his sinning heart and roast it on a spit.'

'Say it right out, brother.' 'Praise be the Lord.'

'And they will grill his liver and eat his kidneys and drink his blood.'

'That's right.' 'Sure will.' 'Amen.'

'And there is no escape. None at all. Because the walls of hell are ten thousand miles thick.'

'That's saying it like it is reverend.' 'Hallelujah!'

'Ten thousand miles thick, my friends. And their livers grilled for eternity. Because the more God cooks the sinner the more he needs to be cooked.'

'Sure does.' 'Praise the Lord.'

'And yet, my friends,' the reverend raised a finger, 'the Lord is merciful.'

'Amen.' 'Praise be His name.' 'Sure is.'

'Merciful and kind. And in his heart he finds room to forgive sinners if only they will accept him.'

'Hallelujah!'

Gopal thought the preacher was looking at him and wondered if all this wasn't getting a bit personal.

'Once, my friends,' the preacher went on, looking occasionally at Gopal, 'once I was a sinner too. A Godless miserable suffering creature.'

'Praise be to the Lord.' 'Amen.'

'Fornicating and drinking, living a Godless life, with no place for the Lord in my heart.'

'Amen.'

'But one day, I was a drivin down the street, just a drivin down the street.'

'Hallelujah!'

'And I had stopped at a red light. That's right. Just a stopped at a traffic light.'

'Praise be to God.'

'That's right. And I heard a tapping at my window, that's right.'

'Amen.'

'And it was Jesus.'

'Hallelujah!'

'And he was a knockin at my window and sayin "Let me in, brother, let me into our car."'

'Praise be His name.'

'But I just drove my car away. Because I was sinner and I was afraid.'

'Amen.'

'But Jesus, he just ran right alongside the car, tappin at the window and sayin "Let me in, brother. Let me into your car." Until I opened the window and let Jesus in, into my car and into my heart and into my life.'

'Glory to the Lord.' 'Hallelujah.' 'Amen.' 'Praised be the name of the Lord.'

Gopal gathered this might not be an opportune moment to enquire if Jesus had encountered any difficulties in getting his cross through the window.

The congregation burst into song. After it finished Gopal assured Tom that he was deeply moved and they left. On the way out he congratulated the reverend on his inspiring speech.

'I hope we'll see you again in our midst soon.'

'Certainly, most certainly,' Gopal assured him with all sincerity. 'I am having wonderful time.'

The reverend beamed. 'We all have a wonderful time in the Lord's house.'

They left.

Dearest Brother,

Kindly convey greetings to Respectable Parents.

So, what all is cooking? With me, good times are prevailing. I am knowing all many things about America now. I am finding Mexican place to eat where for five dollars you are eating all you want, so I am until I am full filled and well fed up. The staff are gathering and giving such looks I cannot tell you. It is serving them right. Now whenever I am going they are turning even more white. But, Brother, Mexican food is tasting so much like Indian that what to do?

Anyway, I am learning many important things about Americans. Biggest thing is language. It is earlier making many problematics for me, because like everyone I am thinking Americans are speaking English. But, Brother, it is not English, it is American. I am facing so many embarrassings on this reason.

Once sitting with Good Friends, we are making good times. Saying jokes and laughing but when I am also saying good joke, they are saying, 'get out of here'. I am going home and not sleeping that night I am in so much fury. Now I am finding that it is also joke to say that. They are having many such sayings.

Once I am chatting with lady at College Office and she is saying, 'Get off my back.' Now really, Brother, how anyone can say I will leap on their back in middle of afternoon in office? One more time some of us are going to hospital where my friend Randy's good friend is lying after car crash. We are finding nurse who is telling us he has died. Naturally we are feeling upsets and all that, but as we are leaving, nurse is saying, 'Have a nice day, sir,' I am giving her such look that I feel she is surely catching fire like gas stove. But, Brother, she is only looking sad.

Many times I am meeting girls of good family during study time and they are saying 'so long'. Really, Brother, you are not telling anyone this, but I am blushing. How they can know? And I am assuring you I am only spending times in Prayer and Higher Studies. Then who is spreading this rumour about me, I am thinking. What they are meaning by saying 'so long'?

And once I am hearing fight, one boy is saying 'Give me a break,' other fellow shouting 'Stick it.' So I am thinking this fellow is wanting stick to break other boy's leg. But why other boy is wanting some part of own body broken? I am feeling full of puzzles.

One day one boy is reading Mark Twain book and enjoying. So being friendly I am asking if he is liking Mark Twain. He is replying 'Oh it is something else'. Now, Brother, again I am wondering that if he is enjoying something else so much, then why he is sitting like damn fool and laughing at Mark Twain book?

So many things they are saying. One boy named Mike Smith is confessing 'I am son of gun'. So I am asking, 'Who is Mr Smith?' He is replying in surprise. 'He is my father.' Then I am wondering If Mr Smith is step-father, or his mother is doing something wrong with Mr Gun. Or some other deep reason. I am filling with thoughts.

One fellow is always saying 'I am bushed'. I am feeling he must be big supporter of George Bush. But biggest problem earlier is word ending with 'it'. Someone says 'darn it' and there is nothing to sew. One fellow says 'beat it' and I am eager to beat him but supposing it is meaning something else? Or they say 'sit on it', which is very kind of them, but there is nowhere to sit. On streets, stranger will ask 'Are you with it?' I ask, 'Are I with what?' He says 'Cool it'. Now, Brother, what is this wonderful 'it' everywhere you will ask? Anyway, it is long story and now I am understanding all many things.

I feel my American has improved but my English has deproved.

Hoping you are taking cares now.

Your Brother,
Gopal.

9

Snow and the Christmas vacation descended upon the campus like a mist of silence. The buildings, the grass, everything lay white and quiet. Gopal wandered past the slumbering buildings like a disconsolate ghost. Just a few days ago there had been a wild clamour with cars arriving and departing, farewell shrieks, the thump of luggage being loaded and a general feeling of complete chaos.

In disgust Gopal had shut himself in his room, only emerging when it was night. For the next few days he had delighted in the silence, strolling proprietorially through the campus as though he was its sole inhabitant Sometimes he met other figures and they nodded to each other in an immediate intimacy. He even made friends with the campus security people for the first time.

But a week later, he was restless. The silence was unnatural. Cemeteries should be silent, not colleges, he thought. Even the quiet during classtime was a respite from the normal roar which Gopal realised with surprise was strangely refreshing. Now the buildings brooded, as though hurt. Icicles wept from the eaves. He missed the friends he had made, particularly Randy.

He speculated on how lonely he would have been without Randy. True, he had met other Americans in class, but they never seemed to want to meet him after school. They were friendly and cordial during the day, sitting and studying with him, but his after-hours social life revolved around Randy and his whims. Fortunately there were many of them and Gopal now realised just how lively his life was when Randy was around. But without him, Gopal suspected he would have felt as desolate as the campus now did.

He had heard of some foreign students leaving out of loneliness. In one extreme case a Palestinian boy, who apparently didn't have a home to go back to, had killed himself with a shotgun. Gopal hadn't been able to even imagine a loneliness and desperation so extreme. All his life he had been surrounded by people to a point where he took their existence for granted as much as he did the air. He had simply accepted Randy as another welcome body. Now totally alone for the first time in his life, he realised that not all foreign students acquired such valuable friends.

Gopal suddenly thought that up to this moment in his life, he had always been within reach of someone he could call, or phone, or visit. Now suddenly he was on a desert island. For the first few days it was interesting, even exhilarating to find ways to amuse himself. But he got bored of that very quickly and he began to feel a physical need to meet people. It was as though his metabolism had got used to a drug and demanded more of it.

He began to feel alone and depressed. To make it worse, he noticed that the Americans, the most resolutely independent of all people, had suddenly bonded together in the unfamiliar guise of families. Wherever he walked in the evenings, he saw log fires in homes, Christmas trees, laughing groups gathered contentedly together, silver decorations overhead. He often stopped outside the homes, watching intently. He felt like a spirit wandering unseen through the human race.

Watching, he could almost feel the warmth of a room, part fire, part family and the wind chill would bring memories of his own distant home to make him feel more miserable. The leaves would squelch uncouthly underfoot as he walked away. He often ached for home. His fat mother and her stupid friends, his creaky grandmother with her endless wheezy songs, his busy father shrewdly assessing each moment, his younger brother making a pest of himself. The servants so distantly in the background yet so much a part of the family. His friends, some angular, some confident, their walks through the twilight streets, through smoke and garbage and the intoxicating whiff of jasmine. Overhead the familiar sky of home. And he would trudge for his apartment, snivelling in the hurting wind.

He waited one morning for the ridiculously inefficient bus service to take him to the mall where he intended to spend the day just to be near people. He waited for nearly two hours for the bus to arrive. He cursed to himself throughout about the conspiracy by big American car companies to cripple the mass transportation system so the people would be compelled to buy cars.

The bus, once it arrived, proved to be very comfortable, though Gopal felt guilty having to make the entire bus wait as the driver punched out his change. There weren't many people inside, Gopal noticed, as he lurched his way to the back and squeezed into the last but one row. There were several black ladies of fairly advanced years and a few men who appeared even older than them. Though none was a pauper, all were obviously from the lower-income group. Gopal felt an odd sense of failure at sharing the bus with them instead of going in a car.

He could have bought a car long ago, but he had felt that the process of adjusting to driving on the wrong side of the road and getting a driver's licence was hardly worth the effort, given the short time he was to spend here. In any case, he didn't need to travel much and whenever he had to go beyond walking distance from the campus, someone was always available in the parking lot or the cafeteria to give him a ride.

He began to settle down to the ambience in the bus. He lowered his shield and sensed the air. To his surprise he felt an acceptance of him. No one seemed to be making any judgments about him, nor did there seem any hostility. He couldn't even sense much curiosity. Black people, he thought, seemed to resent foreigners much less than the whites. They may not go out of their way to welcome you, he thought, but at least they don't dislike you.

From the whites, on the other hand, he had found extremes of friendliness or dislike. Even when they ignored him, Gopal felt it was an active kind of ignoring. With the blacks he had sensed an acceptance that was passive and therefore felt more genuine. Perhaps they feel that anyone coloured is to be welcomed as a likely ally on their side in the racial divide, he speculated. Or perhaps at some date a soldier in some racial war.

He could only wonder why there wasn't a continuous violent insurgency by the blacks, given the wealth with which they were surrounded and their own poverty. He also thought it short-sighted of the whites not to have made a determined effort to bring more blacks into the middle class in order to lower the crime rate, if nothing else. After his visit to the Peacock's ghetto, he had tried to educate himself about the situation of blacks in America and had been shocked at the statistics regarding black unemployment and crime. He believed that people in such large numbers could only have turned to crime out of desperation. And Gopal didn't believe that a country as wealthy, as well run, as cohesive as the United States couldn't solve this relatively small problem if they actually wanted to.

Engrossed in the intriguing question of why this problem was allowed to continue in this inscrutable society, despite the insecurity it caused to the entire country, he got off the bus and walked into the mall. Perhaps they want to keep poor people as soldiers for the army, he thought, hesitating inside the doorway. A pair of lips, unmistakably a pair of female lips, kissed him with a smack on his lips and laughed away.

Gopal's brains turned to butter. He felt that by now familiar sense of utter bafflement. He tried to urge his mind, which had closed shop completely, to start itself again. What could explain this? He tried to think of perfectly logical reasons. There are many, he assured himself. None presented themselves. He felt his grip on sanity loosening. Maybe I am imagining it, he thought. He licked his lips and got the sweet taste of lipstick. Why? he floundered. Poison? he started to panic. Racists in the CIA had found a subtle way to kill him.

He saw people around him grin. One said kindly, pointing upwards, 'Mistletoe.'

Gopal looked up and saw some inoffensive leaves. No doubt some potent aphrodisiac, he thought with enormous relief, whose periodic exhalations made American women uncontrollable with desire. It didn't sound terribly convincing, for one if there had been such an aphrodisiac, Randy would have found a way to bathe in it daily, but no other explanation came in sight. This, Gopal decided, is another one of those baffling American mysteries. He carried on through the mall, keeping a wary eye open for lurking mistletoes.

He felt enmeshed soon in songs, gaiety, silver threads. There were people everywhere. Red-robed Santa Clauses stood at regular intervals and though Gopal had heard all about them, he had never seen one before. After his initial curiosity he lost interest in them, deciding they were meant for children. One of the Santas beckoned to him and Gopal approached him grinning.

'Ho, ho, ho,' said the Santa, 'Merry Christmas, Gopal.'

Gopal went into a fright. 'CIA' was his first thought again, his heart racing.

A closer look revealed it was only one of the students from the college.

'Hey, heh, Merry Christmas,' said Gopal sheepishly.

'Hey Gopal, can you take may place for a second? I've got to go to the john.'

'Me?'

'Here, I've got this spare robe and beard in the bag. Don't worry about the padding. There you go, there's nothing to it. Just ring the bell and say "Ho, ho, ho, Merry Christmas?"'

Gopal, wearing a scratchy red robe and a magnificent white bead, and feeling extraordinarily foolish, timidly rang the bell and essayed a few weak ho, ho-hos. Then realising his plaintive bleats were attracting even more attention, he ventured full-throated ho, ho, hos. 'Merry Christmas and things like that,' he roared. These seemed to be appreciated; so he really got into the spirit of the occasion. His bell rang like a buoy in a storm and his ho, ho, hos were positively operatic.

If passersby thought a skinny brown Santa wishing them a merry Christmas in an Indian accent in a shopping mall in Eversville was an unusual sight, they were too polite to tell him.

In a while the other student returned.

'Great job,' he patted Gopal, wincing at the tolling bell's reverberations.

'I can do,' assured Gopal, now really keen. 'Ho, ho, ho and all that.'

'Thanks, thanks.' The man had to shout to make himself heard. 'But if I don't do it myself I don't get paid. Know what I mean?'

'Oh yes,' Gopal's bell wound down sadly. 'I will do again if you want.'

'Sure buddy, any time. Thanks again.' He resumed his duty.

Gopal walked about with a spring in his step, listening critically to the performance of the other Santas. In general he kept his views to himself, but he felt compelled to reprimand one man: 'Useless. Ring bell harder.'

The Santa gave him an evil glare and rang the bell near Gopal's ear.

All day Gopal wandered through the mall. It was Christmas Eve and everyone was finishing their shopping. There were crowds everywhere and for once it felt and sounded like an Indian bazaar. In the anarchic dash to grab the last items remaining, the restraints of civilisation had fallen and the mobs had begun to assert themselves.

There were screams to catch the shopgirls' attention, tugging sessions to gain possession of an object, hefty thumps from the shoulder to clear the way and the elbow had developed into a deadly weapon. Usually dulcet voices sharpened into spears and transfixed harassed workers on the spot. Families with a talent for strategy had brought along large and formidable aunts who trundled like tanks crushing all opposition in their path, while the lighter troops pillaged behind them. The overly civilised and weak were left to wave pitifully and fruitlessly from the back of the crowd.

Gopal gloried in it. He thought it God's wish that people when they encountered such a profusion of goods should burst upon it like wolves introduced to a lamb after a month-long fast. He had long felt that the American dispiritedness in the face of consumer products that fairly begged for high passion, was a sign of dangerous dissipation. He was pleased to see that their year-long languor was the result of excessive availability rather than a softening of that vigorous American spirit that had stolen California from the Mexicans, Louisiana from the

French and much of the rest of the country from the American Indians. When confronted with opposition, he noted with joy, the Americans wrestled, abused and snatched their prizes with a vigour that would have won them applause even in an Indian bazaar and boded well for the future of the Free World.

He drifted comfortably all day, for once secure that no one was looking at him or was even remotely interested. Watching the mayhem, he speculated that American civil defence plans against a possible Russian invasion should include some word about the Reds having evil designs on the local supermarkets. And then, he thought, let the women defend them. If the Russians, Gopal thought pityingly, couldn't keep Afghanistan, what chance did they have of even setting foot in Sears.

As the evening arrived, the shoppers began to leave the ransacked mall. Gopal wished time would pass a little more slowly, so he could delay returning to his little room and the frozen pizza in the ice box which was tonight's dinner. Once again he began to feel lonely. People were leaving in groups, or in pairs, or carrying parcels that showed that they expected to be with other people later in the evening or at the very latest by the next day. Gopal, disconsolate, watched them leave.

He decided he should also go before the bus service stopped, which it was capable of doing at the most inconvenient hours. As he was on his way out, near the exit he saw a huddled figure handing out leaflets embarrassedly, without looking at anyone. He had long hair and was unshaven and kept his eyes fixed on the floor.

As Gopal went past he took the yellow sheet of paper the man held out and balled it up ready to toss it into the first bin he saw. He wondered which denomination was now soliciting funds. Curiosity made him unfold it.

'Swedish Massage,' it read. 'Your favourite massage by our lovely and trained girls expert in fulfilling your every fantasy. Come one come all.'

Gopal grimaced at the last phrase. He began to feel less full of self-pity. It would be better than an evening at home alone. And what a story he would have to tell Randy when he returned. He could casually inform him that he had managed the deed all by himself without any of Randy's help, thank you. And then of course the details. And what details there would be!

To his surprise Gopal found he was already in the parking lot. Cautiously he looked around and then surreptitiously read the message again. A map gave instructions on how to get there and Gopal tried to figure out which bus, if any, went in that direction. Finally he gave up and decided to walk.

It was dark now and he supposed it was cold, though he didn't seem to be able to feel it. He turned away from the main road and following the map's directions went into quiet residential streets. The houses were ablaze with Christmas Eve decorations, but Gopal hardly gave them a thought.

He felt energetic, excited and purposeful. He tried not to think of the house ahead, but his mind told him it was high time he fulfilled, he thought piously, Randy's ambition. They were bound to be nice girls, he assured himself, from good families who had fallen upon hard times. He would be gentle with whichever one he selected, he decided. He thought she would have blond hair and skin whose freshness leapt like the wind. Maybe she would weep a little, he thought, his mind muddled as he took the last turn and walked down the quiet lane. Would his mother like her? He was already a little in love with her. She would look something like Brooke Shields.

The street became darker. At the end of the lane he saw the dim glow of a house. He walked up to it and rang the bell. There were red curtains on the windows which had bars on them. He rang the bell again and it clanged loudly. The door opened and a woman looked out. He could see the chain still holding the door.

'Yeah?' she asked.

Now that he was here Gopal was abashed. The excitement abruptly vanished and he nearly fled. He rustled the leaflet.

'Got it at the mall,' he muttered.

'You want a massage?'

Gopal nodded. The door closed. This was his chance to run. He stepped back and the door opened again. He rushed forward before he changed his mind. The door shut behind him with many clicks and he felt relieved. If there were any ghosts pursuing him in the dark they would have to sit outside.

The woman was extremely plump and wore a shiny blue dress.

'You wanna sit?' she asked.

Gopal saw two rooms on either side with some sort of ornate upholstery on the furniture, but he sat on a plain chair in the hall at the foot of the stairs. The rooms upstairs, he thought, must be where the girls were.

'Sorry for the delay,' the woman apologised mechanically, seating herself behind a table, 'but I've only got one girl working tonight and she's busy with a client right now. What with Christmas Eve I suppose I'm lucky to have anyone at all.'

'Yes, yes,' said Gopal sympathising completely with the problem of finding good help these days.

'The other one just upped and left. Just like that,' the woman snapped her fingers, livening up at a responsive audience.

'Terrible,' Gopal commiserated, hoping to ingratiate himself with her.

'Say,' she asked curiously, 'where you from?'

'India,' Gopal responded at once. 'Very poor country,' he added, hoping it would induce her to lower the rates. 'Ah,' he cleared his throat, 'how much?'

'Depends what you want.'

Gopal thought about this. 'Meaning?'

'Well there's $45 for the Delux, that's for half an hour. $60 for the Super Deluxe, that's for 45 minutes. And $75 for the Harem Special. That's for 90 minutes.'

'I will have,' Gopal salivated, 'Harem Special.'

'Cash in advance.'

Gopal reached into his pocket. The genes of generations of Jajau's most fierce bargainers held him back, even at this delicate moment.

'Any student discount?' he asked.

'Sorry.' She was firm.

'I have many friends,' Gopal hinted.

She paused. 'Well,' she decided, 'not this time. But anytime you bring five or more people maybe we can work something out.'

Capitulating, Gopal counted out the money.

'Margie,' the lady yelled up the stairs. 'There's another gentleman here who wants a date with you. Hurry up. You haven't got all day.'

In a while there were sounds upstairs and a short, balding young man came hurriedly down the stairs. Gopal brushed past him as he climbed up. Behind him he heard the door open and close for the small man. He went up the stairs with trepidation.

There was a door on either side at the top, but the one on the left was ajar. He pushed it open with hands that trembled like mice. The room was empty but he could hear water running behind a closed door. He stepped in cautiously and shut the door. The room was almost totally bare except for a metal table with a rubber sheet on it. Gopal thought it looked like an operating room except for the picture of Madonna in her underwear on the wall and red curtains on the window. A small table near the metal platform held bottles and vials of liquids.

Gopal found he had stopped breathing. He wished the room had been a little cosier for such a historic moment, but no doubt the girl would make up by her warmth. The bathroom door opened and Gopal looked swiftly and looked away. His first thought was that she didn't look like Brooke Shields. His second was that she had stringy brown hair, wore a blue bikini, was thin and short and her face wore a look that would have been vulnerable if she hadn't hardened it. She was pretty in a wan way. His third thought was that she looked familiar.

He looked again and saw the same spark of recognition in her eyes before she turned away. He recognised her as a girl he had seen on campus. He hesitated wondering if the deal was off.

She handed him a towel. 'You can wear this.'

Gopal took it and went into the bathroom and got out of his clothes. In a way he felt better that she wasn't a total stranger. He could even remember sitting at the table next to hers one lunchtime in the cafeteria. He wrapped the towel around his waist, sucked in his stomach, flexed his muscles and swaggered out.

She was squeezing some lotion onto her palm. 'Lie down,' she motioned listlessly.

Careful to keep himself covered, Gopal lay down on his back.

'Turn over,' she commanded.

Gopal flipped around and he felt her pour some liquid onto his back before starting to knead and pummel him. Gopal lay passively for a while, enjoying her small yet firm hands rhythmically working their way over his shoulders. Let her get used to me, he thought.

'How much time you got?' she asked.

'Harem Special.' His voice was muffled.

He lay still for a while longer and then turned around and looked at her directly.

'How much for more?' he asked.

She kneaded his chest. 'Harem Special's the best we got.' Her voice was non-committal.

Gopal turned around and wondered how to broach the subject more effectively. He decided on subtlety. When he felt her hands leave him and go back to the lotions, he turned around and dropped the towel to the floor.

'Your towel's fallen,' she said tonelessly, picking it up and putting it on his groin.

As she started kneading his thighs, Gopal caught her hand.

'I'll scream,' she said listlessly. 'We've got bouncers in the house.'

Gopal let go and closed his eyes. This is ridiculous, he thought.

'What you are wanting?' he asked.

'A good night's rest.'

Gopal turned over again. Nothing like this had ever occurred in either *Deep Throat* or *Penthouse Letters*. In fact he had gathered from these two major reference works that the chief problem faced by males in America was fighting off females. And here he was even paying one and still failing to succeed. Maybe she's new and shy, he thought. Perhaps he needed to gently woo her.

'You are doing anything at all?' he asked.

'Just Swedish massage.' Her voice sounded like it had fallen asleep while her hands continued fluttering like headless chickens.

Gopal caught both her hands this time.

'Not even touching me? I am paying $75 already.' His voice pleaded yet was angry.

'I'll call the cops. That's prostitution.' Her monotone was unchanged. 'This buzzer on the floor connects to the cop station. We've got protection.'

She waited tiredly, her eyes downcast, making no effort to free herself. Her exhausted passivity disgusted Gopal. He turned again on his stomach and lay there viciously. When she said 'Time's up,' he checked his watch.

'Twenty-five minutes more. Keep on,' he demanded savagely.

Wordlessly she continued.

Half an hour later Gopal came storming down the stairs, glowing with health and fury. He flung himself out of the door and raged off in the general direction of his apartment. Some homing instinct guided him because his mind was busy seething. No actual thoughts formed, just a wild fury.

He didn't know how long it took, but abruptly he was at the complex. He took the stairs as though in a single stride. An envelope was taped to his door with Gloria's scrawl on it, probably containing a Christmas poem. Gopal opened the envelope, tore up the single sheet inside unread and put it in his mouth and chewed it.

He raged to the fridge, pulled out a beer, took out the thoroughly masticated letter and threw it into the garbage can. He started to drink furiously. He put on the television and paced up and down, snorting at the beer. 75 dollars, he boiled.

He went back for another beer, pulled out the half-filled plastic garbage bag, knotted it and flung himself out of the room dragging it behind him. As he came down the stairs, Gloria's door opened and she tip-toed out, beckoning to him. She shut the door softly behind her. Gopal walked to her warily.

'Sorry,' she twinkled sweetly.

'Huh?' Gopal growled.

'Didn't you read my letter? I put it on your door.'

Gopal muttered incomprehensibly.

'Well I've met this nice boy Troy that I used to know earlier and he's moved in with me. So I guess our thing's over. Sorry.' She dimpled her fingers at him and left.

'Our thing!' Gopal bared his fangs at her retreating back.

He dragged the garbage sack towards the rear where the garbage bin was kept. On an impulse he raced back and flung the sack at Gloria's door.

Even her, he thought in disbelieving fury. Even her. He whirled around and raced up and down the car park area. I will get married, he thought in wild rage. That will show everyone.

He ran towards the hedge to propose marriage to Sue. He rounded it and skidded to a stop. The same two seater car was parked there and all the lights were out in Sue's house.

Gopal lifted his face to the moon and howled.

The next few days were among the most miserable of Gopal's life. Lonely, hurting, with no one to turn to, he was reduced to calling Anand in desperation. He heard the phone ring and the whirr of the answering machine. 'Hi there –' Gopal slammed the phone down.

With nothing better to do, he took to wandering around the streets, despite the slush and snow. One afternoon he found himself in an unfamiliar road and spotted a shack announcing 'XXX movies. Gadgets. Novelties. Sex aids.' Intrigued, he walked in.

The bell over the door jangled and the man behind the counter looked up. He nodded pleasantly and Gopal relaxed. He was always worried when entering a bar or any other place he thought of as sinful, in case the people there demanded to know what he was doing in such a dreadful place and threw him out. He also nursed a persistent dread that his grandmother would suddenly come hobbling into sight. He appreciated that this was an unrealistic fear since there was very little chance of encountering his grandmother in a porno store in Eversville, particularly since she had never been outside India and now could hardly walk. But she seemed present in spirit on this as on many such occasions, peering over his shoulder at the sex aids and muttering holy songs.

There was no one else in the store and Gopal browsed through the goods, though gaped through them might be a more accurate description. There were all manner of gadgets, many of them of such shape, size and dimension, that it boggled the mind trying to imagine someone putting them to use. Looking at them closely, Gopal felt sceptical at anyone actually using whips, chains, masks, sticks with bumps on them and other implements to which he felt embarrassed at even trying to put a name. Maybe they are just meant for displaying in homes, he speculated. The Yanks were quite capable of it. He tried to imagine the Dean's living room with one of these things on the centre table, while the Dean's wife tried to pass it off as the tusk of an African elephant.

He drifted to the books section and browsed through the magazines. He had seen many of them already, but not so many together. He found that several specialised in particular areas. One was called *Mamas with Mammoth Mammaries*. It was a monthly publication. Others were so explicit that Gopal felt that they were no longer pornography, but were more accurately gynaecology.

He drifted back to the counter and the man behind it, thin, bearded and long-haired, joined his palms together and bowed a 'namaste', the Indian greeting. Gopal, amidst these exotic surroundings, couldn't believe his eyes. Must be having backache or something, he told himself.

The man spoke clearly, 'Namaste.'

Gopal wondered if he was going mad. I am hearing things, he told himself firmly.

'Namaste, sahib,' the man insisted.

Gopal had to admit that the man was saying something.

'Hello there,' he boomed.

'Namaste,' the man repeated; translating, 'I salute the divine in thee.'

'Namaste,' replied Gopal reluctantly, wondering if the spirit of his grandmother had somehow entered into the man.

'I knew it. One look and I said "Here's an Indian."'

Gopal wondered if his Pakistani story would sell here. 'How you are knowing?'

'Spent a year there. Goa, Varanasi, Kathmandu. I seen it all.'

'Very nice,' admired Gopal trying not to look at the shop's wares.

'I'm Tom,' the man stuck out his hand over the counter.

'I'm, I'm,' Gopal groped, till struck with a happy inspiration. 'I'm Anand. My friends are calling me Andy,'

'Namaste, Anand,' the man folded his hands again, 'where's home in India for you?'

'Oh, my home,' Gopal fumbled, 'Madras.' This was some 2000 miles from his house.

'Gee, that's great. I just loved India. I can't wait to go back. Matter of fact I'm planning a trip again next year. Say, why don't you give me your address and maybe we could meet up in India? What d'you say?'

'Most certainly, yes, yes,' burst Gopal enthusiastically, paling visibly at the thought.

He hastily concocted an address for Tom who wrote it down.

'So tell me,' encouraged Tom, 'what d'you like here?' He was clearly touched by Gopal parting with his address. 'Look around, go ahead. Think of it as your own store.'

Gopal winced.

Tom came out from behind the counter to help Gopal regard it as his own store. "Take what you like,' he urged. 'Anything for a friend from India. Maybe something for the family back home?' he asked helpfully.

He began to pluck a gadget here and a thingummy there, like a friendly grocer among his vegetables, before heaping them all into a cardboard box. 'Feel free,' he urged. 'How about one of these inflatable dolls for those winter nights, huh? See, you just blow into this and she swells up nice and good. See?'

To Gopal's horror it began to inflate to female proportions down to the last anatomical detail.

'And then you just remove this stopper and she goes right back into her bag.' The doll deflated with a hiss.

'So how about that, huh?' boasted Tom. 'Take it, take it. A little free something from America for the family. Bet it'll crack them up.'

Gopal didn't doubt it.

'But you will have trouble,' Gopal protested at the door, carrying the bag of horrors.

'No problem. Hey, no problem,' Tom assured him. 'I can handle it. I'll say we got robbed. I'm planning to leave in any case.'

They were outside now and Gopal couldn't wait for Tom to go back so that he could throw away the box. But Tom was clearly intent on playing the good host. He stood outside waving.

'Hey,' he yelled, 'where's your car? Want me to give you a ride?'

Gopal stumbled in fright. 'No, no, just around corner. Bye.'

'Namaste. See you in India.'

Gopal hastened around the corner struggling with the box. He dumped it on the sidewalk the instant Tom was out of sight, shuddering. He wiped his hands on his trouser, feeling them unclean.

'Hey!' said a gruff voice near by and with a start Gopal saw a man who had been raking leaves.

'You want to pick that up?' He pointed to the box.

Without a moment's pause, Gopal sprinted down the road, the man's outraged cries receding behind him.

Sitting safely in his apartment, he wondered what the man would make of the varied contents of the box. But since he lived so close to the shop, perhaps he was used to finding strange objects growing like unusual mushrooms on his lawns. What must his life be like, mused Gopal, never knowing what the dog was going to dig up and drag back home? And supposing he had small children. How did he explain humming bananas to their enquiring minds. And what about the people who actually made the gadgets, what did they say to their children when they came home?

'What did you do today at the office, Daddy?'

'Oh I made eleven dildoes, son.'

'Gee whiz Dad!'

Gopal's mind had begun to race. How about the actors in pornographic films, what did they say to their wives in the evening?

'Have a hard day at work, dear.'

'Whew, Betty, you can say that again. Fourteen retakes of an orgasm scene and a homosexual orgy.'

'Poor dear. Here, have a nice refreshing aphrodisiac.'

And did such a couple celebrate their wedding anniversary by refraining from sex?

Gopal could have carried on in this unhealthy vein if the phone hadn't politely burred, seeking his attention. He picked it up.

'Herb's abortion parlour,' he chortled, 'you are raping them and we are scraping them.'

He guffawed at his witty imitation of a receptionist he had overheard in the Science Building.

There was a silence at the other end.

'Very nice, Gopal,' came the dry voice of the Dean. 'I see the Wolff educational system has been at least as successful as ours.'

'Oh no, no, no,' protesed an abashed Gopal. 'Randy is not saying anything.' He tried to defend his friend accused wrongly for once.

'I'm sure,' said the Dean ironically. 'Well anyway, we're having a New Year's Eve dinner tonight for our friends and I wondered if you would like to join us?'

'Oh yes, sir, yes, yes,' accepted Gopal, extremely touched and pleased.

'I know it's a little late, but it just occurred to me that you might be feeling a little left out of things at this time of the year. So I thought I'd check.'

'Very kind of you and things like that,' mumbled Gopal awkwardly. 'I will certainly be very happy.'

'Great. I'll call Dr Love and ask him to give you a ride. He lives in your complex. Is around eight okay?'

'Very good, sir. Certainly.'

Gopal hadn't known that Dr Love lived in such proximity. He was a chemistry professor and though Gopal thought highly of his professional abilities, he also felt that he looked like a camel. He was tall and supercilious and he hunched a little. When he walked there was a bounce in his step exactly like a camel's, making Gopal want to leap upon his shoulders, whip his posterior and make clucking sounds. Of course he never revealed his dark desires to Dr Love, but greeted him with decorously downcast eyes.

When the bell rang at eight, Gopal was bathed, cologned and oiled. (His mother had packed enough to last a year, plus little more for emergencies.) Dr Love stood towering at the door, his lips parted in an unfamiliar grin.

'Ready?' he asked.

He loped down the corridor, Gopal following, trying to surreptitiously imitate his bouncing gait.

They got into the car and drove off.

'And so,' said Dr Love, clearly making polite conversation, 'how do you love America?'

Gopal glared at him and decided to answer with some chemistry problems. This eased the atmosphere considerably and they managed to get to the Dean's place without mishap.

The house, Gopal saw with surprise, was in one of the more expensive parts of town and was a large, double-storeyed structure fronted by a long, well-kept lawn. Gopal had always thought that teachers were very poorly paid and lived in the American equivalent of hovels. But clearly he had been wrong. His professors rose in his estimation. They parked in the driveway behind a few cars. Some people seemed to have already arrived.

Dr Love rang the bell and it was opened by a lady who was apparently the Dean's wife. Gopal examined her as she and Dr Love kissed each other on the cheek. She was dressed in blue, had brown hair, but wore far too much make-up. She was very attractive, but her skin had roughened and the sudden inexplicable collapse of American women into middle age seemed to have occurred to her. Gopal wondered why it happened so abruptly to American women. Perhaps the blazing freshness of their youth burned their skins prematurely. There was nothing graceful about their middle age, which wasn't even a middle age. One year they had that overwhelming radiance, the next they had slipped into wrinkles and parchmented skin and old age.

However, like most American women, her delight in receiving guests seemed to have increased in direct proportion to her age. While in most other countries, women maintained an even balance between propriety and effusiveness in their greetings to visitors throughout their lives, in America it ranged from one extreme to the other. It started with gum-chewing insolence as teenagers. 'Yeah?' they grunted nastily. Sometimes they didn't even do that, merely raising their eyebrows in disgust. In the more extreme cases, they didn't even bother to raise their eyebrows. They just stared in expressionless contempt. But as they began to grow older, the volume and intensity of their hellos began to increase, till by college it was nearly civil. By the time they began working, it became positively human. At marriage a quantum leap into excessive delight took place. And you knew someone had entered middle age when she opened the door and on beholding you her effusions made you suspect that this was by far the most significant, memorable and thrilling moment of her life.

Such was the case now. It always made Gopal feel wildly insecure, feeling that there was no way he could hope to live up to the hopes contained in that greeting. Such joy implied that the party was dying before his arrival, but now that he was here, his wit, gaiety and verve would ignite it. Then that 'I've heard so *much* about you' was positively frightening. He had tried to analyse it and decided that his fear was caused by, first, the implication that the husband and wife spent all their waking hours feverishly discussing him. And second, the *much* hinted that there was a very great deal indeed which perhaps she ought not to have known about him, but now most certainly did.

The entire package of greetings was designed to make strong men faint. 'And how've you *been*?' was uttered in tones of such solicitude, that it made you feel as though you were recently released from shock therapy following your arrest for child molestation. This was usually followed by 'we've all been just *dying* to meet you,' leading to feelings of alarm at the vision of rows of wives keeling over dead as a result of your cruel absence. To people who were quite accustomed to being cordially ignored at most parties at home, such delirium at their arrival suggested that they were expected to perform amazing feats centre stage, or at the very least, party tricks. Alternately, the hostess's joy suggested that surely you had brought such wondrous gifts as would enthrall all America and be the envy of the civilised world.

After the first few parties and feelings of foolishness Gopal had learned to take along some rubbishy Indian items. This, as always, was accepted by the hostess with such peals of pleasure, such shrieks of ecstasy, that Gopal always feared one of them would fall flat at his feet, her brain circuits overloaded with alpha waves, her mouth foaming, her feet drumming.

As the Dean's wife displayed his little table cloth to her friends with such gloating pride that it made you suspect she had never seen a table cloth before, Gopal galloped to the bar to hide behind a bowl of peanuts. He observed the other women whose reactions of wild bliss and pure envy seemed to indicate that they too had never before seen such a rare and wonderful work of art as that table cloth. Nor, from their paroxysms, did they seem to think it likely that they every would again.

Gopal shifted from behind the peanuts to the cashewnuts, which being larger seemed to offer more scope for camouflage. But he was ruthlessly dragged out and made to stand before a semi-circle of wives who seemed to have achieved a nearly permanent state of orgasm over his table cloth.

'It's lovely,' moaned one.

'It's wonderrrrful,' groaned another.

If a table cloth can do this to them, wondered Gopal, what would happen if they went to the shop I went to this morning. He thought about this. Probably nothing, he concluded.

'Where can I get one from?' begged another, her pleading demeanour suggesting that she was ready to sell everything she possessed, including herself, if only she would be rewarded by a piece of similar table cloth.

Gopal mumbled about India, shuffled his feet and darted back to his peanuts. He stood there recovering his breath. It can be an unnerving experience, for those unaccustomed, to have a roomful of faculty wives orgasming at you in chorus.

Gopal was content in the shadows, watching the room fill. He didn't feel intimidated, since most of the faces were familiar. They occasionally appeared unfamiliar since they were in an unaccustomed setting and at their most relaxed, but he felt comforted at knowing them and feeling accepted by them. He was happy to be a watcher. He was still puzzled by the women. There seemed absolutely no relation between the high school girls he had met and these women who were presumably the grown-up version of those girls. It appeared as though at some stage the high school girls had been lifted away from America and then replaced by the completely different species that was the older American woman.

No one seemed to think it odd. But clearly they were totally different people. There was no sign of the gradual transformation from girl to woman and apparently an entire generation was regularly wiped out. On reflection Gopal felt this wasn't such a bad thing. He wondered what actually became of the girls. Maybe, he thought sadistically, remembering his experience with the high school girl at the drive-in at Springfield during Thanksgiving, they are all taken somewhere and drowned. He chuckled in satisfaction.

And while he was thus preoccupied with such pleasant thoughts, the most momentous year of Gopal's young life came to an end amidst laughter, cheers, kisses and tenured professors in funny hats.

10

It was summer, at last. And as the trees sprouted new clothes, the people shed theirs. Something or the other is always naked here, thought a bemused Gopal. Just as he had adjusted to a warmly attired America, elegantly clothed, fashionably woollen, and sartorially conservative, they suddenly and casually took their clothes off and unselfconsciously began walking down the streets stark naked, almost.

Gopal again relapsed into a daze he thought he could never again fall into given his hard-won sophistication. But it seemed as though the entire nation was suddenly flaunting their legs at him. He suspected that they had all waited patiently to lull him into a sense of security before suddenly taking their pants off. Gopal felt as though everything he had learned about them had been locked away in closets along with their decent garments. He found it extremely difficult to be courteous and respectful to women who wore shorts that displayed half their bottom. And all winter he had been civil to them, he thought in confusion, without once suspecting them of such legs, much less such bottoms.

Bottoms! he thought in amazement. They had blossomed everywhere, like sunflowers. As though they had been lying dormant somewhere all winter, before leaping out in the sunshine. And if the legs and bottoms weren't enough, Gopal happened to pass behind the girl's dormitory one afternoon and was transfixed.

He beheld acres of female flesh, glistening and undulating like a vast water bed. They lay there so naked and purposeless, that it looked like a giant invitation card. No one looked at him, no one acknowledged him, they just lay there quietly, motionlessly, as though the whole lot of them had been waiting for him all winter and now couldn't wait any longer and were therefore offering themselves, letting him make his choice among them.

When Gopal's brain jerked again into wheezy motion, of course it told him that this couldn't possibly be the case, and any impulse he had felt for tearing off his clothes and dashing into them stark naked, like a swimmer into the endless surf, thrashing his arms and legs, powering and churning his way through, should be sternly resisted. This was doubtlessly some insane American rite and he should withhold all action until discreet enquiries revealed its significance. Leaping among those shimmering bodies like a shark, biting and gouging, a predator feeding in these troughs of flesh, might be looked at askance.

If on the other hand this communal uncovering, this mass baring of the unbareable, signalled the start of some Dionysian revel, some orgiastic greeting to spring, then, thought Gopal sighing deeply and breathing even more deeply and unable to think any further. He began trudging back home. Water, water everywhere he thought, and not any drop and such a lovely day. Surely, he felt keenly, a nation that converted its parking lots into platters on which they offered the unclad bodies of their women, thereby arousing among visitors certain ardent emotions, had a duty to satisfy those emotions.

Randy, thought Gopal viciously. Where is damn fool Randy. He will know what to do.

He walked in discomfort to his apartment and phoned Randy.

'Yellow,' rang out the cheerful voice.

'You are coming here or I am murdering you?'

'Wow. What's up, doc?'

'Damn country.'

'Ah, that-a-way. I'm on my way.'

Randy walked in and found that Gopal was not in the mood for subtleties.

'Naked women,' ranted Gopal. 'Bloody damn fool naked women are lying everywhere. Wherever I am going there are damn fool naked women lying everywhere. Why?'

'Yes,' said Randy, 'I agree completely. Ain't it grand?'

Gopal glared at him. 'For you maybe. What about me?'

Randy began to understand. 'No luck still?'

Gopal snarled.

'Wow,' admired Randy. 'Years and years of celibacy. Like Gandhi, huh?'

'Gandhi is not having bloody damn fool naked women lying for miles and miles all around,' Gopal groused bitterly.

'Right. Probably the poor guy didn't know what he was missing, did he? And even if he did, what would he have done about it? Nothing, that's what he would have done, nothing. Zilch. And you know why?' Randy asked. 'Because he didn't have Randy Wolff to guide him. That's why.'

Gopal didn't appear impressed.

'But if he did have the services of the great Wolff, do you know what I'd have done to help score with the chicks? I'd have first got him out of that ratty old towel he wore. Strictly a no no. Then I'd have put him into some cool threads, know what I mean? Maybe some designer jeans and a Lacoste tee-shirt. Nothing too heavy. The chicks don't dig that. Maybe a little of the old gold chain to show that here's a man of substance, right? And those glasses, oh my God, those glasses just have to go. I'd put him behind some reflecting shades. Real cool. How does that grab you, huh? And he's ready to hit Xenon on Friday night. Right on.'

Gopal was not diverted by this nonsense.

'And me?' he asked belligerently.

'Whee,' whistled Randy, enjoying himself thoroughly. 'We're getting demanding here now, aren't we? Oh all right,' he placated, as Gopal began to look homicidal, 'leave it all to Uncle Randy, righter of wrongs, doer of deeds. What're you doing tonight?'

'Having dinner with Brooke Shields.'

'Well she can't come to the party and that's final and I don't care how much she begs. But you are cordially invited to a lake party where I hope you will join us in a genteel evening of chamber music, bonfires, opera and getting into the pants of this bunch of girls that're coming along. They,' and Randy's eyes clouded as he remembered visions, 'got the morals of an alley cat.'

'No morals?' Gopal was cheering up but trying to make sure, not being clear on the social lives of cats.

'Not a one.'

'Let us go.'

'At nine, my eager young beaver, if you'll pardon the expression.'

Gopal would have gladly pardoned him matricide.

When they left that night, Gopal was carrying a little bundle containing his night clothes, his toilet kit and a change of clothes because Randy had warned him they wouldn't be returning till the next day. Sitting in the car Gopal felt feathers of excitement flutter over him. He had but one thought in his head. He cleared his throat.

'Cats,' he reminded Randy.

'What? Cats. What cats?'

Gopal began to worry. 'Cats in alley,' he reminded, anxious in case this whole thing was one of Randy's jokes.

'Oh alley cats,' Randy recollected. 'Sure, lots of those.'

Gopal breathed in relief. 'That is why they are called vegetarian cats?'

'Well that's a new one on me. But if you say so.'

They drove along, Gopal staring sightlessly in front, his brain crawling with cats. After nearly an hour they turned off the highway and drove along a road that got bumpier. The branches became darker overhead and they went into a gap between the trees. They went down a dirt track and stopped among a jumble of cars.

Gopal was out of the car first. The moment he opened the door, he could hear the music and faintly see a fire appearing and disappearing like fireflies through the trees as he walked forward. The trees ended abruptly and he saw a beach with the night resting on it and a lake like liquid dark spilled beyond. A bonfire rose like a hill of flame and a ghetto-blaster stood near, fanning it with its volume.

Several figures lay or sat like careless blobs around the fire. One female form danced in front and Gopal's heart leapt like the flames. He heard Randy scrunch beside him and they walked down to the beach. There seemed fewer people than Gopal had expected, but he decided not to behave like an uncouth yokel peering excitedly at the girls, trying to pick one for himself. There was plenty of time for that, he rebuked himself. The night was young, the girls were willing and strategy was of the essence. Coolness was what was needed, he told himself. He slowed the pace of his eager prowl to a cool saunter.

But his eagerness was severely tested when he heard Randy ask in surprise.

'Where're the girls?'

Gopal's determination to not look around fled into the night. He gazed anxiously around, the anxiety changing first to panic, then to despair. Aside from the dancing girl, he couldn't see a single other female.

Randy went to question one of the boys moping beside the fire.

'Where're they?' he asked and even his coolness had disappeared.

'Couldn't make it,' the boy responded moodily.

'None of them?'

'Well they were all from one sorority. It turns out some big shot from their national headquarters is coming in early tomorrow so they've all got to be there. Sam just came in with the news.'

Randy cursed and Gopal looked at the stars beseechingly. This was truly some cosmic conspiracy. Here he was in America, the acknowledged international home of fornication and still untouched by human hand. It was all too much, particularly in summer. He felt weepy.

'Well,' said the boy trying to cheer them up, 'but Samantha's here.'

Gopal looked with renewed eagerness at the dancing girl. He would clearly have to make a superhuman effort to woo and win her favours given that the competition looked severe, quantitatively at least. He kicked himself for not bringing his certificate. Maybe he could somehow manipulate Randy into going back to get it while he entranced the girl.

All these thoughts hardly took a moment while he absorbed the image of the girl. She danced well, was his first thought. His next was to wonder if she was related to Gloria because she was even larger. He started feeling depressed again. Her face, he noted, seemed to have pieces of fat stuck on it instead of features.

He wandered off to slump on the sand in despair, still looking at the girl in burning reproach. Her arms and hands moved like snakes and Gopal wished one of her fingers would leap up and bite her. He sat quietly, helplessly, awash with a despair as vast as the lake. Randy settled beside him with a six pack of beer and Gopal silently took a can. They watched the moon send a rippling slab of silver through the water. The wind brushed them with a pleasant moistness and it was too lovely to stay depressed.

Gopal couldn't tell how long he had sat there, watching the moon come alive in the water like a mischievous, glowing face. Randy had drifted away and returned many times but had been gone a particularly long time now. Gopal heard him come up again and instead of sitting down he bent over Gopal.

'Let's go,' he whispered.

Gopal looked at him. 'What?'

'Come on, I'll show you. I promised you a good time, didn't I?'

Curious, Gopal staggered up awkwardly and followed Randy. They headed back towards the trees and Gopal noticed that the bonfire was still blazing, the music still blasting but Samantha was nowhere in sight. They walked into the treeline and Randy stopped.

'Samantha's just behind that clump,' he whispered, pointing to a rock. 'The moment you see a guy walk past, go for it.'

Gopal was mystified. 'Go for what?' his voice rose.

'Shh, shh,' Randy hushed him. 'She's taking us all on. Most of the guys are done already. The next guy that leaves, make sure it's your turn.'

Gopal's guts turned to water. 'No, no, no,' he protested weakly, scared yet thrilled, 'how I can?'

'She'll tell you how,' urged Randy. 'There he goes,' he gestured to a figure walking out tucking in his shirt. 'Go on,' he pushed Gopal. 'Git there before someone else arrives.'

Gopal stumbled as he went towards the rock. He felt sick with excitement and fear. He felt himself begin to sweat. He reached the rock and peered around it. Samantha lay naked, facing the lake, almost at his feet. He could see every detail. The snowy legs, the black thatch, the rolls of fat on her stomach, the large breasts drooping sideways. The moon painted her ivory. In the night, alone and still, Gopal thought she looked beautiful. But did he dare? What about all those men before and disease. But she looked so lovely and like a night goddess of the forest awaiting her lover. Gopal took a deep breath and got ready to fling himself on her.

Suddenly feet trampled warningly and a figure appeared from the beach, already unbuckling his belt. Gopal ducked behind the rock. He heard the feet stop and the sound of clothes rustling and he fled wildly through the trees.

He stopped a safe distance away and paused for breath. He looked around and a little distance away could make out Randy's figure poking a stick into the bonfire. Gopal waited a while longer and then walked out. His walk changed to a strut and the strut to a swagger the closer he got to the fire. He scooped up a beer can with a certain style.

'So,' asked Randy with a quick glance and a small smile, 'how'd we do?'

Gopal gargled his beer in answer.

'Great,' said Randy, who apparently could decipher the sounds of beer being gargled, 'at least that's one problem out of the way.'

Gopal found a spot just beyond the arc cast by the fire and curled himself. He could still go back, but he knew he didn't have the guts. He knew he was a fool, but he somehow felt he was right. He fell asleep, relieved.

The next morning as they drove back with Randy giving him meaningful looks all the way, Gopal maintained an external attitude of becoming modesty. Inside, he was kicking himself as though he was made of footballs. Fool, he cursed. You should have leapt on her. You should have thumped your chest like Tarzan. If he had been given to rending his garments, he would have done so, instead he had to be content with rending his soul.

He sulked all day. Visions of his possible performance and tigerish leaps bounded through his mind. Hoarse and loud cries tragically never uttered the previous night, filled his ears. Dialogues, unsuitable for those sensitively reared, arranged themselves on his tongue. But most of all, an overwhelming sense of having been a total idiot suffused him. He felt that when historic opportunity had knocked at his door, he had told her sternly to leave, informing her that he preferred a good night's sleep. How, he anguished, how I could do this so stupid thing? He wondered for a moment if he could arrive at Samantha's doorstep, apologise for being late for last night's distribution of favours and ask nicely if it wasn't too late for him to get his share. Of course he rejected this idea too. And worst of all he couldn't again look to Randy for help, having almost explicitly told him that the deed was done.

Gopal returned to his books like an orphan seeking vengeance for his murdered parents. He wondered briefly if the nearly mythical Indian capacity for achieving high grades in America wasn't due in part to nearly all of them seeking solace from the heartbreaks inflicted by American women. In India itself, away from America and American women, Indians didn't perform half as well. He wondered further if that too wasn't another national conspiracy by the Yanks to urge on their women to devastate foreign students in order to send them fleeing like boat people to their books, with consequences that could only benefit America. Foolishness, he rebuked himself. You are damn fool foolish boy who is always thinking and doing foolish things. He dived into his books like he was Greg Louganis hitting a pool.

He didn't re-emerge for several months. He found the American educational process so exhilarating, so encouraging, so immediate in its rewards, that he found he didn't really need more than academics to keep him content. The classroom, the library, the cafeteria, were the three points of the triangle that comprised his life. The only outside intrusion was an invitation to attend Gloria's marriage to the boyfriend who had moved in with her. Gopal attended and discovered that the other guests included Gloria's children, all of whom were not only older than him, but considerably exceeded Troy, the bridegroom, in age. This young man was apparently still in college and had a part-time job cleaning windows. During one of his jobs in the complex, he had spotted Gloria through the window panes writing. She had shown him her poems and the rest, as the books say, was history. Gopal discovered to his incredulity not unmixed with horror, that Troy was a literature student. It shook his faith in the American education system that the duo should announce their shared love of Gloria's poetry to be one of the pillars of their marriage. But he consoled himself with the thought that Troy was unlikely to graduate with high grades, if at all. At the lunch after the wedding, Gloria informed the guests that she intended to write a poem every single day for the rest of her life to her beloved Troy. The assembled men applauded, the women swooned and Gopal ached for the groom. He feared for the poor man's sanity.

However, he soon had cause to fear for his own, when for some reason he never quite understood, he decided to visit an art gallery where an apparently much-hailed artist was displaying and selling his wares. Perhaps he went out of a sense that there wasn't much time remaining for him in America and a gift of representative art might be an interesting present to take back home.

He badgered a girl he met in the cafeteria into driving him to the gallery and they arrived at the house where it was located. They walked in and entered a vast gallery painted white and devoid of a single canvas. But as they entered, lights began to flash, and he saw projectors, ranged in the middle of the hall, beam images on the wall. He examined them one by one and they were fairly ordinary collages of various kinds.

A bearded man materialized, smiling benignly. Gopal tensed. He had become wary of bearded men.

'Where is art?' Gopal demanded.

The man smiled even more broadly. 'This is it,' he said gesturing modestly.

Gopal examined the projectors.

'This is Sony,' he complained.

'No, no,' indulgently refused the artist. 'The images are the art.'

Gopal began to understand. 'But how someone is to take image back?'

The man tittered. 'You get the projector too.'

'Free?' Gopal was interested.

'Well,' the artist laughed gently, 'almost,'

'How much for this one?'

'9000 dollars.'

Gopal was shocked. He considered this. 'How much if I take projector and leave behind image?'

The artist's eyes narrowed. He began to look less artistic. 'They go together,' he snapped.

'Any concession?' Gopal thought the projector was worth bargaining for.

'What for?' the artist was curtly nasty.

'Well in India they are having many power cuts and electricity failures. Then no one is seeing image, so I must be getting discount in advance for times when no one can see it.' Gopal thought this was one of his better bargaining ploys.

The artist didn't seem to think so. 'Well I can't help it if you got power cuts. And even if you do, you can, you can — tell you what. You buy the whole thing as it is and if you have any problems with it in India, you just write to me and I'll refund part of your payment. How 'bout that?'

Gopal appreciated the attempt thoroughly. 'Wonderful,' he applauded. 'You are please keeping this one only for me. I am going to apartment to get money and collecting from you soon.'

'Great,' assured the artist lying transparently. 'Nobody but you gets this.'

Understanding each other perfectly, they shook hands amicably and Gopal left. He could recognise and respect another businessman when he met one.

The girl who had given him the ride drove him back.

'What d'you think of it?' she asked.

'Junk.'

'Yeah, I thought so too. But he's the new hot shit.'

'Americans,' Gopal sighed. He reflected that most foreigners, after they spent some time in America, began to sigh and say 'Americans', in the same tone.

The girl giggled. 'Say, you do remember me, don't you? I'm Sally.'

Gopal examined her. 'Of course, of course,' he assured her.

'Aw shit,' the girl sighed. 'I've passed you every day and said 'Hi'. I thought you'd recognise me.'

'Americans,' Gopal explained apologetically. 'You are all looking alike.'

Sally laughed and frowned at the same time. 'Sure.' She gave him an amused glance.

They arrived at the cafeteria parking lot.

'Well,' said Sally, 'that was my good deed for the day. And I hope you'll thank all of America for it, considering you can't tell one American from another. And the next time you see me,' she waggled an admonishing finger, 'you better recognise me. You hear?'

'Oh yes, yes,' Gopal assured her, getting out.

A few days later he met her again as she was walking to the library. She was carrying a stack of books.

'Guess,' she urged him as they both stopped. 'Guess which American this is you're talking to? But first,' she stopped him from speaking, 'first let's get the basics clear. Is this a female American or is it a male American or what? I mean can you at least tell the genders apart in this vast melting pot called America?'

Gopal heh-heh-heh'd in embarrassment.

'All right then, movin right along. We've got a good start here. So let's move to specifics. Is this Raquel Welch here, or is it Meryl Streep or, most famous of all, is it Sally Armbruster?'

'Raquel Welch?' hazarded Gopal.

'Right, first time. And the prize for perspicacity is the honour of helping me return these books.'

'Oh yes, certainly.'

'I hope you realise,' Sally carried on as they went in, 'that I've been rehearsing words like "perspicacity" in case I bumped into you again.'

Gopal smiled admiringly, wondering if 'perspicacity' had anything to do with 'perspiration'.

As they dumped the books on the counter, Gopal noticed with interest that one of them was the *Kama Sutra*.

'You are,' Gopal cleared his throat, 'having interest in Indian – ah – literature?' he pointed to the legendary and world's oldest sex manual.

Sally was unfazed. 'You're not the only Indian I know.' She winked suggestively.

Gopal picked up the book and flipped through it. A thought began to form in his mind. He thought it might be worth pursuing alone. Waving goodbye to Sally, he took the elevator to the fifth floor where he normally sat. He wondered if any other country had elevators instead of stairs in libraries. There was no reason why they should not, but it just seemed odd. He got down to studying, but his mind wouldn't concentrate. It kept returning to what he was starting to think of as Operation *Kama Sutra*.

With great impatience he waited for about two hours to pass and then went down to the lobby to the card index. He checked the location of the shelf where the *Kama Sutra* would be available and went there to find if it had been returned to its place. It had. He opened it with excitement, took out a pen and some paper he had brought with him for this purpose and began writing urgently.

A few minutes later, his mission accomplished, he put the book back in its shelf and began to hasten home. Randy spotted him and let out a yell.

'Hey Gopal, c'mere.'

Gopal merely waved at him and galloped away.

Randy looked at his receding back. I must be losing my charm, he thought.

Gopal raced up the stairs to his apartment and nearly collided with Gloria. Even in his fevered state he could see she was glowing.

'Hi there,' she trilled, wiggling her fingers.

Gopal was desperate to get inside his apartment, but he felt a certain courtesy was obligatory.

'How are you? Congratulations and things like that,' he managed a strained cordiality.

Gloria was too thrilled to notice the strain.

'Guess where we spent our honeymoon?' Gopal could have sworn she blushed.

'Florida?'

'In my bedroom.' This time she was definitely blushing, but there was an element of triumph in it. 'And that Troy —'

Gopal felt an appalled sense of panic in case he was going to have to listen to the explicit details of her honeymoon.

'Expecting call from India,' he hastily interrupted her. 'We will talk later. Bye.'

He shut the door behind him quickly.

He sat down at the table and took out that precious scrap of paper. It had dawned on him in the library, that every book there had a card placed in a flap stuck on the inside back cover. When a person took a book out, his identity tag was pressed on the card under a carbon so that his name was stamped on it. This card remained with the library till the book was returned, when the card was put back in its slot in the book and the book replaced on the shelf.

This being so, the lending card in the *Kama Sutra*, it had occurred to Gopal, would contain the names of borrowers who had the following characteristics. One, they were interested in sex. Two, they were likely to be quite impressed by the sexual knowledge and abilities of the ancient Indians, which, it stood to reason, could only have been improved by centuries of practice. And, therefore, three, the girls who had read it were likely to be not merely non-prejudiced about Indians, but perhaps even actively interested.

Gopal had pursued this piece of disgraceful Machiavellian logic by taking down all the female names on the card. The card was unfortunately somewhat new, the old one obviously having become too full of names to be used, and he now had seven female names. Gopal went through the telephone directory and found four telephone numbers that seemed to match the names. The other three were either married and had different surnames, or lived in the dormitory or sororities and shared communal phones, or were unlisted for some other reasons.

He punched the buttons on his phone for the first name and a man's voice answered. Gopal hung up.

An answering machine replied for the second woman.

The third one answered herself.

'Hello,' her voice was young, breathless, lovely.

'Heh, heh, heh,' sniggered Gopal, suddenly realizing that he had absolutely no idea what to say.

What did one say to suggest athletic exoticisms to strangers? 'Heh, heh, heh,' he giggled nervously again.

'Hello,' she repeated. 'Who's this?'

Her voice was so musical Gopal felt he was in love again. But clearly he had to say something quickly, otherwise she would hang up. Something subtle.

'I am,' he burst out in inspiration, 'from India.'

'Hello,' she was shouting, 'from India. Could you speak louder please. The lines are not very clear.' Obviously she thought he was calling all the way from India.

'No, no, no,' Gopal tried to explain. 'Yes, yes, yes,' he contradicted himself, thinking he might be able to keep the conversation going if she believed it was a transcontinental one. 'How you are?' he asked lamely.

'I'm fine,' she yelled. 'Who *is* this?'

'Oh, actually,' he confessed, capitulating, 'it's only me.' He banged the phone down in disgust.

'Stupid fool,' he cursed himself.

He walked around, trying to think up a suitable ploy for the next one.

He called the fourth number.

'Hello,' the voice was female and mature.

'Madam, I am calling from Students Welfare Office. I am helping foreign students adjust here. Your name has been recommended as someone who might be interested in meeting foreign students to give them introduction to life here.'

'Well, certainly,' said the voice unhesitatingly, 'I'd be pleased to.'

'Well, you can meet Mr Gopal. He's from India.'

'All right. When and where?'

'Up to you, madam.'

'Well I take an evening class every Wednesday in the Arts Building, so he could come by at around eight and ask for me any Wednesday.'

'Thank you, madam.'

'You are very welcome.'

The phone clicked.

Gopal was pleased but a bit guilty about his lies. I should have said this to other girl, he thought. On impulse he called her again.

'Hello.' Her voice, Gopal could swear, had the fragrance of soap that he somehow associated with lovely American girls.

'Oh, excuse me, madam,' Gopal launched glibly into his story.

There was a pause at the other end when he finished.

'You don't work at the Students Welfare Office,' she said with certainty. 'You're the guy who called just now pretending it was from India. Who is this?' she asked in annoyance. Gopal put the phone down in fright.

On Wednesday evening he went to the Arts Building and found out the class being attended by Mildred, for that, unhappily, was her name. He loitered around the water fountain and wondered what so many people would do with arts degrees when they graduated. Passing by the rooms, he saw through half-open doors, platoons of women and bearded men (so this is where they are from, he thought) chipping away at blocks of stone and scrawling on paper. Coming from a business family that not only had never produced any artists, but didn't even appear to know one, he felt it was all very exotic, but a bit non-essential. After all art didn't generate employment nor did it create a cash flow, yet, he puzzled idly, art and artists seemed to arouse great respect among perfectly sensible people. Well, he concluded kindly, art probably certainly had its place, though of course it couldn't be compared to selling hair oil in terms of the general good it generated.

Mildred's class was getting over and Gopal bent down, pretending to drink from the fountain, while he watched with one eye. He tried to fit the voice to one of the faces. The young women could be ruled out. Then someone yelled, 'See you next Wednesday, Mildred,' and Gopal fixed on the lady waving back. She looked kind, was his first thought, like somebody's mother. He observed her closely because Randy had once told him that several of the middle-aged mothers provided unsuspected and indeed unimaginable opportunities for endeavours of an intimate sort. But Mildred, Gopal reluctantly concluded, wasn't one of them. Some of the mothers he knew had a way of dressing — expensive, discreet, yet available — and a casual quick glance that left him feeling like razor blades had cut his clothes away. But this one looked so jovial and kind, that Gopal suspected if he tried to have an affair with her it wasn't that she would necessarily refuse, but that she might agree out of pity for him. He slunk away.

After the failure of this attempt too, Gopal decided that the gods were clearly opposed unanimously to introducing him to the world of carnality and he might as well abandon his ambitions. Besides which, to his concern, he found himself feeling a sense of brotherliness towards the American girls he now met. In part this was out of a sense of defeat, but more because he had less than two months left before the term ended and he returned to India.

He confessed this brotherly emotion to Randy who was alarmed.

'Dangerous,' he warned. 'Never felt nothing like it myself, except Tabby of course, but she doesn't count. Not infectious, is it? I mean it could be the end of civilisation as we know it.'

They parted, concerned at the latest threat posed to civilisation.

A few days later Randy grabbed Gopal coming out of a class.

'Feelin better?' He was genuinely concerned.

'Worse. More brotherly.'

'Shit. I was afraid of that. Well, I have the solution. Dr Randy's Cure All. Come one, come all.'

'What now?'

'There's an ice show coming to town. We'll go see that. They'll have hundreds of girls in their panties. Imagine that.'

Gopal did. He began to feel measurably less brotherly.

So they went to the show and as promised there was an army of underdressed young ladies dancing, pirouetting, racing.

There was music, gaiety, colour. Gopal, Randy was pleased to note, was lost in thought.

'So,' Randy dug him in the ribs, 'what say?'

'What?'

'Did it work or what? What're you thinking?'

'I am wondering how they are having ice in summer.'

'Jesus! I don't believe this! And the brotherly stuff?'

'Still prevailing.'

'You mean you're sitting there, in front of a hall full of half-naked women, feeling brotherly towards them and wondering how they make ice in summer?'

Gopal had to shamefully agree.

'Let's get the hell outta here. You're a goddamn freak, Gopal. Know what I mean?'

Guiltily, Gopal followed the fuming Randy.

Outside, Randy questioned him again.

'You sure this isn't some sneaky Indian trick to give the girls brotherly kisses? Know what I mean?'

Gopal denied it.

'All right, all right,' Randy tried to organise his thoughts. 'Let's get this clear. Are these feelings towards all the girls or just some girls?'

'All.'

'Even the big fat ugly broads?'

'Yes.'

'Even Gloria.'

Gopal hesitated. 'Yes.'

'This is dangerous,' exclaimed Randy. 'I should put the Immigration Service after you. Damn Commie pervert.'

Gopal wasn't sure if Randy was joking.

They drove back, Randy muttering. Gopal couldn't help himself. It was like a dream ending. He felt that in a bare ten months he had gone from child to man. More had happened to him in these few months here than had in his previous two decades in India. Perhaps that was inevitable for any traveller, particularly if he came to a society as open, fast moving and aggressive as this. Whatever happened, good or bad, something always seemed to be happening. And the Americans were like debris in the whirlwind. But no sooner did one tempest deposit them, tattered and bloody, in one spot, than they dusted themselves, and bounded off in eager search of another whirlwind to conquer. He ached sometimes just looking at them.

He had for instance given up trying to keep track of Randy's different girlfriends. One day he would find him entangled with a girl in the most public place, like two amorous boa constrictors unable to disengage themselves and later Randy would wax lyrical on her charms and the arrival at last, of true love. A few days later Gopal would barge into his room and find Randy involved in what he once described to Gopal as 'swapping spit'. But this time the spit swopper would have auburn hair while the last one was blonde.

'What happened to blonde girl?' he had asked. 'She was true love you said.'

Randy had searched his memory for the specific true love. 'Oh you mean Sandra. Hey, she was last week. I mean c'mon Gopal, you can't stay in love with the same girl for longer than a week. Ain't natural.'

'You are swapping so much spit,' Gopal had told him venomously, stalking out, 'that you are losing all your own and are having only people's.'

Even the diverse 'other people', Gopal had come to differentiate only with great difficulty. He had not been joking when he told Sally who had driven him to the art show that all Americans looked alike to him. Aside from being white, with light hair and overweight bodies, they insisted on wearing a regulation uniform of blue jeans. Gopal wondered if this was also intended to madden foreigners.

Initially he used to warmly greet Randy's girlfriends as though they were the same person. But comradely continuations of a conversation that had been previously interrupted, caused looks of such bafflement, that Gopal seriously wondered if Randy selected his girlfriend on the basis of her mental retardation. It was a sad thing of course, but it was awkward to have someone so young and pretty stand and gape at you.

Randy, characteristically, once he realised Gopal's predicament, didn't help matters by sincerely insisting that it was indeed the same girl. It was only when a new girl arrived who had red hair, and Gopal realised that whenever Randy was being so sincere it could only mean that he was being thoroughly insincere, that the problem diminished.

Now of course he could laugh at it. But he felt it a pity that just when America and Americans had begun to take on distinguishably individual features, the time had nearly come for him to leave. He sensed that it was going to be not just a farewell to America, but a farewell to childhood. He would go back home to a gruelling work schedule, to a world of business that was ruthless, endless, savage. He could visualize dry afternoons and cold-eyed buyers negotiating deals. He knew it all of course, knew that the world he had been trained for was the real one for people of his inheritance, and this one was relatively a vacation. He knew he would stand for many days on the shopfloor of the factory, amidst the black stains, the oil smells, the roar of men and machinery, sweating in the heat, and the memories of this interlude would wash over him, cooling yet arousing a longing.

He would remember the rust and gold trees, the mists in the winter, the sounds of a bar-room, the rain on an early evening. Those first snowflakes dancing like him, white trees, a white world, and exuberant faces everywhere. It was such a fresh world. But at least he would have the memories, as he went back to his ancient land, to an arranged life and an arranged marriage and everything else so arranged as to be preordained. And as work and family took more and more of his time and attention, the memory too would begin to feel like an illusion. Of course he had promised himself that he would return, visit old friends, meet the professors, but he knew how difficult it would be. Responsibilities called, they would take their toll and who knew when, if ever, he would return. Perhaps he would relive it all only when he sent his son here to study, to learn in their superb systems, to grow and be hurt and yet feel so alive in their strange world, amidst their alien and rude ways that somehow managed to be affectionate. But it would be long time from now, Gopal knew that.

Over the next two months Randy, for all his thickheadedness, sensed some of Gopal's emotions too. He became so alarmingly civil that Gopal had to throw an empty beer can at him. He became somewhat normal then, but persisted in being extremely polite about India. Instead of his normal snide theories about the reasons for India's poverty, he began to express sympathy, going so far as to cluck his tongue in sorrow on reading of the failure of the monsoon rains. Never again did he urge that the solution to India's problems was for the lazy SOBs to get off their butts and work.

Gopal had learned to enjoy Randy's views once he had overcome his fury at the crass simplicity of it all. He had given up trying to make Randy even begin to comprehend the vastness of India, its confounding complexity and the enormity of its successes. It was simply more than Randy could understand or indeed wanted to. His mind, his ambitions, his world view were contained within the boundaries of the United States and anything beyond lay in the realm of black mists where, as the ancient cartographers said, there be dragons. Periodically someone reasonably civilised though unquestionably 'weird' would emerge from that night and spend some time in the sunshine of these United States before disappearing back into the suspicious blackness. Randy was almost unique in that at least he took an extremely keen interest in the antics of the strangers while they sunned themselves in the blessed land, considering that the other Americans were politely but firmly simply not interested. Nothing of any consequence, they seemed convinced, existed outside America.

But even Randy, with all his involvement with foreigners, just couldn't accept the accounts of Indian life that Gopal gave him. It was as though that part of his brain had been benumbed by some process and nothing could spark any life in that portion of his mind. Though as Gopal's departure date began to come near, he began his wholly synthetic sympathy for India.

'Randy, shut up,' ordered Gopal on one occasion.

'No, really, I think it's great the way India's managed to carry on. Really terrific.'

Gopal realised then that the process of disengagement from him had begun. While he was here, he was, for Randy, a temporary near American. He could be joked with, laughed at, needled, set up for embarrassments, yelled at, made to look foolish and have other rites performed on him that are part of the American collegiate way of life. But now that he was leaving, he was becoming foreigner again and more so with every passing day. His views were being listened to and met with polite responses. Gopal knew, the more polite Americans were towards you, the more they regarded you as a stranger. Normality and friendliness with them usually implied some form of verbal assault.

Before Gopal could feel actually sick by Randy's politeness, he preoccupied himself with exams and term papers. He was leaving before the results were declared, because, another sign of the tentacles of India reaching out to reclaim him, he had to reach in time for a wedding in the family.

It all passed in a blur. Exams, packing, the farewell to the staff that he rushed through. He went to say goodbye to Sue but she wasn't home. He pounded fists with the Peacock and promised to write if American football ever came to India. He refused to call Anand. But he did phone his headwaiter friend in the restaurant to thank him for his memorable visit to the church. Randy brought Ann to his apartment and she gave him a long, lingering, regretful kiss.

'You don't know what you've missed, honey,' she told and amazed Gopal.

As he packed the last of his toilet gear in the handbag, he felt like he was putting in the final moments of his life in Eversville. He thought of going to the mall to murmur a farewell to that neon temple and to pray to its gods for a safe journey, but there was no time.

'Let's go, let's go,' Randy was shadow boxing, more upset than he would dream of admitting.

Gopal presented the last of his hair oil to Randy, who accepted it with apparent gratitude.

As they loaded the bag in the car and stowed away the hair oil, Gloria came rushing.

'Here,' she thrust an envelope into Gopal's hand.

She gave him a tight hug. 'Go now.' She turned and ran back.

Gopal shoved the envelope into his pocket and they drove away.

'We're late, I just know we're late,' chanted Randy.

Significantly, thought Gopal, he hadn't said what a disaster it would be for Eversville if I missed my flight and had to stay. I'm a complete foreigner again.

They pulled up outside the airport entrance and Randy helped Gopal lug the bags and check in.

'You better hurry, sir,' the lady said.

She had red hair and something about that stirred in Gopal's memory. But he was busy saying goodbye.

'Well, brother,' he shook Randy's hand, 'thank you for everything. Please thank your mother and father and say sorry from me to Tabatha if I am being rude to her and all that.'

Randy grinned awkwardly. 'No problem at all. I hope you had a good time. Stay in touch now.'

They shook hands formally again.

'I hope I am seeing you soon in India?'

'Absolutely. I'll write you first.'

Gopal thought, he hasn't mentioned a harem.

They shook hands some more.

'Right,' said Randy increasingly ill at ease. 'Be seeing you. Take care.' He waved, walking backward.

Suddenly Gopal remembered. 'Randy,' his voice was loud.

'Are red-headed girls,' Gopal's voice was a loud whisper, 'red all over?'

Randy appeared to buckle. He hugged himself, waved a last time and turned and ran. Gopal thought his eyes had looked wet.

Gopal walked to the passage leading to the aircraft. His own throat felt craggy. Nice boy, he thought to himself as he buckled himself in, but a bit strange. He tasted the salt in his mouth and wept a little.

At New York he got off and was met by Sunil with great warmth.

'So, you're going back home, eh?' How was Eversville?

Gopal struggled with himself, but he stayed cool. 'It is being kind of neat.'

'Great. Glad you liked it.'

Gopal's flight left late at night so they drove to Manhattan. Gopal had been drinking throughout the flight from Eversville.

'So where d'you want to go to, Gopal?'

'Any bar.'

'Right.'

They parked and walked into a bar.

'What would you like to drink, Gopal?'

'Pitcher of beer?'

'A whole pitcher?'

'Two.'

'Right. A pitcher of beer,' Sunil ordered, 'and a bourbon for me.'

Gopal drank steadily, answering Sunil in monosyllables.

Finally Sunil asked, 'So tell me, Gopal, what were the girls like? You have a lot of girlfriends?'

'No.'

'None?'

'No.'

'Shit. What happened?'

Gopal drank some more.

'You mean you're going back after a year in America without getting laid?'

'Yes.'

'Jesus, I hope the Tourist Office doesn't hear of this. It'll ruin business. I mean we can't let that happen, can we?'

'Gods,' Gopal said thickly, 'against it.'

'Oh nonsense,' encouraged Sunil. 'This is America. American gods love it.'

Gopal shook his head groggily. 'No use.'

'Wait and watch. We can't let this happen. America would close down.'

Sunil got up and walked away. He returned in a while.

'There's a blonde sitting in that corner table. The bartender says 50 bucks is what it takes. I've paid him. It's my farewell present to you. Go get'em boy.'

'No use,' intoned Gopal. 'Gods.'

'Go try it,' urged Sunil. 'It's all bought and paid for.'

He helped Gopal to his feet and pushed him in the right direction. Gopal staggered forward and saw the blonde standing beside the rear door under an exit sign. She stepped out and Gopal followed unsteadily. They were in an alley and the blonde walked only a few steps before turning to go down into a basement. Gopal painfully managed the steps. The door at the bottom was open and as he walked in he saw her already taking her shoes off.

'Bathroom?' he asked.

She jerked a thumb. Gopal stumbled in and unzipped himself. Gods, he thought to himself sadly, but he was starting to get interested. He relieved himself and came out. Excitement began to stir in him and his head felt clearer. The girl was half-lying on the bed. She had taken off her shoes, her blonde wig, her clothes and she was quite obviously a man.

'C'mon honey,' the harsh masculine voice grated, 'I ain't got all night.'

Gopal felt weariness seep into him as though it was an intravenous transfusion.

'Gods,' he said aloud. He walked to the door and opened it. 'Hey,' said the rough voice, 'you paid for it. You want it or not?'

Gopal noticed he had black hair all over. Dispiritedly he closed the door behind him and walked up.

Sunil looked at him in surprise. 'That was quick.'

Gopal smiled sadly.

'Well let's go.' Sunil put his glass down with a thud.

On the drive he asked, 'Everything okay.'

'Yes.'

'Did you like the girl?'

'Very nice girl.'

'Great.' Sunil was relieved. 'At least you haven't made history.'

Gopal sleepwalked through check in and walked up to the first class lounge. He sat down heavily and began to drink again. After a while he noticed a woman in a sari sitting opposite, matching him drink for drink. She smiled at him and got up and walked around a bit before sitting next to him. She was in her early forties, had fashionably short hair, expensive earrings, but a pleasant rather than beautiful face.

Gopal warmed to her and almost as though he couldn't stop, related his sorrow at leaving America, to her. He told her of his fears of a boring future, an unknown wife, a strangling environment, and how the freedom of his American experience now made him want to rebel against the way things were at home. He found from her that she was married, had a son studying in America in college who she had come to visit. As they drifted in their mutual alcoholic cloud into the aircraft, they sat on adjacent seats in the first class section. As the great craft rose towards the dew drop stars, they whispered their secrets.

Gopal told her of his disasters with women. She told him of how her husband ignored her and tried to seduce every girl he met. They drank more. Dinner was offered and refused, and now the lights were lowered. They burrowed in the softness of the cushions they had been given. The cabin was nearly empty and with the comforting hum of the engines around them, they whispered and wept to each other. Neither knew how much they had drunk or what they were saying. They clung to one another, afraid of the morrow but able to ignore it in their contentment with each other.

At some point they had begun to kiss while talking. And then they stopped talking. Gopal forgot this was a woman so much older. He felt absorbed by her. He felt his cheeks wet with tears, his and theirs, and when he lurched into the bathroom, she went with him. And there, crouched uncomfortably but heedless, 30,000 feet above the ocean, Gopal at last felt he had truly become a man.

He went back to his seat and fell instantly asleep. When he woke up, the plane was taking off from London and the woman was gone, obviously having disembarked there. Awake yet disoriented, refreshed yet disbelieving, Gopal wondered if he had imagined it all. He stretched and felt something crinkle in his pocket. He fished it out and it was Gloria's envelope. It had his recent companion's name and address on it too, though he had no recollection of taking it down. He opened the envelope and took out the letter. He carefully put the envelope with its address in his wallet. He was determined to see her again. He read Gloria's poem.

I wish we had got some time,
So I could make you mine.
I know you'll find a love as fine,
In some unexpected time.

Gopal laughed. He would write to Randy and tell him about last night. That should get him on the next flight to India. He laughed all the way home.